About the Author

Martha Twine was born in London in 1948. She moved to Surrey in 1956. Educated at Guildford County School, she worked for over forty years in the public sector, mainly in London and the north east, during which time she gained an accountancy qualification, and worked in finance. She is now retired and lives in Haslemere, where she enjoys gardening and singing in local choirs.

Kiss Terror Goodbye

Martha Twine

Kiss Terror Goodbye

Olympia Publishers
London

www.olympiapublishers.com
OLYMPIA PAPERBACK EDITION

A CIP catalogue record for this title is
available from the British Library.

ISBN: 978-1-78830-380-4

This is a work of fiction.
Names, characters, places and incidents originate from the writer's
imagination. Any resemblance to actual persons, living or dead, is
purely coincidental.

First Published in 2019

Olympia Publishers
60 Cannon Street
London
EC4N 6NP

Printed in Great Britain

INTRODUCTION

In my first book, *Terror in Britain*, I described how, in September 2011, the North American mafia and unethical secret scientists joined forces with Al-Qaida and the IRA to launch a covert offensive on Europe, using electromagnetic technologies. They called it the "European Theatre of War", and they created an organisation called the International Unity Guild, to drive forward that initiative.

The objective was to conquer Europe and turn each country into a police state, controlled by electromagnetic surveillance systems. European citizens were to be held in virtual prison camps, with guards operating electronic weapons. Leaving aside the advanced technologies, North Korea would be a good example of how a country might be run under such arrangements.

At an age when I had expected to be putting my feet up in retirement, I was caught up in this terrorist operation, and learnt first-hand what it is like to be targeted. Thanks to the British military and other law enforcement authorities, I survived, and learned how to navigate the covert technologies. As I grew proficient in using them, I was able to defeat my terrorist attackers at their own game, using their own weapons. I also learned many new approaches, which gave me the edge over the perpetrators.

At the end of the first book, the local terrorists in Britain were defeated. But their allies in North America, mainly from Canada, soon returned to the attack. This time, their objective was to capture me and force me to work on their side. They thought they could use my electromagnetic skills as a secret weapon to gain ascendancy in their covert war.

In the meantime, NATO were working together to develop technologies that would exclude the electromagnetic terrorists from operating altogether. At the time of writing, the North American military have made good progress in this direction, and Europe is now catching up.

By accident, I began working with British authorities on space research, and saw, from the inside, some of the personal stories behind the scientific achievements. Despite increased attacks from terrorists, I started to explore stars and planets across the universe, using electromagnetic technologies. The world started to open up for me, when I discovered that technologies that had been used for terrorism held the potential to transform our Earth for the better and to solve many problems in ways that are beyond all human experience.

This book is not all doom and gloom. On the contrary, it became a lot of fun, and the people that I was privileged to meet and work with all had a lot of laughs together. I hope you will enjoy the story, as it unfolds along the most unexpected pathways. I was able to realise my dreams of space exploration, and got to know as friends, some of the dedicated men and women who work behind the scenes to protect us in our everyday lives.

Martha Twine, 31 August 2018

THEY TRY TO TAKE ME OVER

I woke up one night, and became aware that I was lying on an operating theatre bed. To my right, a white-coated man of Far Eastern appearance was sitting at a table. He was holding a tiny piece of metal with a pair of tweezers and heating it over a small flame. The metal was shaped like a staple before it has been pressed into place. I realised that I was about to get stapled with some kind of nanotechnology device.

I reached across and surrounded the man and his table in an electromagnetic envelope. Then I called to mind a picture of a room where British Special Services worked, in association with MI5. I had visited it before to get help, and my contacts there were Bertram and Madelaine. As it was the middle of the night, I did not expect to find anyone in, but in fact, they were downstairs, having a meeting with three other men in a room next to their science laboratories.

Bertram looked up with surprise. An expression of irritation crossed his face.

Is this the time and place for you to barge in? was clearly what he was thinking.

But I couldn't have cared less.

'Help, I'm being attacked by nanotechnologists, and they may have stuck something in my head,' I cried. 'I've got one of them, and his kit. Where shall I put him?'

'Oh, you can put him in the prison complex out at the back,' said Bertram.

I dumped the man and his kit in a large room which had bars across the middle of it. One half of the room was open, and the other half was a prison.

Bertram and the others came in, and stared at the man. Two armed soldiers followed them. The man started shouting at them in a foreign language, which I later learned was North Korean, banging on the bars of the prison.

Then an older man in a white coat, whose name was Elliot, appeared. It turned out he was an American scientist working for NATO in some capacity.

'Come with me,' he said.

He went into the MI5 science research laboratory, switching on the lights.

'Can you sit in that chair?' he asked, pointing to a strange contraption on the opposite wall.

It looked a bit like a dentist's chair, except that the top of the chair was enclosed in a transparent plastic dome. I did my best to sit in it, which was a bit tricky, given that I was not operating in my normal physical environment. A light went on inside the plastic dome.

'OK, now turn your head to the right, and hold still please,' said Elliot.

I tried to do as he asked. Elliot scrutinised the skin behind one of my ears.

'Ah, I see it now,' he said.

He leaned over and pulled something out of the skin behind my ear with a pair of tweezers.

'That's got it,' he said, holding the thing up to the light.

It was one of those staple things I had seen the North Korean nanotechnology operator wielding.

Elliot then checked the rest of my head.

'You're clear now,' he said, 'You can go.'

'Thank you,' I said, and left instantly, returning to my bedroom, where I fell asleep immediately.

The next day, I thought over what had happened. It looked to me as if the terrorists were trying to implant some kind of device in my head. Some years before, they had managed to implant a microchip in the back of my head, which enabled them to track me. I did not know what the staples were for, but I did not like them. Also, I did not like waking up to find strange people trying to operate on my head.

I decided to wear a crash helmet in bed from then on. This might sound a bit strange, but, in fact, it was quite comfortable, and much more supportive than a normal pillow. I soon got used to sleeping in it.

The next night, I decided to return to the place where I had been attacked by the North Koreans. It was an enormous green field, with some old aircraft hangars and what looked like a fifties aircraft inside at one end. There were some purpose-built sixties-style office buildings nearby, where other terrorist scientists were working. They had North American accents. The best thing to do was to return them and their personal effects to the authorities of their country.

After carefully selecting the entire office block, I tuned into the people inside it and tried to pick up the frequency that represented their home town. Then I lifted up the office block, using electromagnetic technologies, and headed out there. As I arrived, I noticed it was daylight. I was hovering over a large dual carriageway, in a rural area with large grey mountains in the background.

Close to the mountains there were open fields. I dumped the office block there, near to the road. In a few minutes, two police cars pulled over and several policemen got out. I went over and explained what had happened. They were a bit surprised, to say the least. To ensure that the police had all the evidence at their disposal, I went back to the green field and brought over the old aircraft. The aircraft had propellers and creaked a lot as I deposited it on the ground. By now there were a lot of police all over the area, and it looked as if they were taking people from the office block into custody in large vans. They were not that pleased to have the aircraft as well. One of them came over to me.

'Are you planning to bring in anything else?' he asked.

'No, that's it,' I said.

'Well, in case you need to contact us again.' he continued, 'Please could you go to the designated area the other side of that bridge.'

I looked across to an overhead walkway which spanned the dual carriageway. On the other side there was a Perspex building under construction. Half of it was below ground level, and outside it on a bank was what looked like a transparent helipad which glowed and flickered with light coming from underneath it.

'OK,' I said. 'Please can you tell me the name of this place?'

'It's Calgary, ma'am,' said the policeman. 'You're in Canada.'

I made one last visit to the green field to check I had not left anything behind. As I arrived, I could see a large beige canvas tented area being set up by some tall men in military uniform. One of them came over to me.

'What are you doing here?' he said.

He had a North American accent. Other military staff walked by, busily engaged in creating a semi-permanent place to live.

I explained how I had been attacked there earlier, and how I had taken some terrorist scientists to Calgary in Canada.

'Are you from Canada?' I asked.

The man smiled.

'No,' he said. 'We're Americans.'

'Where is this?' I asked.

'Ireland,' he replied.

'Why are you here?' I asked.

'We're part of NATO,' he said.

There was a lot more I wanted to ask, but the man was called away to assist with what looked like setting up of electromagnetic shielding for the tented building.

As I left, I remembered seeing NATO camping equipment on Amazon. I ordered ten rubber sleeping mats from Amazon, which were said to be the same as those used by NATO soldiers, and lined my room with them. Then I installed a sun block blind that covered the entire window wall, and got a curtain firm to line the floor and ceiling with the same material. This made it much harder for the terrorists to attack me while I was asleep. I knew it was working, because I could hear them talking about it on their ultrasound communication system, which they called Syntel – short for synthetic telepathy.

'We can't find her,' one complained.

'Use the infrared then,' said another.

'I am,' said the first terrorist. 'But it's not good enough. Can you get a specialist in?'

In due course, they did get specialists in. They gained access through a loosely closed window and constructed electromagnetic architecture that leaned along the ceiling towards my bed. But their scope for attacks was limited to certain types of weapons, and they were never able to see me, owing to the many shielding devices installed.

The North American terrorists referred to themselves as 'Our Group.' Our Group included staff from the US, Canada and the Irish Republic. There were also some British terrorists, who were IRA collaborators. Recently, these guys had fallen on hard times. Their finances were running low, since they fell out with Al-Qaida. They could no longer keep up the payments on their commercial WIFI satellite either, and had to rely on one belonging to a neighbouring terrorist unit.

There was an electronic boundary between the territory of two terrorist groups — IRA operator's group and psychological warfare group, created by two different transmitters in different houses. The boundary ran down one side of my bed. This meant that if I rolled over, one group could hear my thoughts and talk back at me, but the other group could not. This caused them constant irritation. I had the radio on most of the time, which put paid to their verbal attacks. The NATO rubber mats absorbed their electronic weapons attacks. So, when I was in bed, things weren't too bad.

But once outside my bedroom, the terrorists redoubled their efforts, directing electromagnetic fields at me with an array of linked devices known as oscillators. Oscillators alter gravity around you, making parts of your body feel heavier or lighter. They are used by terrorists to destabilise people and knock them off their feet. The perpetrators tried to drag my body back, to prevent me moving, while sniping at me with painful close range laser weapons.

I countered these attacks with shielding devices made of plastic, rubber and waterproof materials. The shielding devices absorbed the impact of the oscillators, but after several years of these attacks, a cumulative effect of extreme fatigue began to build up. It took only the slightest exposure to these weapons for me to become exhausted, and I needed to rest or sleep for an hour in order to recover.

In the months that followed, there was such a barrage of attacks that I sometimes slept half the day as well as at night. This proved counterproductive for the terrorists, as when I was in bed, they could not reach me, and were therefore unable to earn money by attacking me or by subcontracting me out for other terrorists to attack me. The IRA, who had a lot of collaborators in the area, rented out rooms for North American terrorists to use. Now they had to offer financial inducements to get terrorist units to turn up, particularly as, when awake, I became increasingly proficient at killing them, by redirecting the electromagnetic energy of the terrorists' computer systems against them.

When uploaded to their electromagnetic computer system, terrorists became invisible to the rest of the world. They entered the electromagnetic environment. In this state, they could be made shorter or taller. The technical support teams that operated the uploading equipment generally made their staff smaller, to reduce the risk of detection. Height was also linked to rank. Senior staff were made taller than low-level staff. They all looked about four to six inches tall to me. I could make myself any height I chose.

When terrorists attacked me, I would remove the feeling in their arms and legs. This was a painless process, but it meant they were no longer any use as soldiers, and on leaving the electromagnetic environment, the paralysis remained permanently. Colleagues of those I hit had to finish them off with a bullet to the head, after which the IRA had to dispose of the bodies, which was not cost effective from their point of view.

Terrorist groups were booked in by the IRA to attack me every day, in three shifts. The groups came from units holding paid-up membership of the International Unity Guild. It worked a bit like a terrorist version of NATO.

Each terrorist group made the discovery that attacking me did not work. If none of them survived, there would be no one to pass this message on to the wider terrorist community. I began leaving some of them alive to pass on the story. After a while, the IRA had to scour their contacts to find groups that had not heard about me, and who were still willing to take on a poor old pensioner. If no one was willing to turn up, the IRA would have to come out and fight me themselves, and they wanted to avoid getting hit.

The terrorists mainly operated from artificial constructions, either in the form of many-levelled turrets, or an amphitheatre full of buildings. These were portable, and could be inflated in the general vicinity of my house, a bit like a bouncy castle. They were invisible to the naked eye, being contained within the electromagnetic frequency range.

From these electromagnetic constructions, terrorists tried to lean in on me sufficiently to get within range. The perpetrators could be seen travelling around in a camper van, and setting up their parabolic microphones, dishes and switchpack kits on the local hillside. But the nature of their activities was not apparent to anyone looking from the outside. This made detection unlikely except by use of specialist scientific equipment.

The terrorists started running training courses in a purpose-built structure containing a house and garden, fabricated from electromagnetically charged plastics. The idea was that groups of junior terrorists should be sent to practice attacking me, in a confrontational exercise in which senior managers from the North American "Our Group" team and the visitors would try to get as many of the other's staff killed as possible. They could then claim compensation in cash for those killed "in battle" from the International Unity Guild. That way both sides benefited, and the exercise paid for itself.

The house had three floors. The ground floor was allocated to the trainee visitors, who were unarmed. The first floor belonged to the home team, who always had the upper hand, partly because they were armed and partly because female leaders allocated to the visiting team were IRA double agents acting for the home team. The third floor was available for IRA non-commissioned staff and any officers that wished to oversee the process.

The training courses started early in the morning with an attempt to wake me up and void my bladder. The home team knew this was impossible to achieve, as I had lined my room and my bed with shielding devices to prevent their microwave lasers getting through. But they hoped I would be sufficiently angry with the visitors to hit them.

After that, synthetic telepathy trainees from the visiting team were urged into the ground floor, and given crude comments to read out to me. Some of the trainees could barely read, and it was obvious they were not speaking spontaneously. The comments were written for them by IRA non-commissioned officers on the third floor, and were intended to provoke me into killing the visitors.

My policy was to avoid hurting trainees, who were unwitting victims. I looked for ways to release them from the building but the doors were kept locked, and could only be released by the North American technical support team that maintained the terrorist computer systems.

There were three different computer systems: the Canadian system — allocated to the ground floor, the American system which controlled the first floor, and the IRA system, which controlled the top floor.

When the going got tough, the junior staff on the ground floor were pulling at the punch-lock door and swearing, something that all visiting terrorists were strictly forbidden to do in the electromagnetic environment, for reasons that will become clear.

'Why won't this fucking door open?' muttered a junior female visitor, as she struggled to pull it open.

To her surprise, the door swung open immediately, and she and the rest of her team raced out into the garden to safety. I realised that it was the f-word that had released the catch, and crashed the Canadian computer system. After that, if I wanted to quickly rescue junior staff, when, for example, they were being threatened by armed opponents, I would think to myself, *open the fucking door* and the juniors escaped.

The junior staff soon got the idea, and learned to rescue themselves.

The North American Our Group team were also prohibited from using strong language. Their middle management staff soon realised that they could not make any money attacking me, and wanted to escape from their room too. They watched the visitors learning to open their door with the F-word, but it didn't work for the door on the first floor. This was because their door operated on an American computer system, and in America the F-word is not considered particularly offensive.

Then one day, an irate North American shouted, 'Jason, please can you open the goddamn door?'

All of a sudden it was *Open Sesame* time. The door opened as if by magic. It seems that Americans don't like the g-word at all. There were several other words that Americans did not like, and Our Group found them all.

The morning shift ended at midday, at which point the computer punch-lock doors opened automatically. Two staff from the first floor sneaked up onto the second floor, and hid there until the new shift started an hour later. Then they began swearing at the IRA officers' door, to try and discover the secret word that would open it and crash their computer. But it was something of an anti-climax, as the door was controlled by a British computer system, which had an aversion to most swear words, and opened long before Our Group had got as far as the letter f.

CANADIAN CONNECTIONS

Under the direction of their headquarters in North America, the terrorists continued their efforts to take me over, using a two-pronged attack of psychological warfare and electromagnetic weapons. This involved verbal aggression and subvocal emotional threats from their mind control group, while their weapons group launched arrays of oscillators, mind confusion microwave beams, and carbon dioxide lasers at me. The lasers delivered a payload of fine droplets taken from carbon dioxide and carbon monoxide gas canisters, designed to make me too tired and weak to leave the house.

I spent a lot of time disintegrating my attackers. I got through large numbers of terrorists every day. As a result, they began to lose ground. When this happened, they started putting children and teenagers from their people trafficking business in the front line. To combat this, I created a programme which I broadcast on all terrorist electromagnetic computer systems, which meant that no youngsters could ever be hurt by anything I did.

Whenever I discovered youngsters on the front line, I surrounded them with a magnetic envelope, and brought them into H.M. Special Prison Services, where a reception centre was set up to receive them. This became the default location for rescue cases within the British Isles. I had only to remove the invisible "tin-hats" that all terrorists wore to lock them within the electromagnetic system, and the kids flew straight into the reception centre. Often, the children arrived with physical injuries inflicted by their captors, and were unwashed and unfed.

The men and women of H.M. Special Prison Services had kind hearts. They worked overtime to get all the kids in, and attend to their needs. Then they would contact the governments of whichever countries the kids came from, and arrange for them to be repatriated.

When I was on the battlefield, in electromagnetic mode, with bodies flying in all directions, I often found children dressed up as adults, being pushed towards me by the terrorists. When kids and young people appeared, the electromagnetic sky-ceiling above me would open up, and friendly people from H. M. Special Prison Services would look down with concerned faces, saying, 'We'll take them now. Can you pass them up to us, please?'

Most of the terrorists I brought into H.M. Special Prison Services were not from this country. Some came from the Republic of Ireland, but most of those calling themselves 'Our Group' came from Canada. This really surprised me.

Once when I went to the public library to use the free computer room, ten women and children from the terrorist community suddenly appeared and sat around watching me. They had been ordered in to conduct a close-range gang-stalking event.

I was struck by the close resemblance that the women and children bore to each other, as though they all belonged to one family. They were tall fair-haired people, of Nordic appearance. A young child was sent toddling up to my table, carrying a book, which she carefully placed next to me, before skipping back to her mother. I glanced at the book. It was entitled *'Liphook, Bramshott and the Canadians. The story of Canadian troops in Liphook and Bramshott during two World Wars,'* by Laurence Giles.

It turned out that many Canadian troops had been stationed in Aldershot, and worked around Hampshire, Sussex and Surrey during the Second World War. Some Canadian soldiers married English girls, and settled here. Others returned to Canada with English wives, at the end of the war. I was interested to learn about this, but at the time I did not get the unspoken message that the terrorist women were sending me...

'People from *our* country were here.'

We have several Canadian friends, and I couldn't understand how terrorists could have got a hold in that country. French-Canadian terrorists told me there were IRA sympathisers among minority extremists within Canada, some of whom had come from Ireland originally. They joined up with the US mafia, unethical North American scientists, the Canadian mafia, the IRA and Al-Qaida to launch the terrorist initiative called the European Theatre of War. There was also a group of criminals from the Caribbean, who boasted descent from French colonists, who linked up with the French Canadians.

US initiatives to crack down on crime had an increasing impact. As a result, terrorists, gangsters, drug dealers and people traffickers started moving over to Canada, because, unlike the US, Canada does not have the death penalty. So there was a growing population of disaffected people within

Canada, whose numbers were added to by terrorists posing as asylum seekers from Asia and the Middle East. Familiarity with the French language was a significant factor, as Canadian terrorists were able to work with Al-Qaida in Algeria and Tunisia, where French is spoken.

I was starting to work out where the electromagnetic terrorists came from, but there were gaps in my knowledge, particularly about how the American scientists got involved. I decided to go and look for someone who would be willing to talk to me.

The European Theatre of War relied extensively on the work of secret scientists behind the North American terrorist movement. From what I observed, some of their work dated back to the 1950s. The American military are known to have carried out research into a range of advanced technologies, after the Second World War. I suspected that the original scientists behind the North American terrorist movement might have been around at that time.

I decided to try and find one of them, by surfing the terrorists' computer systems. My mental "internet surfing" catapulted me into the study of an elderly man in a terrorist building on the Canadian border with the US. He was wearing shielding devices to conceal his identity, including what looked like a semi-transparent ball over his head. When he saw me, he dived under the table.

'It's all right, I'm not going to hurt you,' I said. 'I just want to ask you some questions about the past. It's for a book I'm writing.'

The man, whose name was Derrick, looked at me suspiciously for a moment, unsure if this was a trap, but I just stood there. Then he indicated with his hand towards an easy chair, and I sat down.

'Are you one of the original architects of the Our Group computer system?' I asked.

'I was one of them,' said Derrick. 'There were several. There aren't so many around now.'

'Did the technology come from the US military?' I said.

Derrick sighed.

'Well, you could call it military research. After the Second World War there was quite a lot of work for us. But then the American Military decided they wanted to go in a different direction. So, there we were, looking for work. We set up our own private business, as consultants. Now the type of clients we got, you wouldn't have to be too fussy about. But we worked at it, and built up our business. We got ourselves quite a reputation — mainly mafia assignments, or South American bosses running their own countries. Occasionally, a rich eccentric would call on our services.'

I raised a question that had been in my mind for some time.

'Did you work with the Nazis at all?'

'No,' said Derrick. 'We had already started our research before the Second World War, and it was strictly government funded then. That's not to say we weren't aware of work that the Nazis were doing. Later on, after we became a commercial enterprise, I met Joseph Mengele in the US. He was using a different name, of course. But we didn't really overlap in business terms.'

'Our Group seem to rely on external technical specialists for psychological warfare work. Is that something to do with you?' I asked.

Derrick leaned back in his chair. He was beginning to relax now, and he opened up somewhat.

'We trained the psychological warfare group, and designed the student courses that they now run themselves. In fact, the psychological warfare group hold direct responsibility for Our Group.'

'But they do not seem to run Our Group,' I said.

'Right,' said Derrick. 'But they ought to, as they have delegated powers from the International Unity Guild to do so.'

'Does that mean the psychological warfare group supervise Our Group and are accountable to the International Unity Guild for their activities?' I asked.

Derrick nodded.

'What exactly is the International Unity Guild?' I asked.

'I don't know if you've ever seen the United Nations building in New York?' asked Derrick. 'Well, from the outside, the International Unity Guild building looks quite similar. It's an electromagnetic architecture construct, accessible only via our technology systems. Flags of all the participating bodies are flying outside, and several committees with different responsibilities work inside, with representatives from all participating agencies.'

'Oh,' I said. 'Is that the place which has an agreement that if a member needs troops to help them, they can call the Guild to arrange for forces from another organisation to assist them?'

'You've got it,' said Derrick.

'And every member has to pay a fee towards the overall upkeep of the Guild?' I continued.

Derrick laughed.

'Well, that's the idea,' he said. 'But not all members are up to date on the payments. If it wasn't for one or two large donor members, the Guild would not operate.'

I now had information to answer a lot of my questions. I thanked Derrick for his co-operation. He looked relieved as I left. I was genuinely grateful to him. Maybe I didn't have the whole truth or even part of it, yet, but I could see some of the jigsaw pieces coming together.

BLACK MOON

Back home, terrorists from North America and North Africa were redoubling their efforts to attack me. I was killing them in increasing numbers, and I needed to find a suitable place to dump the bodies. In a moment of madness, I had an environmentally unfriendly thought, What about the Moon?

I searched my mental archives for an image of that first moonwalk by the US spacemen, and got a photo taken from within their space transport after it had landed. The sky was dark, with white sparks of light, and the Moon rocks shone a brilliant white. My intention was to get myself to that place by looking at the photo, and tuning in to the frequency of the location I wanted to visit. Then I could mentally adjust my Global Positioning Satellite address to that frequency, and by default, that is where I should be.

The next time I had bodies to dispose of, I tuned into the Moon photo and found myself in a rather bleak landscape, with no plants or trees, only rocks. It was a bit like an overexposed black and white photograph. In some places the light was blinding, but where the rock cast shadows, it was black. I looked around me. About fifty yards away there was a sheer drop of at least one hundred and fifty feet into a large flat area. I guessed I was looking into an ancient meteorite impact crater.

On the other side, there was a series of rocky step-like extrusions going down to a plain below, and above behind me, were some higher rocky cliffs.

I dragged and dropped two villains, who were attacking me with electronic oscillators, on to the rocks. They lay motionless where they fell.

'Fine,' I thought, 'This is my new recycling tip.'

Then two Algerian Daesh genetically modified dwarves attacked me — I had met them before in my previous mission. I deposited them on the ground, and left them. Later, when I next dropped some terrorists off, I noticed that the dwarves were not lying prone like the rest. They were sitting on a rocky promontory, swinging their legs over a short drop. They seemed completely absorbed in their own conversation.

Later still, I dropped another Daesh dwarf off nearby. He lay on the ground not moving. His friends saw him, and came over to him.

'Why are you lying down?' asked one of them.

'Because I'm afraid I may float away,' he replied.

After that, I dropped some men over a two-hundred-foot cliff, and watched them descend in a gentle, almost leisurely, fashion until they rested on the ground below. It seemed that the Moon's lighter gravity had something to do with it.

'Why had the Daesh dwarves not died from lack of oxygen like the rest?' I wondered.

That afternoon I was attacked by two heavyweight black men from the IRA's London Metropolitan Regiment. I dropped them off on the lunar landscape, but it seemed they had no intention of dying either. One of them sat on the cliff looking out over the massive panorama below him.

'Hey, man, look at this,' he said to his friend. 'We're in a large crater. It must be at least a hundred and fifty feet down.'

His friend was not that impressed by the view.

'Mm,' was all he said.

Then he got up and walked off to explore the steps down the other side, where the first two Daesh dwarves were now sitting.

I decided there might be a better outcome for them, since they no longer exhibited aggressive tendencies.

'I know, I'll return them to Al-Qaida's North American research centre in Algeria,' I decided.

I dragged and dropped the dwarves into the science research part of the centre, in front of a couple of Canadian scientists in white coats. The scientists were familiar with my occasional visits to the research centre, to rescue some children from the terrorists in the UK. I explained where the Daesh two had come from.

'How interesting,' said one of the scientists. 'I would like to see how these little chaps stood up to all that. They're from here, you know.'

One of the Daesh two was lying on the floor.

'Are you unwell?' asked a gowned orderly.

'No,' replied the dwarf. 'Everything seems so heavy here. I don't think I can sit up.'

He was having trouble adjusting to the Earth's heavier gravity. An orderly wheeled the dwarves off for observation on a ward in the research section. I looked in later, and saw one of them tucking into a large meal, so he had obviously acclimatised OK.

I explained to one of the scientists that most of the men I dropped on the Moon died immediately.

'I don't suppose I could see a couple of the bodies,' he said. 'It would be interesting to examine the state they are in now.'

'OK,' I said, and went off to my lunar recycling tip.

I selected a man and woman lying on the top of the rocky promontory.

'Here they are,' I said. 'They've been there for about fifteen to twenty hours.' Then I left the scientists to their investigations.

Later, I became aware that the scientists were trying to attract my attention with a high-pitched whistling noise.

'What is it?' I asked.

'Come and look,' said a scientist.

We went into a private ward with two beds in it. The man and woman were sitting up in bed, eating and drinking, just as fit as they were before I removed them to the recycling tip.

'What does it mean?' I asked.

'Simple,' said a scientist. 'They were in a state of suspended animation — stasis. We're still checking them out, but they appear to be unharmed.'

I mentioned that the black London terrorists had been able to survive the lack of oxygen, just like the Daesh Algerians.

'There is so much more we want to know about all this,' said the scientist. 'Thank you for your assistance. Perhaps we can call on you again sometime?'

Considering the unethical nature of the Al-Qaida research carried out on site, particularly genetic engineering of humans, I had no wish to assist them further. As I left, the words of a song by Kenneth L. King came to mind:

'And if you really want to, we can get together soon,

Next time I see you on the Moon.'

I was still curious about how the black terrorists had managed to survive on the Moon. A few days later I saw one of them, when I was depositing the bodies of some drug traffickers up there. He was sitting outside a cave in the rock.

'Hi,' I said. 'How come you survived up here? There's no air and no water.'

The big guy, whose name was Wayne, shrugged his shoulders.

'It's OK,' he said. 'I like it here.'

'But you must get hungry,' I persisted.

Wayne beckoned me into the cave, and pointed to the side of the wall. There were some marks that looked as if someone had scraped the rock with a knife, and next to them were what looked like rock bubbles or small indentations in the wall. Wayne scraped one of the bubbles, and after a while the top came off, and there was liquid inside.

'See, this is all I need,' he said. 'We can go without eating or drinking anything else so long as we have this.'

We looked out of the cave across the stunning lunar landscape.

'Have you been down there?' I asked.

Wayne pulled a face.

'I haven't wanted to really,' he said. 'At midday the sun is beyond blazing, and down there there's no shade for us. We could die from the sun's rays.'

I had a thought.

'Maybe your skin colour has helped you to survive,' I said. 'I doubt if the whites could cope with that amount of solar radiation. It seems rather hazardous here. I expected you to be dead, but since you're not, do you want to return home?'

31

Wayne smiled at me.

'Look out there,' he said. 'It's all mine now, and I won't have to share it with anyone.'

'But maybe you're missing family and female company,' I suggested.

Wayne laughed.

'Well, it so happens that women aren't really my thing,' he said. 'Now, my mate down there,' he added, pointing to the other black guy, who could now be seen about a hundred yards further down the slope. 'I can't speak for him. But he hasn't complained so far.'

I said goodbye and left them to it. It was hard to make sense of any of what had happened. A few days later, I was being attacked with laser weapons by terrorists from the Metropolitan Regiment, urged on by a couple of sneering black female terrorists.

'Aha!' I thought, looking at the females. 'I know a better place for you two!' I transported them immediately to the lunar landscape.

Next day, I looked in, just to make sure they were OK. They were sitting outside a cave. Sure enough, they had sussed out about the liquid in the walls.

'Oh, there's some water in there at the back, enough for us to drink,' said one. 'But where can I do my washing?' she asked imperiously, pointing to her pop socks.

I was a bit irritated that she would expect me to solve all her problems.

'Look here,' I said. 'I am not a launderette!'

She laughed in a good-humoured way.

'OK,' she said. 'But there is something you could help with… some male company would be an advantage.'

My mind went to a black guy called Dean, who worked as a security guard in one of the London gangster hideouts. All the men were afraid of him, because of his large build, and exuberant personality. He seemed to live full time in his work place. Maybe he didn't have anywhere else to go.

Shortly after that, I gutted the building where he worked and dropped many of the men, who were hell-bent on attacking British citizens, in the Gobi Desert, from a height of about five hundred feet. But I rescued Dean, and brought him to the place where the two females were living. One of the girls was out there. The Moon seemed to have a positive effect on Dean.

'Hey, babe, come here!' he shouted, removing his clothes. 'I am so ready and waiting.'

He wasted no time in demonstrating the truth of this statement. The girl had not seen any men for some time, and she enthusiastically responded to his invitation. Then the other girl turned up, to cries of welcome from the big guy, and they all seemed to be getting along fine.

As the weeks went by, there were times when I caught up with the Moon's new inhabitants, or added to them. I lifted an entire houseful of Daesh black dwarves up there, using a kind of "copy and paste" effect to replicate the house they were living in. This particular group of dwarves were so naïve and unprepared for life in the world outside, let alone terrorist activities, that they appeared to have been conscripted from a kindergarten.

I heard them complaining about their lot to their IRA slave masters — Why were they here? Why were they expected to attack people with weapons, and why would no one explain anything to them? Knowing they were able to live in the Moon environment, I decided to give them a second chance of a better life.

Things worked well for a while, and the dwarves seemed completely satisfied with each other's company. Then one day, one of them hailed me.

'Excuse me, Miss,' he said. 'We need paper.'

'What kind of paper?' I asked.

'Paper to stick on the walls, and bigger than this, please.' He held up a shop receipt, which seemed to be the only paper he had on him.

'OK,' I thought. 'I know where to get that. I'll go to the terrorists' stationary cupboard, where they keep all the paper for printing fake dollars, and see what's in there.'

There was plenty of A4 and some A3 paper. I took the lot and put it on the table in the dwarves' front room. They were delighted.

'Can we use both sides to draw pictures?' they asked.

I assured them they could. Later, I peeped into their house and saw they had created a strange kind of wallpaper out of the sheets I had given them. Why? Not a clue, but at least they were happy.

I continued to reflect on how blacks could breathe so well in the Moon environment.

'Maybe it's because we are operating in an electromagnetic version of the environment,' I reasoned. 'But if so, how come whites can't handle it?'

Unable to answer this question, I left it. Some months later, I heard of a new movie called 'Hidden Figures,' about the pioneering work of three black women scientists, at NASA's Langley Research Centre in Virginia. Mary Jackson was NASA's first black female space engineer. Dorothy

Langley became the first black, female supervisor at NASA's Langley Centre, and Katherine Johnson, a space trajectory expert, calculated the trajectory for America's first space mission in 1961, manned by Alan Shephard, and the flight path that put Neil Armstrong on the Moon in 1969.

'How timely that the movie should be honouring the achievements of black women scientists now,' I thought.

That week I checked out several US mafia gangster hideouts in the London area. From what I could gather, their job was to carry out protection rackets, arrange drug and people trafficking, terrorise local communities, and wait for the time when they would rise up to join Al-Qaida in winning the European War.

All the hideouts followed the same format. The penthouse office belonged to the boss, with an adjoining committee room. Each building had four or five work rooms packed with men staring at laptops, and there was a basement where food was prepared by black women. The organisation was totally patriarchal, and treated women as servants. But where were the black men? There weren't any.

'What about Al-Qaida's motto "WHITES OUT! BLACKS IN!" I wondered.

This was so strange that I asked a black female terrorist, who worked in the kitchen, where her male compatriots were based. She spent a long time going through her cell phone address book, to see where the black gangsters were holed up. At last she found one building.

'Here it is,' she said, showing me a photo of some male friends of hers.

I tuned into the frequency of the photograph and found myself in what seemed to be a very crowded locker room full of black men rushing in and out, changing coats, jackets and sports gear. I went upstairs. The building was similar to the others I had seen, but it was not clear what work the employees were actually doing.

It turned out that they were offering short-term call-off contract services, filling in for white gangsters when they needed extra men. The black men were being marginalised even in the mobster community, and forced to live in a segregated building. I felt sorry for them. They were keeping themselves fit, and were ready for any work, but their opportunities were limited. OK they were criminals, but they did not seem particularly sinister or malicious.

In the middle of the chaos of the men's changing room, one man caught my eye. His name was Daniel. He wasn't rushing about. He was moving slowly, taking his time as he put on his waterproof jacket. His gaze was constantly moving upstairs, where he could just see the blue sky and the light outside. I looked again at his building.

'I wonder if this would work,' I thought, as I "dragged and dropped" the house into a particularly beautiful lunar crater.

The crater had two levels. Inside the main crater, there was a small mini crater, lower down, right in the middle of the bigger crater. I stood in the lunar crater, looking at the house in its new surroundings. Then I saw Daniel's head and shoulders silhouetted as he came up the stairs from the locker room. He looked out of the door, gave a gasp, and stepped outside. Then he wandered off, and sat down against the wall of the crater. A couple of young men came out of the building. Their faces lit up with amazement and pleasure, as they took in the beautiful scenery and refreshing environment.

There was a lot they needed to know, so I went to the next crater, where Wayne and the other men and women were living, and asked if he would go over and explain things. He agreed, and I transported him straight across. He saw Daniel sitting against the crater wall and went straight over.

'Hi, man, what's new with you?' he said.

Daniel had been in a kind of dream state. He looked at Wayne with amazement, not expecting to see another human being. Then he got up and patted Wayne on the back.

'Are you alive, or are we both dead?' he said.

'I promise you, man, I am very alive,' said Wayne. 'And you are too. Who are these dudes?'

By now most of the men were outside the building looking around. They were trying to make sense of what had happened. Wayne went over to the men and explained how I had brought him to the Moon, and how he was now enjoying a life of unbelievable freedom. The new arrivals were greatly encouraged by what Wayne was telling them. They clustered round him, as he explained about finding liquid contained within the rock, and how drinking that was enough to provide all they needed instead of food and water.

The sun was, by our standards rather hot, but the men seemed to be enjoying it. Wayne started an expedition down to the little valley in the centre of the lunar crater. Then he shouted to the rest of the men 'There's water here!'

Everyone went down to investigate. The mini crater acted as a drain for liquid seeping from the high rocks of the Moon mountains in the area. Not that the liquid could actually be described as water. H_2O it was not. But it could be heard dripping down into something like an underground pool. The men collected it in containers and refreshed themselves.

In the days that followed, they completely altered their lifestyle. There was no rushing around at the beck and call of bosses. They were enjoying their new-found free time, exploring caves, and climbing up out of the crater to explore the rocky landscape.

'Would your life be better with some ladies?' I asked.

'Well now,' said Daniel. 'Some black belles would be just fine, but it's not essential.'

I thought I ought to do something about it, so I went back to the helpful black girl who had put me in contact with the men. She was highly intrigued by the whole thing.

'I know several gals that would be up for it,' she announced. 'Just give me a little time.'

Three hours later she had assembled a group of eleven young ladies, all of whom understood the score, and were willing to give it a try. When I arrived, they were sitting on comfortable chairs and settees. A middle-aged couple with a young baby, arrived at the last minute. I lifted them all, and the furniture with them, and set them down outside the men's house on the lunar crater.

The men welcomed them courteously. They enjoyed socialising, but did not feel driven to pair off with the new arrivals. The girls soon settled into their new environment. Initially, they adopted housekeeper roles, but they quickly took their places as Moon explorers, often in a women's group.

They discovered a special cave, where liquid was readily accessible. The cave led down into a large underground space the size of a cathedral. Last I heard, they had made it their own. The vaulted cave received some light from the entrance above, but much of its contents remained mysteriously in shadow. I would have liked to join in the exploration, it looked so inviting.

As I was coming out of the cave, I saw the middle-aged couple — David and Jesalynn, standing together. Something was wrong. Jesalynn was crying and David, was comforting her. One of the girls was looking after their baby for them.

'What's up?' I asked.

'We didn't expect to be going anywhere when you picked us up,' said David. 'We just dropped in for a minute to say hello to my friend, when suddenly we were here.'

'It's not that I don't want to be here,' sobbed Jesalynn. 'But our two sons were at my sister's house playing football with other kids, and I miss them.'

'Do you have someone I could contact to find your sons?' I asked.

David pulled out his cell phone, and pointed to a picture of a friend of his.

'This is Thomas,' he said. 'He worked in the same office as us, but he was out when the building went up. He knows my sister, and I'm sure he would be willing to help us.'

I tuned into Thomas's photo and went off to find him. He was walking along the street, in the centre of London, with people pushing past him on both sides.

'Thomas,' I called.

Thomas looked round, but couldn't see me.

'I'm here, Thomas,' I called again.

Thomas located me, his eyes widened. Then he turned into a side street. I followed.

'I know who you are. Has David sent you?' he whispered.

'Yes,' I said. 'He said you could tell me where his sons are. He wants me to bring them to him.'

Thomas gave me a look of complete comprehension.

'Right,' he said. 'OK. Now let me see what's best. I know… the local football stadium.' He showed me a picture of the stadium on his cell phone. 'Can you be there on Thursday evening at 7 pm.'

'Yes,' I said. 'Is that where the boys do their training?'

Thomas nodded.

'OK, I'll be there,' I said.

I made a note on my calendar for Thursday at seven p.m. When the time came, I called to mind the image of the football stadium, and arrived outside. There was a lot of noise going on in there, so I went in cautiously, not sure what to expect. As I walked down the concrete path, the stadium came into view. It was full of people — fathers and mothers carrying suitcases, children running about, men standing in groups talking, and women laughing together. They looked as if they were getting ready for a church picnic.

Thomas came running towards me.

'We are all here,' he said, smiling broadly.

'Where are the boys?' I asked.

Thomas dived into the crowd, and emerged with two teenage boys, dressed in suits.

'Do you think I'd forget them?' he laughed. 'Jesalynn would never forgive me.'

Everyone was looking at us now.

'Do all these people really want to come too?' I asked.

'YES, WE DO!' the crowd shouted.

'OK, GET READY THEN!' I shouted back.

Then I picked up the whole lot, and brought them straight over to the lunar crater where David and Jesalynn were living.

There were cries and cheers as we arrived. It was daytime now, though it had been night a moment ago. People in the crowd shouted and waved to friends they recognised around the crater. Wayne came forward to greet everyone. He led them down the little valley, so they could all drink the life-giving water. I looked for Thomas, and the boys, but I could not see them. Then I caught sight of a small group at the back of the crater, almost unnoticed, away from all the commotion. They were hugging each other and crying.

Jesalynn waved to me, her arm around one of her sons.

'Thank you, thank you,' she said.

In the days that followed, I dropped in on the new arrivals from time to time. They settled in easily. Some of the new group decided to move to a smaller crater nearby. I provided things that they asked for, including tents, drinking mugs, pillows and duvets. But soon the new group stopped asking for things. They had learned to create whatever they needed, within the electromagnetic environment, by using their minds. They were now Moon people.

RED PLANET

Wasn't that a crazy trip! I wasn't the only one who thought that. A number of local terrorists, who were monitoring my activities, thought so too.

'What about Mars next!' I heard a woman terrorist whisper to her friend.

It was like watching a movie for them. As soon as she said it, I could picture in my mind, the photos of the little remote-controlled buggy, curiosity, bravely trucking along on the dusty red surface of Mars.

'Well,' I thought. 'In principle, there is no reason why not, so let's give it a go.'

Next time an elderly male terrorist tried to void the contents of my bowel, using close-range telemetry and an electromagnetic device, I thought, 'Right, you've asked for it,' and I dragged and dropped him to the exact spot in the photo where the Mars buggy was parked.

Mars was nothing like the Moon. For a start, the sky had colours, and you couldn't see the darkness of space. It was clearly daylight and rather nice. As I dropped the aging terrorist off, he did not lie prone, as his compatriots had done on the Moon. He tried to sit up and look around. At that moment, I caught site of the shadowy figures of two large men who emerged from somewhere that looked like an underground garage, with the door pushed up and back, revealing an entrance to a subterranean area. From above, you would never guess it existed. It just looked like rocks and earth.

The men acted so quickly that it was over in no time. They picked up the terrorist and took him into the underground garage. Then they came out to talk to me. I was beyond excited to see humans. The fact that they seemed to be breathing normally without special equipment just washed over my head in the amazement of the moment.

'Hi, great to see you! We love you!' I said, surprising myself at my emotional response.

'We love you too,' they replied in American accents.

Then one of them said, 'If you can do that, could you bring some younger people. That grandad you brought is a bit old. We need young people.'

He paused for a minute, and his friend added, 'Particularly, fit, well, female young people. They don't have to be anything special, just fit, well and female.'

'I can't promise anything,' I said. 'But I'll see what I can do.'

I went back to the local terrorists, who had been watching enthralled.

'What do you think?' I asked. 'Have you got any young people of either gender who are well behaved, fit and preferably have some skill to offer?'

The terrorists looked at each other.

'Go to Mars?' giggled one of the females.

'What about those young, virtual reality kids,' suggested a man, 'You know, the Chinese ones.'

A message was sent to the overcrowded living quarters of the terrorists' Chinese/Philippine community, and two well-scrubbed twelve-year olds, a boy and a girl, presented themselves.

I cross-questioned them a bit about their I.T. skills, but I was already aware of their proficiency at hacking, computer gaming and virtual reality special effects. I lifted the kids into the Mars environment and deposited them on the ground. They were immediately taken into the underground facility and given special shoes like the ones the Mars men were wearing. I saw them fitting the shoes on the young girl.

'Thanks,' said one of the Mars guys. 'But they are a bit young. Haven't you got any er... lady people, you know, like grown up.'

'I'll try,' I said.

I honestly couldn't think of any clean-living young ladies within the local terrorist community. Over a certain age, they all became malicious criminals breathing fire at anyone within range. Then I thought of the children that had been in the Al-Qaida batch kids programme. Not all of them had gone through the soldier training programme, as they were needed to look after the younger kids. They were in their early twenties, and spent their time doing household duties. I went to the house where they worked.

There were three of them in the kitchen area of their safe house, busily employed in cooking and washing, with little kids running in and out of the garden outside.

'Hi,' I said. 'Would any of you like a fresh start on the planet Mars, assisting some nice astronaut men?' They just laughed and got on with their work.

'Seriously,' I said. 'There is a vacancy if any of you are interested. I think there's a shortage of young women up there.'

'Well, I'm free,' said one young woman called Trisha, patting her hair. 'If it's assisting nice men you're talking about.'

My heart sank, I feared I had landed yet another young harlot. They were two a penny in the IRA outfits I had visited.

'Actually,' said one of the male terrorists, reading my mind. 'She isn't like that, she is quite suitable. We ought to have made better use of her ourselves.'

'Well, you're not paying her much at the moment,' I replied.

This was an understatement. They were not paying her at all, just board and lodgings. You could say she was a slave, but she had grown up within the terrorist unit, and knew no better.

Trisha stood proud and tall.

'I want to go, and I'm ready now.' She said.

'OK,' I said.

I carefully surrounded her energy field and lifted her out of her environment and into the Mars red earth environment. As I laid her on the ground, I heard the voice of one of the American astronauts, 'Well now, that's more like it!'

He dashed forwarded, lifting Trisha up in a chivalrous manner, and took her inside. Trisha's expression was one of sheer disbelief. She was speechless, but her shy smile said it all. She had known nothing but abuse in her short life, and meeting a nice, normal human male was as unlikely to her as landing on Mars. As I left, I caught site of her having special shoes put on her feet. The world was all before her…

On my next visit, described later, another astronaut told me that Trisha was doing well. She had settled in and picked up the skills needed to make a good contribution to the work of the team. Everyone liked her, and if I knew of any others like her, well...

But sadly, the chances of finding another industrious well-conducted female from within the terrorist community were nil.

IN THE SCIENCE LAB

After my trip to Mars, I started to wonder if the type of scientists that work on space travel might have insights into how I could deal with terrorist electromagnetic attacks. I had heard of the European Space Agency, and knew that work relating to the International Space Station programme was carried out at various universities in Europe. I looked up one in the UK, the Surrey Space Centre, and checked out photographs of it on the internet, selecting some that looked like science labs. Then I tuned into the frequency of one of the photos, and arrived instantly in what looked like a large cupboard with lots of switches and wiring in it.

From the cupboard, I found my way into a research lab containing engineering equipment. I went through a door, and down a flight of stairs into a corridor with two main laboratories on either side, one of which was partly viewable through a glass partition. There was CCTV in every room.

I decided to leave a message, which I hoped would be decoded by scientists clued up in electromagnetic technologies. I copied a photograph of the Moon, and superimposed it on the CCTV record in the first room I had visited. Then I left and went to cook my evening meal. After dinner, I was relaxing on the sofa, listening to music when I heard a woman's voice whispering, 'Look, there! It's the same person we saw on CCTV.'

'No, it isn't,' said another woman's voice. 'Her hair isn't the same.'

By now, I was wearing a parker, with the hood up, partly for shielding reasons, but mainly because it was warmer.

'Do you think she needs help?' asked the first voice. 'I saw two people with weapons of some kind pointed at her when we arrived. But now they've gone.'

'Maybe we frightened them off,' said the second voice. 'Anyway, go on then.'

'Err, excuse me,' said the first voice. 'Was it you that tried to contact us? We saw you on CCTV and traced your image here.'

'Wow!' I thought.

There was a lump in my throat as I said, 'Yes, it's me, and I was wondering if you could help me, so I left the picture.'

'Is it about those men with weapons?' asked the woman.

'Yes,' I said.

'Well, why not come on in and meet us?' the woman continued.

So, I did. I found myself in a very large room with brown wooden panels. Round the room there was a strange contraption that looked like an air conditioning duct, attached to a large glass case with what looked like measuring equipment in it. A very pretty young lady of ethnic Chinese extraction, wearing a white coat, was busy attending to the equipment.

The room was divided into two sections by a wooden partition about four feet high. On the other side of the partition were six young women in white coats, holding note books.

These, as I later found out, were international postgraduate students from countries allowed to participate in science training courses. The two women who invited me in also wore white coats. They were both tall with brown hair, tied in low pony tails. They pointed to some chairs round a wooden table, offering a seat for me. I could tell that they were the senior managers of the section.

'I'm Alison,' said the one who invited me in. 'And this is my sister, Bronwyn.'

I introduced myself and explained about the terrorists who were attacking me.

'We don't have any trouble with them,' said Bronwyn.

She picked up a metal device that looked like a fire lighter and putting on some dark goggles, scanned round my body. Every so often she pulled the trigger on the fire-lighter, and, within the electromagnetic environment, I could see men falling onto the ground, and lying there like dead flies.

'Thank you,' I said, feeling greatly relieved.

'Why did you leave a picture of the Moon?' asked Alison. 'Is it because of our work?'

'Oh, I don't know anything about your work,' I said. 'I just put up a picture on your CCTV to see if you could figure out how I did it. If you could, then I thought you would probably have the kind of technologies to help me.'

'Well, we have all kind of technologies,' said Alison. 'But why did you pick the Moon? You do know this is a space research facility, don't you?'

'Yes,' I said. 'Since the terrorists started attacking me with electromagnetic weapons, I've found a way to explore the Moon and Mars using the electromagnetic technologies that I'm connected to. Do you have anything like that?'

There was a silence.

'Are you saying that you have visited the Moon and Mars like you are visiting us?' said Alison.

'Yes,' I nodded.

I explained how I started off trying to dump terrorists off the planet, to get rid of them, and how I found that some people could live on the Moon.

'Did you go to Mars, then?' asked Bronwyn.

'Yes,' I said. 'But not as much as the Moon. I just dropped a terrorist off there at first. Then some men came out of what looked like an underground garage, and took him inside.'

'Did you talk to the men?' asked Alison. Her voice had gone very quiet.

'I met some Americans,' I said. 'And they asked me if I could bring young people to join their community.'

'And did you?' continued Alison.

'I brought two ethnic Chinese youngsters who were good at IT, and a young lady from the terrorist community who wanted a new start in life...' I replied.

My voice trailed off. Alison put her head in her hands. She leant against the wooden panelling, her shoulders shaking as she sobbed. Bronwyn went to comfort her, putting her arms around her.

'It's all right, it's all right,' she said, trying to sooth her sister.

Alison lifted her head, tears pouring down her cheeks.

'I could never have that chance,' she sobbed. 'And now other people can go, just like that.'

'Well, I could take you,' I said, trying to cheer her up.

Alison grabbed my arm.

'Could you? Could you really?'

'Sure,' I said. 'When would you like to go?'

Alison stopped crying and started laughing.

'I must just go and check a few things,' she said, wiping her tears.

Grabbing a contraption that looked a bit like a cell phone. She dashed out of the room.

Bronwyn came over and sat beside me.

'Alison's husband is up there now,' she said. 'He is not due back for another year, and Alison is finding it hard.'

She paused.

'And my friend is up there, too,' she added.

'Well, I could take you as well,' I said.

The young Chinese scientist came over to me.

'Hi, I'm Annette. Did I hear you say you could take people up to Mars?'

'Yes,' I said.

Annette looked enquiringly at Bronwyn.

'If I could be spared...' she began.

At that moment, the six postgraduate students on the other side of the room started shouting, 'And we all want to go too. If Annette goes, it's only fair that we should go too.'

'We can all go!' laughed Annette clapping her hands.

'Now, hang on a minute,' I said. 'Shouldn't you check first with the people up there? They might be rather busy, and there might be rules about that sort of thing.'

At that moment, Alison came running into the room waving her arms excitedly.

'I can go! I can go! It's arranged!'

All the women began laughing and chattering at once. They made so much noise that the door to the laboratory opened and a tall kindly-looking elderly man in a white coat, looked in.

'Bronwyn, can I have a word?' He spoke with a strange accent that I couldn't quite place.

'What is going on?' he asked.

As Bronwyn explained what had happened, the expression on his face changed from puzzlement to disbelief, and he burst out laughing. Then he went out.

'That's Lars,' said Bronwyn. 'He doesn't work with us. He runs courses for postgraduate foreign students in astrophysics, as well as his own research.'

At that moment, there were sounds of a scuffle outside, as if several people were trying to turn the door handle at once. Five men in white coats, from the Far East, put their heads round the door. They took in the scene, talking fast in a language I didn't understand, and looking inquisitively at the women, who were, by now, racing round the room tidying up, as if in preparation to depart.

'I wonder when all these trips to Mars are supposed to start,' I said to myself. 'Even if the trips are approved, the Mars people won't want everyone at once.'

Then I remembered how pleased the American astronauts had been when even one young lady arrived.

'Mm, there again...' I thought. 'They are all young, fit and female...'

Alison came over and sat next to me.

'It's been agreed that I can go for a week, while Bronwyn holds the fort here,' she said. 'And then it's Bronwyn's turn to go for a week. Annette can do some of our work while we are both away, and after that, she and our six students here' — she waved in the direction of the young women, 'can all go together for a weekend. They won't be allowed into the research facilities, but there is a visitors centre where they can socialise with the locals, and get shown a few things.'

'Great,' I said. 'How soon can you be ready.'

Alison looked at me with a mixture of hope and fear.

'I know it's a bit short notice,' she began.

'Oh, you want to go now, of course, don't you,' I said, smiling.

Alison clutched a small overnight case.

'If possible, please,' she said.

'Let's go then,' I said.

I surrounded her magnetic field with an electromagnetic envelope, and lifted her up, turning my consciousness towards the underground garage entrance I had visited previously on Mars. As we arrived, I placed her carefully in the doorway of the garage. A tall, fit man in his thirties reached out and grabbed her, picking her up and swinging her round in his arms. He went inside the facility and I could see them, arms tight around each other, laughing and crying at the same time.

Another man came forward to me. He picked up Alison's overnight case.

'Can you return at the same time in eight days to collect her?' he asked.

'Sure,' I said. 'And I will bring her sister, Bronwyn, as well. See you then.'

I left and returned to the science lab, where the other women were just leaving. I agreed times and dates for the other visits with Bronwyn, and went home to bed. It had been an emotionally draining day.

YOUNG, FIT AND FEMALE

The day before I was due to go back to Mars to pick up Alison, I went back to the science lab to check with Bronwyn that everything was still going ahead as planned.

Bronwyn said that everything was fine, but as I was going, Annette said, 'Excuse me, Martha, Lars would like to ask you something.'

'OK,' I said.

Annette led the way to the white-haired scientist's room across the corridor. Lars's room was the same as the other lab, and was also divided into two parts. Lars's desk and books were on one side, and through the wooden partition, I could see the same equipment as in the other lab, that looked like air conditioning ducts attached to a clear glass box with measuring equipment inside. Lars was sitting at his desk, writing.

'Oh, hello,' said Lars, not looking up from his work.

'The lady is here, Lars,' said Annette.

'Yes,' said Lars.

He pushed a piece of paper towards me. It had yellow powder on it.

'Can you go and find me some more of that, out in space, please?' he said.

'Well, I don't know,' I said, looking at the yellow powder. 'I can give it a try.'

'OK, then,' said Lars, and he returned to writing notes in his log book.

I fixed my gaze on the powder. I tried to tune into the frequency of it, and archive the memory. Then, I turned my consciousness into whatever "space" might mean, and started to search for a frequency match to what Lars had shown me. At first, it was all black, and then I was staggered to see the unmistakeable image of the planet Saturn loom into view.

'It's the rings,' I thought. 'I'll see if they match.'

They did. So I dived into the rotating wheels of rocks and dust and grabbed some stuff. I mentally created a transparent plastic bag and dropped the stuff into it. Then I returned to Lars's work room.

'Is this any good?' I asked, putting the plastic bag on his desk.

Lars turned to Annette.

'Can you see to that, please.' he said.

Annette picked up the bag and went into the corridor, in order to get to the side of Lars's room where the air conditioning ducts were. I followed her to see what she would do. Annette opened the transparent glass case, and using a metal spoon, placed some of the powder on what looked like a weighing table. Then she went to a control panel and activated some equipment.

There was a roaring noise, and a yellow material with the consistency of hard fudge came out at the other end of the ducting, onto a large tray. The powdery rocks that Annette put on the weighing table measured about a quarter of a teaspoon, but what came out of the ducting was a flat material about three feet long, and one inch high. Annette cut a small slice out of the material, using a laser, and took it into Lars's room. She laid it on his desk.

'Ah,' said Lars. 'Now let's see.'

He switched on a machine on his desk which lit up. Lars placed the material inside it. Annette went to another piece of equipment at the side of the room, and activated it. Some A3 size papers came out of a printer. One contained a table with a list of variables and rows of numbers, and the other showed a spectrum of colours which provided the visual equivalent of the numeric table.

Lars studied the table and the spectrum of colours carefully. Then he opened a draw in his desk, and drew out a similar set of papers. It looked as if he was comparing the two sets of papers.

Then he smiled and looked up at me for the first time.

'Good,' he said. 'You seem to have brought back what we wanted. Now, can you go back again, and this time, please can you only gather material from the inside rings.'

'OK,' I said, and off I went.

When I came back, Lars was much more forthcoming. When the printouts were produced, he put on his glasses, and muttered things to himself, in another language. Then he removed his glasses and turned to me.

'That is very interesting,' he said. 'Thank you. Are you willing to get other things from time to time?'

'Oh, sure,' I said, glad that what I had brought back was OK. 'I'll see you around,' and I left.

Afterwards, it occurred to me that Lars already knew the specifications of the first sample that I brought him, as he had them in his desk draw. He was just testing me to see if I had really gone out and done what he asked. After all, I could have picked up some yellow stuff from anywhere. He needed to be sure about the validity of what I brought back and about my reliability.

Next day, I collected Bronwyn from the science lab and took her to the Mars base. She was thrilled by the whole experience. Her partner was standing in the gateway of the underground entrance, waiting. When she arrived, he took her hand and they just stood together, making the most of that moment. Then he put his arm round her and they quickly disappeared from sight.

Then, Alice and her husband came out to the gateway together. They must have said their goodbyes already. They held on to each other until the guard murmured that the time had come. Alice turned her face away, to hide her tears, and her husband gave her a last sad look, before turning back into the underground entrance. I picked up Alice and her suitcase and deposited them back in the science lab. Alice immediately left for home, and did not come in to work for the rest of the week. I heard she was visiting her husband's family, to let them know how he was, and to pass on personal messages.

At the end of the following week, I took Bronwyn home. She was much happier in herself than Alice had been, and said she had really enjoyed her week "away". Alice was back at work now, and Bronwyn took some time off. Seven days later, it was the turn of Annette and the six science students. When I went to collect them, they were buzzing with excitement, all smartly dressed, as if they were going to a party. And that wasn't far wrong, as it turned out.

News of their impending arrival at the predominantly male Mars base had created quite a stir. I could see men looking out of portholes inside the underground walkway as the girls arrived. A senior officer came out to welcome them formally to the base. As they went in, they were laughing and waving to the welcome party, stopping for a moment to take in the alien landscape, before they disappeared from view.

They were still in high spirits two days later, when I returned to collect them, waving goodbye to their newfound friends and promising to pass on messages to families back home. They bounced back into the science lab and dashed off into the outside world. Physically, they had returned, but it was several days before they really came down to earth.

When I went to collect the girls back from the Mars base, a senior officer asked me if I would mind making just one more trip to bring someone from Earth the following day. I agreed, and returned the next day. The senior officer was waiting. He beckoned forward a young man called Natal, who turned out to be from Spain. Natal took out his mobile. It probably didn't work out there, but it had pictures of friends and family on Earth. Natal showed a picture of himself with another young man. The two men were smiling for the camera, with their arms around each other's shoulders. I looked at the image of the other young man.

'Is he expecting a visit from me?' I asked, thinking it could be rather a shock if he had not been warned in advance.

'Yes,' said Natal, smiling broadly. 'He knows what to do. He is waiting.'

'OK,' I said. 'I'll be right back.'

I recalled the image of the young man in the photo, and focused on it, as I turned back towards Earth. In a few seconds, I was in a pleasant kitchen-diner. There were bookcases everywhere. Sun poured in through wooden venetian blinds, and I guessed I might be in Spain. For a moment, my eyes were blinded by the bright sunlight. Then I could see the young man, leaning back against the wall. He looked expectantly into my face.

'Hi,' I said. 'Your friend has sent me. Do you know about that?'

The young man took a deep breath and nodded.

'Yes, I am ready,' he said. Then he shut his eyes.

I quickly picked him up and transported him to the entrance of the Mars base. As the young man opened his eyes, Natal's arms were already around him, holding him tightly. They walked together down the underground walkway, in a dream. The senior officer came forward again.

'Very many thanks for your assistance. You will not need to return to collect the young man. In this case it is a one-way trip.'

As I left, I caught sight of men working on the surface of Mars. Some of them wore transparent, protective clothing over sand-coloured boiler suits and sand-coloured hard hats. They were holding what looked like Geiger counters. In the background, there was a mechanical digger, the same colour as the sand, apparently scouring out a hole in the ground.

I returned home, and took some time out in the garden, which had turned into a jungle, owing to my recent lack of attention.

Next week, Alice was on day shift. I looked in to see if Lars wanted anything, and found Alice bewailing her fate, surrounded by Annette and the six students.

'I just can't stand it,' said Alice. 'I can't focus on my work any more. I'm going out of my mind. It's no good telling me I will see him in eleven months. I want him now, and he's not here.'

The girls tried to boost her morale.

'Eleven months is a long time,' said one girl, sympathetically.

'If I were you,' said another, 'I would just go out and get yourself the proverbial. I'm sure your husband would understand.'

The other girls burst out laughing at this, but Alice still did not cheer up.

Then a scuffling noise could be heard at the top of one wall, where there was a small, opaque glass partition adjoining the next room. Annette went over to investigate. She seemed to be talking to someone through the partition.

'What is it?' asked Alice.

'It's one of the Indonesian male students from Lars's group,' said Annette. 'He says if you're serious about needing temporary support, he is offering his services.'

At this, the girls all laughed even more, but Alice did not see the funny side of it.

'Right, that's it,' she said, grabbing her bag. 'I'm going home,' and she walked out, slamming the door.

She did not reappear for several weeks, and I heard she had gone into therapy. In her absence, Annette was temporarily promoted to her post, and I saw quite a bit of her, as she also worked with Lars on his outer space exploration work.

Lars called me in to his room. He wanted me to go to a planet I had never heard of. He wrote the name down on a bit of paper. It said: '55 CANCRI e.'

'Can you go there and get some rock, please?' he said.

I went home and searched for it on the internet. Apparently, it had been discovered in 2004 and was in the Milky Way, quite nearby. What made it interesting was that some scientists believed that it was made up mainly of carbon in the form of diamonds and graphite. Some reports suggested that at least a third of the planet could be pure diamond. Other reports suggested that was most unlikely. But there was nothing on the internet that I could use to get me to the planet.

I returned to Lars's office. The scrappy paper was still on his desk. Lars looked up when I arrived. I pointed to the scrappy paper, and shook my head.

'That means nothing to me,' I said. 'I must have a photograph, otherwise I can't find it.'

Lars called one of his students in, and asked him to bring a large ring binder full of photographs. Together, they leafed through it until they found the right page. Then, Lars pushed it towards me, so I could see. What I saw was a photo showing the blackness of space, with lots of lights, some small and some large, some bright and some dim.

'Please can you circle the right one,' I said.

Lars drew a white circle round one of the smaller dimmer lights.

'Oh no,' I thought. 'How will I find it?'

But I said I would do my best, and off I went. I focussed on the image in the photograph, and aimed at it as hard as I could. I really hadn't a clue what to expect, or how far it was to the ground, when suddenly, I had landed face first and bumped my nose.

'Well, at least I've hit something,' I thought, as I drilled down into the ground. My mission was to bring back some rock, so I hacked a large chunk off. But it was going to be too big for laboratory purposes. I put it in a bag, found a place in space that I could return to by memory, and stuck it there. Then I cut a much smaller piece off, put it in a plastic bag and returned to the science lab. With my mind, I sliced the rock up into very thin pieces, and placed one on the glass weighing table. I left the plastic bag inside the glass case.

Lars asked Annette to activate the ducting machine. What came out at the other end was quite a surprise. It was hard, shiny and reflective, much more glassy than natural diamonds are, when found in the earth. Lars was quite pleased with the results, but not ecstatic. He confirmed that it was a very hard material. I wondered if the material could have industrial applications, but Lars was not particularly interested in that. However, a few minutes later, I saw Annette in the other science lab, wearing an absolutely blinding diamond on a chain round her neck. When she moved, the light flashed from every facet. She looked stunning.

'Did you make that just now?' I asked.

'Yes,' she said.

'How?' I asked.

'I can use this equipment to do many things,' she said.

I suspected that she had created a blueprint, programmed it into the machine, and produced the finished product at the touch of a button. But Annette did not reveal how she had done it.

'Give me one too,' said another girl student.

'I don't think you should,' I whispered to Annette. 'This research must carry a high classification. Even if the students have been cleared to work here, they ought not to take samples home, as the UK would lose its unique selling point — access to a resource unavailable to any other country in the world.'

I was already thinking of manufacturing possibilities for Britain. But Annette wanted to please her friends. She privately made pendants for all of them. Lars couldn't care less either. He was busy writing performance appraisals for the Indonesian research group that he supervised. I began to wonder whether the security arrangements at the science lab were all that they should be. I mentioned my concerns to Bertram, at the British Intelligence Special Services office.

Shortly afterwards, a security officer was appointed to work specifically inside the science building. He tightened up security procedures quite a bit. There was more locking up of sensitive things at night, and more checking of access rights to certain parts of the building. You might think that this had already been fully covered under existing arrangements. The rules certainly existed, but compliance had lapsed a lot, partly because scientists are very focussed on their work, and not so interested in red tape. Then I heard that one of the male students from overseas had been asked to leave. It turned out that he had several different passports, and was not what he appeared to be.

An added bonus of this enhanced security was my introduction to a military research specialist called Max. He wore a white coat, like Lars, but his work was exclusively to do with weapons. I knew nothing about what he did, but occasionally he would ask me if I could match a particular stone somewhere on Earth.

On one occasion, after delivering some rocks to him from the Bering Straits, Max asked me to go over and sit in a clinical chair. It looked like the one that I had seen in the MI5 research lab, when Elliot removed a Nano-device from behind my ear. A bright light went on, and he unwrapped a needle from a container. There was silence for a few minutes, during which Max was doing something to my head. It did not hurt. Then Max switched off the light.

'Thank you, you can go now,' he said.

He was examining the needle under a microscope. I could see a tiny device attached to it. Max had removed the microchip that the terrorists used to track me with, and was studying the serial number on it.

A few days later, Lars asked me if I would get some material from somewhere called Kronos. He wrote it down for me, and I looked it up on the internet. According to several reports, Kronos was a binary star, with a partner star called Krios. What was special about Kronos was that it had devoured about fifteen planets. There was a good photo of it on the internet, and I was able to find it from that.

I harvested some of the gas from the star, and cooled it to the point that it crystallised. Then I took a large crystal to Lars's laboratory and placed it on the glass weighing table. Annette operated the equipment, which enabled the material to retain its properties within the Earth's atmosphere. A grey stone with marbling and coloured streaks came out of the process. I guessed that the reason the material came out bigger than it went in was to do with the different air pressure and gravity on Earth.

Several research students in white coats were hovering around waiting for the output to appear. I cut six thin strips off it, using a mental laser, and the students took it to Lars, for him to analyse using a spectrometer. They crowded round him, and scientists from other parts of the building joined them. The results confirmed that a wide range of metals were present in unusually large quantities, suggesting that Kronos had indeed eaten a lot of planetary rocks.

After that, Lars asked me to carry out several more assignments, collecting rock samples from the planets, Uranus, Neptune and Pluto. I loved exploring the solar system. Neptune had a bluish glow, and Pluto looked a bit like a cappuccino with chocolate powder sprinkled on top. But Uranus was spectacular. There was a pale blue-green glassy sea, with transparent blue-green glassy rock formations on it. I used to lie on a smooth flat rock, looking at the light of the sun shining dimly through a natural glassy arch. It was very restful.

Annette liked the rock samples from Uranus as well. She produced a beautiful blue-green pendant in the shape of a wish-bone, which she wore on a chain round her neck. It looked amazing. I remembered Annette telling me that she had done her PhD in a European university, and spent eighteen months working with NASA. She was seriously high-powered.

HER MAJESTY'S SPECIAL PRISON SERVICES

In the book *'Terror in Britain'* I described how, thanks to enhanced technology upgrades, some UK prisons were able to detect terrorist electromagnetic activity, and how dedicated men and women prison officers had worked in their own free time to rescue me from terrorist attacks, and to capture thousands of terrorists. This work continued, but things changed when the terrorists started to import young children and youths into the front line.

In the old days, members of the International Unity Guild had received money from Al-Qaida to bring up batches of child soldiers. But in 2014, Al-Qaida cancelled that part of the contract with the IRA and its associated terrorist groups. The terrorists continued to use kids in child brothels until the age of eight, after which they got no income from keeping them. The terrorists tried to get the kids killed by dressing them up as adults, magnifying their height, which is possible in the electromagnetic environment, and forcing them to operate electronic weapons in my direction.

It was not hard to spot the kids, usually in groups of twenty, looking terrified and confused. As soon as I saw the kids, members of H.M. Special Prison Services would pick up what I was seeing and would make contact with me. They would suddenly appear, looking down from a hole in the sky of the electromagnetic environment, and ask me, 'How old are they?'

If the kids were about twelve years old or above, the prison officers would ask me to bring them into their area, where they would rescue them. The way I did this was by selecting one of the kids first, bringing him or her into the Prison Service's electromagnetic area, and removing the invisible metal hat that all participants in the electromagnetic environment wore to keep them in that state. When I did this, all other kids linked to the same computer I.P. address were automatically pulled in. They flew in through the air, landing in a row behind the first.

My main contacts in the Prison Service were Mike and Tanya. Mike was a warm-hearted man, tall, with brown hair, in his late thirties. He wore a dark brown uniform designed for working in the electromagnetic environment. Originally, he had been in charge of the technical side, but with so many kids constantly arriving, he began to develop new skills. The kids were often very traumatised, and Mike would quickly gauge what they needed. If the kids could get up and walk, he would usher them into a reception centre dedicated to victims of electromagnetic attacks. If they needed stretchers, he would call in the rescue team to assist him.

The rescued kids were mainly boys, but if there were any girls, then a woman prison officer called Tanya would come running out and take them by the hand, leading them to safety. Tanya was a tall, motherly woman with fair hair, in her early forties, wearing a white uniform with a fitted top and a full skirt. She always found the right words to welcome the kids, as if they were her own, putting them at ease. When the kids saw Mike and Tanya, their little faces lit up. You could see that they now felt safe in the company of adults, perhaps for the first time. They instinctively trusted their rescuers.

If the kids were under twelve, the Prison Service was not permitted to accept them. But by now I had found a way to protect them from being used in the electromagnetic environment. I would purge all the microchips and cranial implants from their bodies, using a beam of energy from my mind, and I would disconnect them from the terrorists' WIFI communications and ultrasound synthetic telepathy system with a series of criss-cross gestures. When I did this, a transparent X mark appeared on the foreheads of each child, between their eyebrows. That mark prevented the terrorists' computer systems from registering the kids. They could never be forced to work in the electromagnetic environment again.

One evening, I looked into the terrorists' area of operations, and down into their underground pathways. I could see over twenty small bodies lying limply on the floor, supervised by an African terrorist, like those I had seen in Lesotho. I quickly removed the terrorist and went to see what had happened to the children.

'Are they dead?' I wondered.

I saw a child slightly move its head. Then I caught sight of its leg. It was manacled in a kind of man trap device. If the child pulled against the manacle, it tightened further, until the child was in agony. I gave a cry of horror. The good people of H.M. Special Prison Services immediately heard me and looked in. One of the women prison officers gave a gasp. Then there was a rush, as I and all the prison officers, raced to release the children.

It was not all that easy. The manacles had to be carefully removed to avoid hurting the children more. Tragically, some of them already had broken ankles. The emergency rescue team brought stretchers. The children were taken into the Special Prison Services reception centre. They were all Canadians. There was no explanation as to how the kids came to be there. They may have been child brothel batch kids, formerly funded by the Al-Qaida programme, who were sold by Canadian terrorists to African traffickers, once they were over eight years old.

Sometimes, children would arrive packaged in cases like Egyptian sarcophagi, several kids to each. It was not easy to extricate them, and I brought them into the Prison Service. Mike and several other men would run forward, carefully opening the packing cases, and untying the arms and legs of the children. The kids were usually very young, having being imported to provide child brothel services to the terrorists. The kids were sometimes in a bad state, and it was very stressful for the men of the Special Prison Service, having to help get the kids out. In these cases, it didn't matter what age the kids were, the Prison Service took them in.

One day, I brought some extra-large packing cases into the Prison Service. Mike helped me to open the first one. As we looked in, we saw several children tied in a sitting position, their legs bent under and secured to small wicker chairs. It took a long time to disentangle the children's legs from the chairs. Jack, another prison officer, came to help. The children were unable to walk, and needed immediate medical attention. We were all very shocked at what we saw. Jack clenched his fist.

'I know what I'd like to do to those monsters,' he said.

I agreed with him. It turned out that the reason the children were packaged like that was so that their traffickers could claim they were younger than they actually were, and therefore, worth more money. The packing cases were designed for small kids, but the terrorists were determined to squeeze older children in.

I did not see Mike for a while. Then one day, when I was bringing in a group of teenage Canadian boys rescued from the battlefield, I saw him. He was training a team of men on how to untie the legs of kids from wicker chairs, using plastic doll-like figures for practice. Later, I heard that he led a team of prison officers who searched for kids in packing cases within the terrorist electromagnetic environment, rescuing hundreds. Mike became a child rescue specialist, and resources were found from within the Ministry of Defence to fund this work.

As well as rescuing children, the Prison Service's electromagnetics team were able to repatriate them to other countries, by arrangement with NATO allies. There were a lot of youths from Canada needing to be returned home, and an equally large number of younger children from the Irish Republic. Occasionally, we would get groups of kids from Lesotho and The Democratic Republic of Congo.

Sometimes, the prison officers were too busy to repatriate the kids, as they had many other duties to attend to. When that happened, I would gather the children up into an electromagnetic envelope, and take them back to their country. When I took kids back to the Irish Republic, I took them to the United States NATO people I had met in the first chapter. They arranged for the children to be handed over to the Irish Republic.

When I took kids back to Canada, I went to a place in Ottawa where I knew the Canadian military were hunting terrorists and taking them into custody. Their priority was to rescue Canadians who had been forced into terrorism, and pass them to Government agencies who could rehabilitate them. Whenever I went there, they were always very supportive.

It was a different story when I went to Lesotho. I was not sure where to repatriate the kids. I had seen terrorists operating in the jungle near a main road. On the other side of the road, there was a high wire fence, containing a secure Western compound. It looked official, with modern red brick buildings, so I delivered the children in there. A white Caucasian man came out and thanked me for returning them to safety. He had a Canadian accent. All seemed well, but the kids were not happy at all. They looked at me as if I had betrayed them. I wondered if the Canadian was all that he should be. One way to find out was to see if I could select him using electromagnetics. If I could, he must be one of the terrorists. So, I tried that, and sure enough, I was able to pick him up.

I went straight to where Mike was working, and told him what had happened. He directed me to some Special Service people who worked in the building next door. It was a hot, sunny day, and they were sitting outside, working on a terrace, because their building had no air conditioning. Len, the man in charge, asked me to deliver the Canadian to them, so I deposited him in front of them, and withdrew. Five minutes later, they were back to me.

'Could you please go to the place in Lesotho where you picked up the man?' said Len.

I went straight there.

'Just stand there, please,' said Len. 'We need to get a fix on the location.'

Then I heard another man saying, 'Right, we've got it. OK, thanks, you can go now.'

'Fine,' I said.

As I was leaving, I could see Special Service personnel reaching down through the sky of the electromagnetic environment. They were grabbing people from the building which the Canadian terrorist worked in. There were terrorists running out of the building in all directions. It turned out that these villains had been posing as a charity helping African children in Lesotho, while running a trafficking racket to European destinations. The place was closed down, and the children were taken to a place of safety by the British Special Services team.

After that, Canadian and Irish terrorists began attacking me constantly. I countered these attacks by selecting perpetrators in large groups and shouting, 'Return to sender!' This created a whirlwind, which picked them up and deposited them in a British military collection centre. The centre was manned by electromagnetic technical specialists who worked alongside H.M. Special Prison Services. They closely monitored electromagnetic threats in the UK, and kept an eye on my welfare.

These Special Technical Service people created a force field which pulled all the terrorists out of the whirlwind and into an electromagnetic well, where a sifting process identified any terrorists wearing an electronic tag put there by the authorities.

The tags were checked and entered on a computer system, to update counter-terrorism records. Whatever happened to these people had to be recorded. The terrorists arrived in an unconscious state, in their electromagnetic miniaturised form. If they were to be removed from the planet, an electronic system directed them to a wire fence on the roof, which was charged in such a way that it dematerialised them. If you have seen the movie '*Whose Afraid of Roger Rabbit,*' it worked in the same way as the dissolving fluid that disintegrated cartoon characters in Toon Town.

Despite these arrangements, the volume of terrorists was getting a bit much. At the time of writing, in most countries, electromagnetic terrorist activities were not covered by any laws, which meant that procedures for dealing with them had not been formally agreed.

I knew a local British Army garrison near where I lived, that was able to see electromagnetic terrorists and detect their activities. I had spoken to the major there before. I checked his office, and he did not seem too busy, so I knocked and went in.

He looked up, and his face fell on seeing me. He looked sad and ashamed. I expressed my frustration.

'I've got hundreds of terrorists every day to deal with, and what are you doing about it?' I said.

The major looked extremely uncomfortable. His orders were to maintain a watching brief but not to intervene, because terrorists who were nationals of allied countries — Ireland, Canada and the United States, were involved.

'You'd better take the Canadians to the place across the road,' he muttered.

'What's that?' I asked.

'It's the Canadian NATO building,' he said.

'Ah,' I said.

I thanked him and went across the road. There were some large locked gates leading to a compound. There was a small door in the side of one of the locked gates that looked as if it might open, so I knocked on it. A man in military uniform looked out.

'Can I talk to someone about Canadian terrorists, please?' I said.

'Come in,' said the man, and he escorted me inside the hallway of the main building.

A few minutes later, a tall man with reddish hair came out.

'Nice to meet you, at last,' he said. 'There are some new developments which may interest you. From now on, there will be Canadian military staff operating in an electromagnetic force field adjoining the terrorists' main field of activity, near where you live. We are offering all Canadian terrorists an opportunity to return home, if they go there. All they have to do is arrive, and we will immediately transport them back to Canada.'

'Does that mean I can pick up groups of Canadians and drop them off there?' I asked.

'Sure,' he said. 'You can start now.'

'Great,' I said. 'Thanks very much,' I left.

I went back to the terrorists' main operating area. It was an electromagnetic architecture construct, containing several buildings on both sides of a small road, which ended in a cul-de-sac. It was a miniature version of the real world, and when the terrorists operated within it, they were correspondingly reduced in scale, the idea being that they would not be detected within an area that took up no more space than a large room.

On one side of the road, was the 'Group One' psychological warfare headquarters. It was a square building

74

with a flat roof, housing three floors. Originally, psychological warfare had been intended as work for women terrorists. The Group One computer system would not accept people into the psychological warfare area, unless they were wearing a dress as their uniform, whether they were female or not.

The ground floor of the psychological warfare building was used by low-ranking staff, IRA child brothel managers, and their children. The first floor was used by IRA staff, supervisors — some trained in scientific and technical research assassination skills, synthetic telepathy operatives and Non-Commissioned IRA Officers. The top floor was occupied by IRA unit staff, IRA mafia henchmen, and senior IRA officers.

When I woke up in the morning, I often found myself on the first floor of the psychological warfare building, where IRA staff wearing headphones, addressed me and each other via microphones, using synthetic telepathy. They could tell if I was mentally present there, as they had what they called a "light box". This looked like a glass sphere resting in a black container. It contained a CD of my biodata. When I was awake, a light would come on in the sphere. The technicians in charge of the cameras in my eyes would connect my internal gaze to whatever the light box was pointing at. They would try to keep my interest in this internal scene, and engage me in abusive conversation. If I chose, I could appear in an electromagnetic form, clearly visible to the terrorists.

On the other side of the road was the 'Group Two' weapons division. These people lived in a modern building, where electromagnetic weapons were stored and supplied to the troops assigned there. The men all wore black wet suits, covering everything except their faces. The suits were designed to give them shielding against electromagnetic radiation and electronic weapons. A lot of Canadian terrorists, aged eighteen to early twenties, worked there.

Weapons Group troops lived below ground in three large rooms leading to an underground electromagnetic pathway that connected them with terrorist units up and down the country. In one room, men were stored in "stasis", a state of suspended animation which could be easily reversed by flicking a switch. The other two rooms were for men to come round from stasis, get washed and dressed. The Canadians were kept here, before they were ordered out onto the main field of operations.

I wondered where the Canadian military were operating their force field. I looked up the road to the cul-de-sac end. The road ended in a large tarmac turning area. There was a flight of stairs leading down from that area into a garden. On the other side of the garden were two flights of stairs leading up to a veranda with two electromagnetic portals. A man and woman in Canadian military uniform were standing there.

'Is this the place to bring the Canadian terrorists to?' I asked.

'That's right,' said the woman, smiling. 'Just direct the Canadians to come here, and we will do the rest.'

'Right,' I thought. 'Let's try this out.'

I went back to the Group Two building and down into the basement. There were twenty young men about eighteen years old, getting kitted up in their black wet suits.

'Any of you want to go back to Canada?' I asked.

Some of the men looked up, questioningly at me. It was clear that they knew who I was.

'Your military have a doorway here to take you home, if you want to go,' I continued.

'Can you fix for us to get there?' said one of the young men. 'We can't get out by ourselves, we are locked in.'

'I can take you all there now,' I said, 'Just gather together in the centre of the room, and I will pick you up.'

The men hastily gathered into a group, and I lifted them up and dropped them off in the tarmac turning area. They looked a little disorientated.

'Just go down the steps,' I said.

The men cautiously began to walk down the steps.

'Hi there everyone!' called the Canadian military man. 'This way down.'

The men came down into the garden and stood looking at him.

'You'll need to take off that gear,' he said.

'But we've only got underwear on underneath,' said one of the men.

'Oh, let them go through like that,' said the Canadian military woman.

'Let them have suitable clothes that they feel good in,' I thought to myself.

To my astonishment, the young men's clothes were immediately transformed into all kinds of warm casual gear, leather jackets, big, baggy trousers and boots. They pressed round the staircases.

'Can we go home now,' they asked.

'OK, guys, this way,' said the Canadian military man.

The men filed up the stairs to one of the doorways and walked through. I watched where they went. Inside, there was a walkway about five yards long, and at the end you could see another doorway leading to daylight. As the men went into the light, they emerged out of the electromagnetic environment onto the pavement of a Canadian road, where several large coaches were waiting. The coaches were going to different parts of Canada. A military man was asking each of the youths where they used to live in Canada, and directing them to the appropriate coach. Several smiling Canadian soldiers stood nearby. Some of them were armed. They were taking no chances with the former terrorists.

MAGICK TABLE RESTAURANTS

An unexpected effect of the NATO technical enhancements was an increase in my ability to control the electromagnetic environment. I had only to think of something I wanted to happen with focussed intent, and it happened.

The day after the first group of Canadian youths were rescued, I looked along the road to the Canadian military portals. I was amazed to see a queue of blue coaches, each capable of carrying forty people, stretching back down the road and out of sight. Young men wearing white running gear were getting off the coaches, and sprinting the last few yards to the Canadian portal point. The coaches were turning round in the tarmac turning area, and edging their way carefully back down the narrow lane, now packed with vehicles.

Down in the garden, the Canadian military were directing young men up both staircases to the two gateways. The place was packed with returning Canadians. There must have been several hundred of them. Some of the coach drivers had driven through the night from all points in the British Isles. They looked exhausted.

'What they need is some coffee and food, and washrooms,' I thought.

Then I remembered how the Canadian men had been given new clothes, when I wished for them. I looked for a suitable point where refreshments and facilities could be located. It had to be on the opposite side of the road to where coaches were parked. I selected a suitable place.

'Let there be a place where people can get any food and drink they want, and where they can sit down, with nearby toilets.' I thought.

It wasn't a clever, well-considered command, but it did the job. I spoke to the driver of the first coach in the queue.

'If you go and stand over there, by that niche in the bank, and think what you want to drink or eat, it will be there,' I said.

The driver looked across the road. A young terrorist was watching with interest.

'I can get it for you,' he said. 'What do you want?'

The driver laughed.

'What do I want? Well now, what I really want is steak and chips, and a takeaway coffee. Can you do that for me?'

He was a man of little faith, but the young terrorist was not. He went confidently to the niche in the bank and thought about the food the driver had specified. A plate of steak and chips appeared there, with a knife and fork, wrapped in a paper napkin, together with a plastic cup and top, filled with coffee. The boy took the food and handed it up to the driver. The driver said nothing at first. He just got on with eating the food, and drinking the coffee. After he'd finished, he sighed.

'That was good,' he said, and he gave the boy a small tip. Then he started up the engine of his coach, and went to the turning point at the end of the cul-de-sac. As he came back the other way, he smiled and gave me a wave. Then he and his coach disappeared.

The next coach drove to the head of the queue, and the driver looked out.

'Where's the food, please?' he asked.

The young terrorist leaped up with alacrity. He had found himself a gainful occupation.

On the ground floor of the psychological warfare building, a young Irish mafia male, dressed as a woman — a requirement for those who worked on the psychological warfare side, pressed his nose against the window.

'They are having food,' he said.

A number of elderly tramps, who had once been low-level terrorists, were hanging around the compound in case they could earn a few pence lifting and carrying equipment. They emerged from a hut and made their way across the road. The young lad showed them how to get things to eat and drink. One of them ordered a whole roast turkey. It came on a huge plate, with a carving knife and fork. The tramp staggered with it to a table, and began working his way through it. Afterwards, he went to sleep on the ground.

I realised that the terrorists made no provision for feeding their staff during working hours, and some staff had no official method of getting food at all, relying on the good will of others who lived nearby.

That night, the terrorists sent in waves of perpetrators to attack me with lasers and electromagnetic oscillators. I removed them all. Then the Group Two underground staff delivery system, which looked a bit like an airport luggage carousel, disgorged another wave of "warriors" wearing black "Darth Vader" uniforms. They were not very tall, and I suspected they might be child soldiers. I selected one and removed its uniform. Inside was a child of about eight. He was pale and terribly thin with a mop of unkempt hair. He was shaking with fear.

I mentally selected the rest of his group and removed their uniforms. They were all from the Republic of Ireland. I heard two of them whispering to each other.

'Where are the sausages? They promised us sausages.'

It was clear that the children were only interested in one thing — food, and they had been lured into the terrorists' trap with the promise of it. Having had a little success in creating food before, I immediately designed a modest restaurant with wooden tables and benches.

'Let the tables give people whatever food and drink they think of,' I announced. 'And let anyone who sits down at the tables be released from the terrorists' computer system, with all microchips, cranial implants and tracking devices permanently removed,' I added.

'Sit down, everyone,' I said to the kids. 'Now look at the table and think of whatever food or drink you want in the world, and it will be there.'

One of the kids sat down. He felt the release from the computer system, and his shoulders straightened as if a heavy burden had been lifted from his shoulders.

'Look at the "magick table",' I said, 'The table will give you whatever food and drink you think of when you look at it.'

A plate of sausages and mash appeared in front of him, with a knife and fork, wrapped in a napkin. The kid tucked into the food.

'It's good!' he announced to the others.

Two seconds later, the tables were full of kids eating as if for dear life. I was a bit worried that they might not be able to absorb the food, having been on starvation rations.

'Take your time,' I said. 'There's no hurry. No one can hurt you or make you work here ever again. You can always have more if you want to.'

'Can we have *anything* we want to drink?' asked one kid.

'Sure,' I said.

I guessed he wanted alcohol, to be like the grown-ups. Sure enough, a mug of beer appeared in front of him. He took a sip.

'Hey! Guys! You have to try this!'

The others all immediately had beer mugs as well, and their little faces lit up as they tried the exciting new drink. I knew it was OK, as the magick tables I had created operated at a much higher frequency than the terrorists were used to. So whatever they ate or drank had to be good for their bodies. Whatever they thought they were getting, the high frequency energy would translate into protein, calcium and vitamins. And if it was good for the body, it could not be a poison at the same time, so what they took to be alcohol would be perfectly safe. But the table would make the drink taste like whatever the kids wanted it to taste like. And they could drink as much as they liked without getting drunk or overweight!

It turned out that the kids were on one meal a day, to toughen them as child soldiers. After eating as much as they wanted, they all felt sleepy, because their bodies needed to rest and digest the food. So I said, 'Let's have appropriate sleeping accommodation — whatever they like best, and make it and the kids invisible, so they cannot be hassled while they are asleep.'

A whole lot of giant bean bags appeared, and all the kids crashed out on them and went to sleep. I also created showers and toilets, invisible except to the user. Whenever a kid wanted a bed or a washroom, it would appear before them, as new, and would disappear when no longer required, so that the beds and washrooms were new every time and never needed cleaning.

Later, I noticed the kids pulling something out of their mouths and going to drop them in the toilets. It looked like two tea bags connected by a small string. I wondered if it could be a method of carrying drugs without detection, but a terrorist told me I had it all wrong.

The kids were routinely offered to Asian soldiers as child brothel slaves. An Al-Qaida contract specified that Asians should receive some of their wages in the form of access to children. Those unspeakable monsters did not care if the children lived or died, and children often died of suffocation. Child brothel managers, wanting their slaves to remain alive, issued the teabag contraptions to the kids to fix round their back teeth, to protect their breathing.

Next day, I selected all the Irish children and took them back to the Republic of Ireland to the place where the United States NATO base was located. The Americans were happy to take the kids and pass them over to their contacts in the Irish Republic. After the first group of children was rescued, word got around about the magick tables. When children got rescued, the first thing they asked was, 'Where are the magick tables, please?'

'How do you know about them?' I asked.

'We've seen the video, and we've been promised we can go there after we complete our work,' they replied.

It seemed to me that the food and drink from the magick tables helped to improve the kids physical and mental health. The terror in their eyes quickly disappeared after they began eating and drinking, and they became relaxed and content.

I decided to set up two magick table restaurants within the terrorists' main building, one for lower ranks, and the other for officers. That might seem strange, but I figured that it might help the terrorists to become more peaceful and less aggressive. There was no shortage of terrorists wanting to try the new tables. For a start, the food, and more importantly, the drink, were free, and they could drink as much as they wanted to without getting drunk.

Soon after that, three senior terrorists, an Irishman and two Canadians, arrived in the officers' restaurant. All the men in the restaurant immediately stood to their feet as a mark of respect. The three unit heads, Brian, Liam and Antoine, sat down at one of the tables, and a self-appointed waiter bustled up to explain how it worked. Brian, the most senior of the men, told all the men to sit down. Then he looked at Liam and Antoine.

'Here goes,' he said with a wink, and thought of the most expensive meal he had ever heard of.

A huge plate of food appeared, taking up most of the table. It had slices of meat, fish, seafood, and poultry, with various sauces and a side plate with different types of bread and salad on it.

'Is that what you expected?' asked Liam.

'Mm,' said Brian, his mouth full.

He made a circle with his thumb and forefinger to indicate his approval. Antoine, a French Canadian, then thought of a very rare vintage red wine. It appeared with a glass, and the waiter poured it out for him, officiously. Antoine sniffed it cautiously. Then he passed it to Liam.

'What do you think?' he said.

Liam took time to appreciate the fragrance of the wine. Then he created another bottle and glass for himself. Both men drank the wine in silence.

'I wonder if it's possible to get a cork for this,' said Antoine.

A suitable cork immediately appeared on the table.

'Do you have a carrier bag?' asked Liam.

The waiter disappeared for a minute and came back with two large carrier bags. Antoine and Liam thought of more wine and corks, so that they could fill the carrier bags and take them back for their friends and families.

'Don't you want some wine, Brian?' asked Antoine.

Brian was, by now, in conversation with two officers standing nearby.

'They think I should try the real ale,' he said, as a large mug of beer appeared on the table.

There was a silence as the men watched him taste the beer. Brian looked up. There was a light in his eyes. Then he laughed.

'Ah,' he said. 'This is the real thing.'

There was a loud roar of approval from the men, who were convinced he would see things their way. After a while, the three senior men got up and left. There was no further fighting that day, as everyone in the restaurant was enjoying themselves too much.

Next day, two senior military men in uniform from the Kent terrorist training academy, one with the rank of brigadier, asked if they could speak with me. The Kent regiment's main activity was training boys from senior families in academic and military studies up to the age of eighteen, after which they "passed out" and were appointed to administrative posts within the terrorists' electromagnetic environment. Their work included operating the technical equipment that enabled terrorists to enter and leave the electromagnetic area, peacekeeping between terrorist units within the electromagnetic area and apprenticeship to senior people involved in the development of military strategy.

It was a requirement of the Kent regiment that all their men were turned into eunuchs at the age of twelve. This sacrifice gained them the right to work in the inner circle of terrorist committees, where they acted as trusted clerks and private secretaries.

'Would you be kind enough to consider providing our establishment with restaurant facilities?' said the brigadier.

To me, this seemed like an opportunity to bring a more human element into the terrorists' most elite group. I was convinced that "higher spectrum" food would help to make these people more peaceful.

'OK,' I said. 'Can you show me where you want the restaurants.'

Using electromagnetic technologies, the two military men teleported themselves to their academy. I tuned into their frequency and followed them. The building they walked into looked like a large Victorian red brick mansion, with mock-Tudor chimneys and red tiled roofs. The large double doors led through a dark lobby with oak wall panels into a vaulted hall with skylight windows in the ceiling. There were rows and rows of tables with benches on both sides.

'This is where our students eat,' said the brigadier.

I had seen some of the classrooms on the way in. There were old-fashioned wooden desks with rows of boys wearing grey school uniform. Teachers wearing military uniform were writing on blackboards. I looked at the tables in the food hall and waved my hand across them all, while I mentally turned them into magick tables providing food and drink on request.

'That should work,' I said. 'Would you like to test it?'

The brigadier's assistant went out into the corridor and nabbed a couple of students. They followed him in obediently.

'Now then, boys, sit down at the table,' he ordered.

The boys looked at him inquiringly.

'Look at the table, and think of a small snack you would like to eat, and a bottle of pop,' he instructed.

The boys did as they were told, and the table produced two sandwiches from a well-known food store, and two fizzy drink bottles.

'Is that what you wanted?' asked the brigadier.

The two boys nodded.

'Well, that all seems satisfactory,' said the brigadier. 'Shall we go to the officers' mess?'

He led the way up a flight of wooden stairs with polished banisters, into another oak-panelled room filled with tables and chairs. I quickly turned it into a magick table restaurant. This time, the brigadier's assistant invited a waiter to sample the food. The waiter thought of some pasta and a coffee to go with it, and pronounced it excellent.

'We also have a bar,' said the brigadier, walking into an adjoining room.

I fixed that for him, and he and his assistant sampled the magick table's famed real ale.

The two men thanked me, and I left. It might seem a strange way to behave, creating food for terrorists, but it paid off to some extent. No terrorist that ate or drank from the magick tables ever attacked a British citizen again. The down side was that most terrorists were not permitted anywhere near the tables. However, on our local battlefield, where terrorists constantly attacked me, I created two magick table restaurants.

I set the parameters so that the act of sitting down at the tables freed everyone from the terrorists' computer systems and left a transparent X on their foreheads, which prevented them from being put onto the computer systems ever again. This made it possible for victims that had been forced into terrorism to escape, if they could get near the restaurants. I provided magick ladders around the terrorists' main buildings. which also liberated victims from the computer systems if they climbed onto them, enabling a steady stream of soldiers of all types to make their way out of the buildings to the nearby restaurants.

The terrorists tried to remove the ladders, so I made the ladders replicate themselves automatically. That worked pretty well. Escapees took extra ladders to other buildings, to help their friends climb out. After that, all of them made their way to the magick table restaurants for a meal, before accepting the help of the Canadian and British military, now discreetly stationed at the bottom and top of the battle field area.

The terrorists came mainly from NATO countries, whose governments wanted to rescue as many of their own people as possible. NATO technical specialists were working hard behind the scenes on ways to solve the problem of electromagnetic terrorism. I could sometimes see them in the distance.

As mentioned earlier, HM Special Prison Services spent a lot of time rescuing kids, who were often in a half-starved condition, so I offered to create a set of magick tables in an out building in the Special Prison Service garden. This went down well with the kids, and the tables were also patronised by some of the prison officers, after they were off-duty. Their rules specified that they were not to drink alcohol while on duty. I pointed out that magick table alcohol did not make you drunk, but rules are rules, which have to be obeyed, so that was that.

One day, I had just transported a group of Irish kids to the Special Prison Service, and watched them troop into the magick table building, when Tanya and Pam, another lady prison officer, came forward, holding a photo album.

'Martha,' said Tanya. 'We would really like to be able to make magick tables like you do. There are so many places we know about, where the tables could make a difference. We have some photos of possible locations here, if you would like to choose one. Can you show us how to do it?'

'Great idea,' I said.

Selecting the ladies in an electromagnetic field I said, 'Let both of you have the same abilities as I have to create things from mind, and in particular to set up magick tables and all that goes with it.'

Then I asked where they would like to go first. Pam turned a few pages in the album and pointed to a photo of a dingy, run-down looking village centre somewhere in the British Isles.

'Can we go there?' she asked.

Enveloping them both in my energy field, I tuned into the photo. We arrived on the street, in the rain, with no particular reference points to guide us.

'How do we start off?' asked Tanya.

Looking round the village, with its rows of plain grey-roofed bungalows and boarded up shopfronts, I couldn't see how it could be done. Then I had an idea.

'I know,' I said. 'Let's just select the whole village and say "Let every kitchen table in every house now be a magick table".

Pam and Tanya did that.

'Now,' I suggested, 'Let's add, "Where convenient, let there be a plate of food and a drink, that the occupants will like, on each table. Then let them discover how to use the table"

Pam and Tanya did that.

Then as an afterthought, I added, 'If necessary, expand the size and number of tables to meet requirements.'

That was quite a mouthful, but we did it anyway.

'How will we know if it worked?' asked Pam.

At that moment, we heard a woman talking loudly through an open window in a house nearby.

'John, did you put this food here? What's going on?'

'What're you talking about?' came the reply.

A man in his late fifties could be seen moving past the window. He looked at the food.

'What's this, Deb?' he said.

Then he picked up a mug full of beer.

'I think I know what this is,' he said. 'But how did it get here?'

John gave the beer mug a sniff.

'Mm,' he said. 'Smells good,'

'Be careful, it might be poisoned,' said Deb.

But she was too late. John was already downing the contents of the mug.

'Well,' said John. 'If the food's as good as the drink, I think I'll just finish this off,' He started eating what looked like a plate of steak and chips.

'What about me?' said Deb.

Tanya rang the bell of the house. Deb, a lady in her early fifties answered the door.

'Can we come in, please, it's about the food.'

'Oh, so you're the one to blame for that, are you? You'd better come in,' said Deb.

Tanya invited Deb to look at the table and choose her own food and drink. John watched intently as she ordered steak pie and mushrooms, washed down with red wine.

'Well,' said Pam. 'You seem to have got the hang of it. Can you let other people in the village know how to use the tables?'

'No need for that, dear,' said John. 'I'm just emailing everyone I know about it.'

We all smiled with relief. That would be a lot easier than going round all the houses. John's mobile was already ringing, and he walked into the next room to take the call. We could hear him explaining to someone how to work the magick tables.

We took our leave of the couple and I returned us to the Prison Service garden.

'I think we understand what to do now,' said Tanya. 'Can we call on you if we need to ask anything?'

'Oh, sure,' I said, waving goodbye.

That evening, I began thinking about places in the world that might need help with food. There were so many, but you have to start somewhere, so I picked Venezuela and a province in China, where I had heard that it was not always easy for people to get food. I had seen pictures of a prison in Venezuela, and used the photo to get into the main kitchen area. Even though I do not speak most languages, there doesn't seem to be a problem if you're using the electromagnetic environment, where communications can be made at the sub-vocal gut reaction level, or, as clinical research technicians call it, the "evoked potentials" level.

Soon, the Venezuelan prison kitchen tables had become magick restaurant tables, and the prison catering staff understood exactly how to use them. I went on to include the surrounding town, as we had done in the British village. I could have done the whole country, but that might have attracted the wrong kind of attention, particularly in repressive regimes. It seemed safer to start small.

I looked up a map of China on the internet, and selected a remote area in Sichuan province. The province had been a heavy industry manufacturing centre, but it had fallen on hard times. In the driving rain, I could see people planting rice on the hills. I started off by creating tables with food and drink on them, for the entire locality, and then moved into a two room shack nearby. The house was surprisingly tidy and fresh-looking considering how basic the accommodation was. I saw a plate of seafood and noodles on the now magick table, accompanied by a mug of beer. A grey-clothed, middle-aged man came in from a side door that led into the back yard. Seeing the food, he sat down at the table. He took the beer, poured some of it over the food and started eating fast.

The man's wife came in, and watched him. I knocked at the door, and explained to her what had happened to her table. She went out and called excitedly to two other men, who came in. Then they all sat down and began creating food. They were very quick on the uptake.

The first man said, 'I don't want this,' and he chucked the rest of the beer out of the window.

Then he created what looked like rice wine and poured that over his food instead.

'Mm, much better,' he announced.

The three others were talking rapidly and eating at the same time. Then the lady said to me, 'Does it do clothes as well?'

'Do you have a wardrobe?' I asked.

The lady shook her head. I created one, and asked her to open it and think what clothes she wanted. The men gasped, as a smart dress and shoes appeared.

'I want one too,' said one of the men.

'Let the wardrobe replicate itself whenever someone wants another,' I said.

Another wardrobe appeared. The man got up and looked inside. Some casual khaki clothes and boots appeared. At this, the first man, who had now finished his meal, jumped up.

'Can we replicate the tables as well?' he asked.

Before I could say yes, he had replicated the table. Then he picked it up, and carried it outside. He began creating more tables.

'There are poor people with no tables, down there,' he said, pointing into the valley. 'We can give them all tables now.'

Replica wardrobes began appearing as well, and the men drove trucks up to the backyard, picking up the furniture and transporting it around the town.

'Is there anything you can do for the car?' asked one man.

'Well,' I said. 'I could make the oil, gas and water always stay full up.'

The man jumped into his car and switched on the ignition, to activate the indicator panel.

'Do it then.'

It was more of a challenge than a command. He didn't quite believe it would happen, but it did.

'How can I pass it on to another car?' he asked.

'Stand, touching both cars and wish that the power will pass from one to the other, or connect both cars with jump wires and do the same thing,' I suggested.

It was only a suggestion, as I didn't know if it would work. The men tried both methods, and they both worked. By now, the backyard was a hive of activity.

'We can sell the furniture,' said one man.

I had always been cautious about selling food from magick tables, as I thought food should be free to everyone. But furniture was different, as it could be replicated, and if many people had replicas, the price would soon be low and easily affordable. I did not know whether the magick would stay in the furniture if it was sold, but I could see no reason why not. Really, it was up to these enterprising Chinese people how they played it.

After that, I regularly visited areas of the world that needed food, if they had a sufficiently developed electromagnetic environment, to see if it was possible to help with a magick table. I visualised the world as a map in front of me, and looked to see if any places stood out as needing food. The first time that I did that, another part of China, Xinjiang province, above Tibet, stood out like a beacon. I zoomed in on the location, and found myself in the village junior school. It was mealtime, and the kids and their teachers were sitting round the table eating rice — just rice.

I turned their tables into magick restaurant tables, and then appeared in front of them, explaining how the tables worked. The teachers looked a bit shocked when I appeared, but when I explained about the magick tables, their faces broke into smiles.

'Yes, we heard about that in Sichuan province. Can we do that with our table?'

The teachers started creating meals on the school table, and showing the kids how to do it. Then I produced a magick cupboard. Shen, a man of about thirty, immediately stood up and went to the cupboard. He began producing clothes for all the children. The kids jumped up from the table, laughing and waving their arms, as they queued to be given their clothes. Shen was rather gifted at clothing design. He gave all the boys white T shirts, long camouflage shorts, and trainers with matching camouflage trim. Then he did a T shirt for himself. It was white, and said something across the front in Chinese characters, which loosely translated, read:

'It is always better to be happy.'

He gave himself an adult version of the kids' clothes, and a new haircut. The hair was shaved except on the top of the head, in a fashion known as a Short Pompadour. He looked really stylish. The he took the little kids for their sports training in a nearby field. They all lined up at a traffic light, waiting to cross. A car pulled up at the lights, and the driver and passenger wound down their windows, and stuck their heads out.

'Wow! Look at that cool gear!' they shouted.

Shen led the kids across. They were skipping and jumping. I watched them playing football in the field.

Back in the schoolroom, the women teachers were making more magick cupboards and tables, and loading them into trucks. All seemed to be going well, and I was about to leave, when I saw a very elderly woman, bent double, being assisted into the schoolroom. She had heard about the food, and had come to see if there was a chance that she could eat some. Along the street outside, several other really elderly men and women, hardly able to walk, and terribly thin, were trying to make their way towards the schoolroom.

I quickly created some wheelchairs, and helpful passers-by pushed the old people into the school room. I made another table, designed for wheelchairs, and the old people sat round it. They were desperate to eat, and the women teachers were helping them. Some of the old people were accompanied by their working age children, who started feeding their parents with spoons.

Although the village was poor, I had not realised that food was as scarce as this. Chao-xing, the daughter of one of the old ladies explained to me that it was not just a matter of having enough to eat, but of having food of the right quality. Old people did not do well on the food available. Everyone knew about the magick food in Sichuan province, and had worked out that there was more to it than met the eye. People got better from ill health conditions when they ate it. This was why the old people rushed to the schoolroom. They hoped the food could help their health.

I looked at the old lady who was being fed by Chao-xing.

'How old is your mother?' I asked.

'Sixty,' said Chao-xing.

To me she looked about eighty-five. I produced a "mini cupboard" — it was like a small, oblong wooden box, with the inside hollowed out.

'Can you put your mother's finger in the space in the box, and your finger as well, and think, 'My mother is fit and well and in the prime of her life' I said.

I had never tried this before, but I was hopeful. The mother was not capable of understanding much, which was why I asked her daughter to do the thinking.

Chao-xing did as I suggested. Immediately, her mother stood next to her, now a woman of about forty, the same height as her daughter, with dark hair in a long bob.

'Mama!' cried Chao-xing, hugging her, while tears poured down her face.

A man in his early thirties tugged at my arm.

'My father, please,' he said.

His father looked well over eighty, very frail and unwell. I made another mini cupboard for him, and showed him how to do the same as Chao-xing had done for her mother.

A tall fit man with dark hair appeared next to his son. He had a dignified air about him, and a lovely smile. The son knelt at his feet, sobbing, 'Papa, Papa has come back.'

I felt very upset, seeing the suffering of the old people, and thinking how easily I might have missed the possibility to help them. But it was heart-warming to see what could be done with this electromagnetic technology. The wider implications were too mind-blowing for me to take in at first. The good thing was that the teachers fully understood what to do, and would be able to help their village.

As I left, two of the teachers were on their way to the little hospital which served the community. I was sure that they would pass on what they had discovered to local people across Xinjiang province, and that no barriers would prevent the benefits of the technology spreading after this.

The plight of people behind the Bamboo Curtain does not receive that much coverage in the Western press. I had no idea how desperate things were for some people until I started visiting places where magick tables could be useful. North Korea has been covered in my previous book, and journalists have reported in depth on the real shortage of food there. After I discovered about magick tables, I visited that country again.

One image from North Korea still remains with me from my second visit. I went to a village of extreme poverty, on the border with China, which I had heard about on the radio, and created magick restaurant tables, placing them over the villagers own modest tables in every home. A man came into his house after finishing work, and saw his family eating a substantial meal round the table. He knelt, weeping beside the table, thanking God, again and again for saving them.

THE CAR-A-VAN SCAM

One day, I picked up a particularly gross overweight IRA paedophile called Sam, who was harassing kids. He was so obese that his uniform had to be a grey sheet with a hole for his head. I dumped him with his hands and feet loosely tied, at the bottom of the hill, while I rescued some Canadian children.

The Canadian military now had an office with a portal at the bottom of the hill, as well as the one up the road. I escorted the children into the new Canadian office. The Canadian Military objected, understandably, to the paedophile being dumped outside their door. To get him out of the way, I created a wheelchair, loaded him into it, and pushed it down into the mezzanine area, which was a vehicle pick-up and drop-off place for the outside world.

Once the Canadian children had been taken into the Canadian portal, I went to look for Sam. He had some money on him, and was trying to get a taxi to take him to a place where he could be readmitted to the terrorists' computer system. A white van pulled up in front of him. It had a sign on the side which read 'CAR-A-VAN,' meaning that the van was also a taxi.

The van was operating illegally, as it had not been registered as a taxi for business purposes. The driver, an

African, got out and came round to where Sam was sitting in his wheelchair. Sam's tied hands and feet were covered by a rug. The African opened the back of the van and pulled out a wheelchair ramp. Then with some difficulty, he pushed Sam up the ramp and into the back of the van, securing the wheelchair with a makeshift seat belt. I caught sight of a CCTV camera attached to one of the pillars supporting the concrete ceiling of the mezzanine area.

I decided to follow Sam's progress to see where he went. As the driver was about to shut the doors at the back of the van, two suspicious-looking characters with beanies and dark glasses jumped in with Sam. The African appeared unconcerned by this. He got into the driver's seat and accelerated out of the pick-up area.

In the back of the van, the two men were taking out Sam's wallet and stealing his credit cards. They had knives and hand guns. Sam was able to detect my presence.

'Get me out of here,' he whispered under his breath.

'Where do you want to go?' I asked.

Sam visualised the place he wanted to get to in his mind, knowing that I could see it. I recognised the place. It was a well-known terrorist safe-house known affectionally to operatives as the Parking Hut. It was run by a number of Asians who regularly worked as terrorists within the electromagnetic environment.

I picked Sam up and took him out of the van in his wheelchair. As I did so, I heard the sound of a police siren. When the van driver heard it, he put his foot down on the accelerator and sped away, which was not the wisest thing to do. Two Hampshire police cars gave hot pursuit, and the van was soon in a lay-by. The three robbers — the African and two

Asians, got out and stood against the side of the van, while two armed police put cuffs on them. They had been done for speeding.

'Where's the wheelchair passenger?' demanded one of the policemen.

'What passenger?' said one of the robbers.

'We've got you on video,' said the policeman. 'We know you had a wheelchair passenger.'

I could see the way things were going, and wasted no time in untying Sam and depositing him and his wheelchair in the drive outside the house known as the Parking Hut. As we arrived, two Asians were standing out there, and behind them was a white van, with the sign CAR-A-VAN on it.

Sam jumped out of the wheelchair and greeted one of the Asians warmly.

'Hi, Isaac, how're you doing? Can you give me a lift to the top of the hill? I got chucked off the system by the HerMan — *A name given me by some of the terrorists, who were convinced I must be a male if I could beat them.*

'Did she just drop you here?' asked Isaac, looking a bit worried, in case I was still around.

At that moment, the two police cars we had seen earlier arrived in the drive. The three robbers had confessed everything at the police station, including the address of their place of work... which happened to be the Parking Hut. But they had not been able to explain the disappearance of the wheelchair passenger.

One of the policemen got out of his car, and spotted the now empty wheelchair.

'Look, there's the wheelchair!'

Sam whizzed round the side of the house, and pressed his large body against the wall, hardly daring to breath.

'Just get me out of here! Quick...' he prayed.

It was not clear who he was praying to, but I picked him up and placed him a little below where the British military now had a portal. Then I returned to the Parking Hut to see what had happened.

One of the police officers had phoned for a van. The other had got the two Asians lined up against a wall, with cuffs on. A large black van came up the drive. The police secured the two Asians inside it, and it drove off. A few minutes later another white CAR-A-VAN sped up the drive and parked before spotting the two police cars. Three Asian men got out, wearing berets and dark glasses.

One of the police cars moved to block their exit, and the two policemen challenged the Asians to put their hands up. The Asians looked a bit ashamed at being caught red-handed. Then one of them foolishly went for his gun. He was immediately tasered in the arm by one of the policemen. The other policeman radioed for help.

By now, a woman police officer was in a car outside the drive of the Parking Hut, next to the main road. She noticed yet another CAR-A-VAN vehicle. It slowed down, indicating that it was turning into the drive of the Parking Hut. Then the driver caught sight of the police car, and changed its mind, turning back into the traffic, causing another car to swerve. The woman police officer took the number plate of the van, and reported it back to HQ. Soon, two more police cars were speeding down the road, sirens blaring.

Half an hour later, it was all over. The Asians CAR-A-VAN business had folded. It was only a matter of time before they would have been caught anyway. Two earlier victims of robbery had reported incidents to the Hampshire police, which was why CCTV had been discretely installed at the vehicle pick-up point.

The entrance to the Parking Hut was cordoned off with red and white police tape, and a number of police cars were parked in the drive. Several policemen were inside the building, ransacking the contents. They emerged carrying a large number of electromagnetic weapons in plastic bags. Then, representatives of the Counter Terrorism squad arrived. They were there for several days. It was clear that not only the British and Canadian military, but several other law enforcement agencies were closing in on electromagnetic terrorist operations in the UK.

TERRORISTS IN PLAIN SIGHT

The electromagnetic environment enables terrorists to prey on civilians freely without detection, because the perpetrators are invisible to the naked eye. A basic rule of survival, obeyed by all electromagnetic terrorists, is that they must never bring their activities into the real world outside. Despite strict rules, however, there were three occasions when I witnessed this happening.

The first time it happened, a group of terrorists based in Devon were determined to break what they saw as the logjam of unsuccessful attempts to control me. They planned a physical ambush on me, as I was walking back from watching a movie at our local cinema. They knew in advance that I had reserved a ticket for the show. Their boss authorised a long-frocked senior male "manageress" to take forty pounds in cash and give it to the perpetrator who was to carry out the intimidation attack. The perpetrator's job was to give me a fright by following me along the road to my house, exposing himself in front of me. He had two look-out men to back him up, and a supervisor to verify that the job had been done. They all got a small share in the forty pounds prize.

It was a dark evening in November, and I was trudging home, feeling quite sleepy, when I heard someone walking along the road behind me. The footsteps were faster than mine, but that is quite normal, as I am a slow walker leaning on a stick, so I took no notice. The person walked on the other side of the single-track road, and overtook me, just as we reached a street light. I looked up to see who had overtaken me. It was a man about five feet nine. He turned and looked back along the road, before surreptitiously undoing his jeans. I could tell he had practiced the move before. He wasn't wearing any underwear.

My first reaction was disbelief.

'My God! It's a flasher!' I thought

Then I looked at the man more carefully. His blue jeans were at half-mast. He wore a black top, black beanie, black balaclava and matching black gloves. Clearly, he must have got kitted up nearby, as his gear looked highly suspicious. I wondered what he was going to do next. He paused, as if wondering the same thing. I noticed that his skin was pale white, that he was slightly paunchy — I'd put his age at about thirty-eight, and that he was uncircumcised. Also, despite his best endeavours, he clearly was not pleased to see me!

'Why should I stand here waiting for him to do something?' I thought. 'I know what I want to do, so I'll get on with it.'

I raised my stick and aimed it at his private parts. He danced back a couple of feet, like a boxer in the ring. I tried again, moving in, but missing him. Then I hit his body but not in the right place. I could tell he was mad at me, as he was moving in with a right punch, and I had to step to the side. But at the last minute he pulled his punch, probably thinking how it would look to the police if he was caught hitting an old lady in the face. At the same time, I began to wonder how it would look to the police if I hit him with my stick first, and he didn't hit me. Would I end up in prison instead of him?

The man stepped backwards three paces.

'Oh, give over gurrl,' he said, half laughing.

Then he turned and ran back down the road.

I could tell from his accent that he had spent the early part of his life in Devon before moving to Hampshire. I was sure he belonged to the terrorists, though he was not registered on any of their computer systems at that moment. The best thing to do, I thought, was to prevent him working again, by wiping all the microchips, cranial implants and other WIFI communications from his body. I mentally selected him, although by now he had disappeared, and cleaned out his electronic connections.

I followed his progress along the road. The tall man in the long frock, with the rank of manageress, walked towards him, and gave him a bundle of cash in a plastic bag. It was the kind of bag that banks give you if you ask for change, and it contained £40 in two-pound coins. The perpetrator threw the bag to an operative behind the hedge. The operative handed him a small suitcase, containing his normal clothes, and he slid behind a bush and got changed, reappearing in casual clothes and trainers. His assistant took the bag of cash, selected a few coins from it and resealed the bag. Then he turned down another road to where a tall man, wearing a black mac and hat, was standing. The tall man helped himself to a few coins from the bag. The perpetrator appeared at this point and took the rest of the cash. Then they all hurried away into the darkness and disappeared.

I was walking home, watching this mentally. After I got back and had a cup of tea, I thought, 'This really is a bit much.

I'm going to report it to my contacts in H.M. Special Prison Services.'

I went to where they worked, and stood in the dark in the back garden. They were all busily employed in the building, which was full of lights. A minute later they had detected my presence. Mike came out.

'What is it?' he asked.

I told him what happened. His face darkened.

'Leave it with me,' he said, and he went inside.

I went to bed, and fell asleep. A couple of hours later, something woke me up. I could hear terrorists screaming. I looked to see what was going on. There were several men from H.M. Special Prison Services standing around the terrorists' miniaturised hideout. They sliced open the building as if it was a beehive, disclosing all the floors. As I watched, they cleaned out the entire top floor of the building and all the terrorists in it. They seized the top man, who was sitting in his private office. He shouted and waved his arms, as they deposited him in a container. Then they walked off. There was silence. All the lower level terrorists had left the building, and were hiding in the darkness. Their managers and their top boss had gone.

My next encounter with terrorists in the real world was less traumatic. It was mid-morning on a lovely sunny day. There were wild flowers in the grass verge and birds singing, as I walked back from my music lesson towards the bus stop, up a side road. A balding man in his fifties, with long, grey unkempt hair in a pony-tail, emerged from a house on one side of the road, and crossed over, before disappearing into a house on the other side. The man was wearing a long brown leather apron with a dragon painted on it. In his arms he clutched twenty electromagnetic weapons. They were black hand-held "pointer" devices, used to bring targeted victims into range from remote locations linked by WIFI. Typically, they are operated from parked cars.

The whole thing was over in two minutes. I made a note of both houses. They were in quite a high price range. I reported what I had seen, with details of the Hampshire house addresses, to MI5. Two months later, I saw the same man, this time more normally dressed, in our road. He was parked outside a known IRA safehouse, opening the boot of a battered orange Ford. I suspected that he was delivering another batch of electromagnetic pointers to local terrorists for use in their many training courses.

The third time I saw terrorists out in the open, I was walking down my road, when several men came running along it, followed by others in cars. They all turned into a side road, leading to a footpath. The men were shouting and gesticulating. One of them stood at the end of the road, directing cars into the side road. I recognised him as one of the terrorists I had seen in the electromagnetic environment. What was going on?

I found out later that there had been a dispute between two groups of terrorists, and one group had kicked the other group out. They moved into a trailer park area at the end of the next road, and set up camp there. The first group of terrorists were well-heeled IRA families, who provided rental accommodation to members of the International Unity Guild, whenever they requested it. The second group were a band of Irish mafia criminals, not part of the IRA, but supposed to be working in cooperation with them. They stole from the IRA whenever they could, and were prone to heavy drinking and brawling at night. In the end, it got too much for their hosts, who expelled them.

BACK TO THE MOON

From time to time, I went back to check up on how the Moon people were doing, in case they needed anything. One day, I saw a young Chinese couple, Bill and Chloe, and Luke, a youth of about fifteen, walking up on a ridge. They had been IT technicians working for the terrorists, and I must have dumped them there during a battle, along with a lot of others, at an early stage before I realised that it was possible for anyone to live on the Moon. At first, I was surprised to see that Chinese people had survived, as well as ethnic Africans, but I remembered reading that thousands of years ago, there were people living in what is now Nigeria, who left Africa moving East, and eventually settled in China. If the Chinese are related to people from Africa, it might explain how they are able to live on the Moon.

I went up to the group and asked how they were doing. Bill and Chloe said they were fine and doing well. Luke — that was the Western name he used, said, 'You're the person who put us up here, aren't you?'

'Yes,' I said. 'Are you missing your family? Would you like me to take you back to Earth?'

'No,' said Luke. 'I like it up here, it feels like home now.' Then he frowned.

111

'I get on OK with the others here, but I need a girlfriend. Can you do anything about that?'

'Do you know anyone back home who is suitable?' I asked.

Luke shook his head.

'We could go to my old place, and see if there are any girls there who would be interested,' he said.

He sounded unconvinced, and lacking in confidence.

'Where do you want to go?' I asked.

'You could try Soho,' said Luke.

'OK,' I said. 'Let's go.'

I surrounded Luke with an electromagnetic field and landed with him at the gates of the Chinese village in Soho. Luke felt faint at first. It took him time to adjust to the Earth's heavier gravity. I had to send electrical energy through his body, and create a "designer water" energy drink, to get him grounded. When he had recovered, we walked through the village, to the centre and stood there.

An old man and woman came out and walked towards us. I could tell they were elders within the Chinese community, and bowed to them.

'Why have you come?' asked the old man.

I began to feel uncomfortable. How could I explain?

'I have brought one of your sons, who no longer lives on the Earth. He is looking for a Chinese bride,' I murmured.

I felt stupid saying that, and not sure how to go on. The old woman's face broke into a smile.

'Yes, we know all about the Moon,' she said, 'It is sacred to Chinese people, and we know what goes on there.'

A group of Chinese men and women were watching from a respectful distance. The old man spoke to them in Chinese, asking them if they had any daughters who would be interested in Luke and in living on the Moon. Several attractive young girls appeared and had a good look at Luke. They stood whispering and laughing. Luke stared at the ground, looking embarrassed.

The old man said, 'It seems that the young man is not considered suitable, because of his age. Our girls prefer more mature men.'

It had to be admitted that fifteen going on sixteen was a bit young, especially for such an important decision as choosing a partner. Also, the girls looked fairly sophisticated. I could see it wasn't going to work.

'I'm really sorry, Luke,' I said. 'Is there anywhere else you would like to go?'

Luke shook his head. I thanked the Chinese elders for their time, and prepared to take Luke back. Suddenly, I heard a shout, 'Wait! Wait! don't go yet, please...'

An extremely pretty, young girl with long black hair came running out of a nearby house. She was all of thirteen. She turned to Luke.

'I would like to go, that is, if you like me,' she said, with a confidence that belied her years.

'What is your name,' said Luke.

'Layla ,' said the girl.

Luke took both her hands.

'Layla, I like you very much,' he said.

At that moment, a young couple, about eighteen years old, came running out of Layla's house. They bowed in respect to the Chinese elders.

'That's my sister, Stella, and her boyfriend, Gary ,' said Layla.

'You're from the Moon, aren't you?' Gary said to Luke.

'We'd love to come with Layla,' said Stella.

Together they turned to address the Chinese elders.

'May we have your permission to go with Layla?' said Stella.

'Are you really sure you want to go?' said the old lady.

'Yes,' they both said.

'It feels like this is the right thing for us,' said Gary.

'They can always come back if they change their minds,' I added.

The Chinese elders smiled and raised their hands in blessing.

I thanked them, and transported the four young Chinese people back onto the Moon. There was much laughter and surprise as they met the other Chinese couple, Bill and Chloe. I left them taking a look round their new home. Like many of the other Moon people, Bill, Chloe and Luke lived in a cave slightly underground. The views from the ridge above their lunar crater were fantastic. Incredible cliffs, with rocky outcrops framed the background and a wonderful glow lit up the evening sky.

As I left, I wondered if Layla and Stella would become pregnant, and if they did, how all that would work on the Moon. Four months later, I went back to see if they needed any help. Both the girls said they were pregnant, but it was a bit early to be sure. There again, how long would it take for a baby to develop on the Moon?

Two months after that I looked in on the Chinese group. Luke had matured a lot since meeting Layla. He got on well with Gary, and was very concerned about the health of both

Layla and Stella. By now both girls looked pregnant. I began to check up on them more frequently.

A few weeks later, I found Layla lying on the ground, with Luke holding her hand.

'Is everything all right?' I asked.

'Look at me,' said Layla.

Her stomach had swelled up rather suddenly, and I wasn't sure if this could be normal.

'Are you in any pain?' I asked.

'No,' said Layla. Then she gave a gasp and a sigh and fell back against Luke.

'I feel so strange,' she said.

'Don't worry,' said Luke, putting both arms around her. 'I'm here.'

I was quite worried now, so I sent a surge of electronic energy up her body, in the hope that it would help. At that moment, it seemed that Layla's waters had broken. But that couldn't be right so soon. Then a moment later, Layla gave a cry, 'The baby's coming! I can feel it!'

It was as if the baby floated or slipped out as the waters broke. Now, I am no midwife, but I do know that babies floating out as the waters break is not possible. But that's how it happened. I produced a towel and some wipes. The baby's cord seemed to have separated from the placenta at the moment of birth, and did not need to be cut. I did my best to make Layla comfortable. Then I wrapped the baby — it was a boy — in another towel and waited for the afterbirth to emerge. But it didn't come.

'Something's wrong,' I thought.

But Luke and Layla were cuddling the baby and talking to it, completely absorbed in it. I suggested that they should bring some of the liquid from the Moon rocks and put it on the baby's tongue. After that, the baby seemed to be even more alert and responding. They named him Ralph. The three of them were so happy, I did not like to interrupt them further.

'I expect the afterbirth will emerge in its own time,' I thought.

Two hours later I checked back. Luke and Layla were holding the baby upright by its arms, and it was walking. The afterbirth never emerged. I think it was reabsorbed into Layla's body. Things are very different on the Moon. All that people have to live on is the liquid that exudes from the rocks. For a mother to build up a placenta must take a lot of doing. It may be that the reabsorbed placenta helps the mother get stronger after the birth. The baby could not have been more than seven months in the womb before birth, and yet it was fully developed, healthy and normal.

I wonder if the different gravity on the Moon might have something to do with it. Certainly, the lighter gravity made it much easier for the baby to walk. It was walking with help from day one, and within a month, could walk about by itself. Not that it needed to. Luke and Layla were constantly with it, walking with it, holding its hands, carrying it and playing with it. Luke had changed from a shy teenager into a proud father.

Gary and Stella's baby, a little girl, arrived a few days after Ralph. I wasn't there at the time. They told me the birth happened in exactly the same way as Layla's. I went back to Soho, to inform the two elders of the good news. They greeted me warmly and told me that they knew all about it. The old lady asked me if I would take some gifts for the family. There were baby clothes and a necklace of semi-precious stones for each of the mothers.

I went back to the newly developing Moon community, and presented the gifts. I thought the fathers also deserved acknowledgment, and asked what they would like. They smiled and pointed to their smart casual gear.

'We really don't need anything,' said Gary. 'You can see that we know how to provide for ourselves.'

'Of course!' I thought. 'They've worked out how to create things by thinking, and it works for them too.'

It is over a year now since the two Moon babies were born. So far, there is no sign of either mother becoming pregnant again. It is a bit of a mystery how things work, but since everyone is doing well and is happy, there seems no point in worrying further. Last time I checked in, Luke was playing ball with Ralph, and Ralph had already developed good coordination.

SCARY STUFF

It was early morning. I was half asleep, when I became dimly aware of a room with pale grey walls, and alcoves along the walls. A man in a white coat, and his assistant, were leaning over an elderly man on an operating trolley. The man had an arm missing. Another assistant brought a grey limb from another room, and the three clinicians secured it to the man's body, with the hand tucked into his jacket. Then I heard the sound of a fine drill or electric saw. One of the assistants left the room and returned with a moulded wooden frame, with an arched top, about three feet wide by four feet high. The three clinicians bent over the man's body, fitting, adjusting and pushing limbs and clothes into place. One of them took a large bottle of resin and sprayed it all over the frame and its contents.

Then the staff stood back to survey the results of their work. One of them held up the framed "portrait" for the other two to look at. The frame was reminiscent of those surrounding Renaissance paintings of the Virgin and Child. The top half of the man who had been on the operating trolley was now encased within the frame, looking forward, his eyes open, but glazed, with one arm across his body, rather like paintings of Napoleon with one arm in his jacket. Two of the staff carried their new creation to one of the niches in the wall, and set it up there.

One of the assistants left the room, and returned, leading in another elderly man. The white-coated leader pulled back a curtain, to reveal a niche with a plinth supporting another resin creation, this time of a woman. He started lecturing the man on how lucky he was to end up as a work of art. Then, using a pointer, he began to run through the procedure used to achieve the 3-D human portrait. The elderly man watched as the steps were explained to him. Then, one of the assistants brought him a ceramic mug containing a liquid. The assistant told the elderly man to drink it. The man did as he was told. He became totally paralysed. Then the two assistants lifted him, unresisting, onto the operating trolley, and pushed him out of the room. As he left, I caught the man's eyes. He was awake, could feel everything, but was unable to move.

After the man had been wheeled out, one of the assistants prepared some paperwork, which included a disclaimer limiting clinicians' liability, should any harm befall the patient undergoing certain procedures. The patient's signature was forged by the assistant.

Then it was my turn. The white-coated leader ran through the procedure that I was to undergo, and an assistant brought me a ceramic mug, containing some liquid to drink. I put the mug to my lips, and raised it. As I did so, I smelled something nasty in the liquid. Then I thought, 'No, I don't think so,' and I put the mug down.

'Shit, she's refused,' I heard the malicious voice of a mafia woman.

I started to come out of the gas-induced trance and realised what was happening. The "mad scientist" was

119

standing looking down at me, with cold, staring eyes. Then I hit him in the face.

'Select all, arms off, legs off,' I shouted.

All three clinicians fell to the floor, the nerves in their arms and legs non-functioning.

I rose out of the skylight of the building, over the roof and up into the sky, trying to work out where I was. I looked for landmarks. Then I recognised the Rocky Mountains. I was near the Canadian military's Calgary base. I landed on the illuminated helipad outside the base.

'Help,' I cried. 'They are dismembering live people without an anaesthetic near here.'

One of the Canadian officers came out. He listened carefully.

'Go back and we'll follow you there,' he said.

As I returned to the building, I could see several terrorists hurriedly pushing equipment on trolleys, carrying cardboard boxes, and pieces of electrical equipment. They were trying to remove the evidence of their creepy operations. When they saw me, the terrorists scattered in all directions. At that moment, Canadian soldiers ran in through the lobby of the building, carrying semi-automatic weapons. More of them were on the roof, and came in through the skylight. All the terrorists were rounded up and taken away in a large unmarked van.

The Canadian officer thanked me for my help in reporting the incident, but did not offer an explanation for what had happened.

'I know that terrorists want to kill people,' I thought. 'But what was all that about?'

Later, terrorists from the Psychological Warfare Group based in the UK, told me that what I had seen was a set piece used on people they wanted to recruit, to make them believe they were under terrorist control. They assured me that real people were not involved, and it had just been a virtual reality video beamed into the back of my eye, something they often did to scare victims into submission. They said that people from the Toronto mafia had organised it.

I suspected that the Canadian mafia were involved. I knew that the Canadian mafia belonged to the terrorists' International Unity Guild, and that some of them were involved in attacks on British citizens in the UK. I had met Canadian terrorists from Vancouver, working in collaboration with members of the IRA, who had infiltrated a counter-terrorism unit in Greater London. There had been a rather nasty high-profile murder case in Toronto in December 2017. Some of the terrorists where I lived thought the Canadian Mafia had done it.

'Who are these guys?' I wondered.

Thanks to NATO technical enhancements, it was much easier for me to connect to terrorist WIFI across the world these days. In my mind's eye, I hovered across North America, tuning into the terrorist frequencies. I was trying to find the people behind the virtual reality show, put on for my benefit. I picked up a strong signal in the Toronto area. Latching on to it, and making myself invisible, I dived down into the source of the signal.

I found myself in what looked like a stone castle. Terrorist technicians can construct electromagnetic architecture in any format, and some of their creations are like movie sets. There were winding, spiral stone staircases, rooms which you stepped up into, with tapestries on the walls and over the doors, and tiny glass window panes. I climbed up a turret staircase, and near the top, came onto a landing. A doorway led into a circular room, with what looked like a throne on a stone platform raised above the floor. A richly clothed man with shoulder-length hair and a kind of crown on his head was sitting there. A woman in a long dress with a low-cut bodice, wearing an extravagant white wig, walked past.

I could tell they were terrorists, presumably with a taste for costume drama. The man on the throne was issuing orders to some younger men dressed as page boys. Apart from that, nothing much was happening, and the action was obviously somewhere else. I could hear a discussion going on in a nearby room. A large man, heavily disguised, was deep in conversation with three hardened-looking men in their fifties. They were talking about money and international deals.

'Probably drug dealers,' I thought.

They may have been drug dealers, amongst other things, but on this occasion, it sounded as if they were discussing pharmaceuticals. I decided to bring them in to the Calgary military. So, I lifted them all up, and tried to deposit them on the military helipad. Three of the men materialised, but their heavily disguised mafia leader would not appear. There wasn't enough electromagnetics on him for me to get a hold. That meant, amongst other things, that he was not registered on the terrorists' computer system.

I struggled to land the guy, but he just wouldn't shift. Afraid of losing him, I shouted to the Canadian military, 'Can anyone give me a hand? This one's just not coming.'

A Canadian military officer appeared.

'Hold on!' he said, 'We can deal with this. Just keep holding onto him.'

The man struggled like a large fish on the end of a line. For a moment, I glimpsed an array of Toronto terrorist technicians, wearing black wetsuits, working intently on laptops, to hold the man in place. The Canadian military were running towards a room in their underground building with a large piece of kit on wheels, which looked as if it could emit a broad radiation beam. They switched it on. Then everything went blurry. The light was dazzling, and I couldn't make out what was going on. The mafia technicians increased the power of their equipment, which was humming and making a high-pitched sound.

Then suddenly the Canadian military gave a shout, 'Got him!'

Everyone burst into a round of applause. I relaxed my hold. Looking into the military building, I could see several glass-walled rooms, with two corridors meeting at the near end. The big fish that the Canadian military had landed was lying in a large glass room, on the carpet, clutching an electronic weapon. His head was heavily masked. Outside the glass, military men and women were clustered staring in, and talking to each other excitedly.

The mafia technical team had magnified the man's size to well above normal, in an attempt to prevent him being captured. He looked huge. Then I heard gasps and shouts of astonishment. The big shot had removed his mask.

'No! I don't believe it,' said one man.

'It can't be him, it can't be!' said another.

'I'm not coming out!' shouted the Mafioso, raising his electronic weapon.

By now, the glass room was surrounded by military personnel with various types of electronic equipment, shielding devices, and a communications device which broadcast into the glass room. A trained negotiator was standing on a platform, interacting with the terrorist. The corridor was cordoned off, and armed soldiers stood along one side.

It looked like a long haul, so I went home, intending to check on developments later. When I got back home, I could hear the local terrorists buzzing along their ultrasound communications line, camouflaged with a tape of bird song. Their chatter whizzed back and forth. It seemed that the captured terrorist was a well-known Canadian criminal who had given the authorities the slip and gone missing about five years ago. He was now the leader of a gang of four mafia chiefs that ran everything in the Toronto-New York area.

Having caught one of the gang, I decided to try and locate the other three members. I found a terrorist unit in Toronto, located in a side street on both sides of the road. But it only contained low-level terrorists. I went back to the mediaeval castle, and climbed up to the very top. There was a gantry with a look-out man on the top of the tower.

'What for?' I wondered. 'Was there something up above in the sky?'

I looked up and saw a strange contraption like a floating Pringle. It was a light potato-crisp colour and curved in a concave way. The electromagnetic aerial craft hovered over the outskirts of Toronto. I went inside it, and found myself in a large, airy corridor, with doors leading to rooms on both sides. I opened one door, and saw rows of technicians working on desk-top equipment with plasma screens. Tuning into my in-built WIFI navigation, I recalled the frequency of the Toronto big shot, and searched for similar matches. Then I picked up something directly below us, underground. I dived into the underground area, and into a dark, smoke-filled room. The other three gang members were in there. The floating Pringle was their private method of transport.

This time, I had no difficulty in bringing the other three mafia bosses into Calgary. As I landed on the helipad with the three men, soldiers came out and took them inside. I followed, and saw the big criminal, now in a smaller glass room, under armed guard. When he saw his three compatriots being led away, he stared at the ground, careful not to display any emotion. It seemed likely that these guys were funding some of the UK terrorist activities. I went to the military front desk, where a man was sitting.

'Can I help you?' he said.

'Please could you ask the officers to get the terrorists' bank account details and stop them making payments,' I said. 'It could make a difference to wider terrorist operations.'

The man said he would pass on my request. I returned a couple of hours later to check on developments. The big criminal was sitting in his room, with a notebook in front of him, copying out rows of numbers. In another room across the corridor, the three other mafia bosses were sitting talking to a couple of military personnel, and reading numbers out of their diaries.

Next day, I learned that a number of bank accounts in different parts of the world had been closed at the request of the Canadian government. Our local UK terrorists were now being paid in cash, on a temporary basis, as all their personal accounts had been closed. This was satisfying, but I knew that by the end of the week, other bank accounts would have sprung up to replace them. Stopping the terrorists' funding was never going to be that easy. I wondered where the brains behind the finance side were located. Focussing on the intricate network of terrorist banking systems, I tried to tune into the centre of the network.

Then, suddenly, everything went dark. I found myself in an underground cave, with light coming in from a doorway reached by steps. The cave had two levels. I looked down into the lower level, where I could see two strange figures, about eight feet high. As my eyes became used to the darkness, I noticed a small stove which gave off a slight red glow, and standing next to it, there were two creatures, not human, but alive and capable of thought. They looked a bit like T Rex dinosaurs, or huge lizards. One was dark brown, with a lighter brown belly, and the other one was yellow all over. They seemed to be talking to each other about their work.

'Only eighty dead today,' said the brown lizard.

'Not good really,' said the yellow lizard. 'I only got seventy.'

I noticed a strange, eerie blue light coming from the level above me, and realised there was a tall oval glass tank filled with liquid, dimly illuminated from the base. The tank was about twelve feet high and four feet wide. Half way up the tank, there was a dark grey shadow, covering the entire width of the tank. It looked like a huge tadpole. It *was* a huge tadpole. It had eyes and a mouth, and a strange wistful expression.

'Hello,' said the tadpole. 'Have you seen my friend?'

'What friend?' I asked.

'Can you see a lizard down there?' said the tadpole.

'I can see two lizards,' I said.

'Is there a yellow lizard?' asked the tadpole.

'Yes,' I said. 'And a brown one.'

'The *yellow* lizard is my friend,' said the tadpole.

'What work are you doing?' I asked, realising that I was talking to some kind of artificial intelligence construct.

'I kill people,' said the tadpole. 'I'm very good at it, much better than the lizards. I can kill four hundred at once.'

'How do you do that?' I asked.

'Easy,' said the tadpole, 'I just go KILL, KILL, KILL.'

The tadpole thrashed its tail for a minute, emitting, blue sparks.

'But there's no one dead here,' I said.

'No,' said the tadpole, 'But I control the minds of four hundred people, and when I do that, they carry out my orders.'

'So, it's a WIFI transmitter, emitting impulses to cranial implants, by the sound of it,' I thought. 'And perhaps the lizards are earlier prototypes. But why use artificial intelligences to do the job, when a computer could do it? Why go to the trouble of creating personalities for these creatures, and why make them so lifelike?'

At the time, I could find no explanation for the strange events unfolding before me. It was later explained to me by some North American terrorists, that a lot of work had gone into replacing supervisors of low-level staff with artificial intelligence creations. The supervisors were prone to corruption, and had low productivity, whereas these artificial intelligence creations were reliable, and cost less to maintain.

The early prototypes could only handle a few cases, and had a limited range of instructions, whereas later models could manage a large number of staff via WIFI links to their cranial implants. They could give orders and administered electric shocks to the head, for motivational and corrective purposes. The creatures were lifelike because genetic modification of existing life forms was the preferred method selected by unethical North American secret scientists, notably, those working in Al-Qaida's Algerian research base. The creatures were human-reptile hybrids with electronic implants.

The artificial intelligence machines could be used to organise terrorist low-level staff into carrying out set schedules of attacks on a regular basis. Their targets were people whose movements were predictable, for example, elderly people living alone or in nursing homes, who always sat in the same chair, or lay in the same bed. A daily schedule of invisible electronic and electromagnetic attacks could be mounted, such as involuntary bowel and bladder movements, sharp pains in different parts of the body, chronic pain targeted at joints and sleep deprivation.

Why didn't the terrorists just kill their victims outright? One reason was that sudden deaths of numbers of elderly or disabled people would arouse suspicion. Another, was money. The perpetrators' objective was to make their assignments last as long as possible, claiming the maximum amount of payments they could get from their terrorist paymasters.

But the appearance of these artificial intelligence creations had distracted me from my main purpose. I was looking for the centre of the terrorists' finance network, and I seemed to have come to a dead end. I climbed up the steps leading out of the cave, and into a mild spring day outside. The change in season and climate gave me a clue.

'I bet I'm in one of those terrorist scientists' "Near Earth" architecture constructs,' I thought.

I had been in one of those before. It was like a huge Eden dome, with cities and countryside inside it. It was created on our Earth, from an electromagnetic substance, and interpenetrated our Earth. The last time I visited one, there was a hypersonic monorail that terrorists used to move between our Earth, and the Near Earth.

About one hundred and fifty yards away from the cave was a vast Louis XV mansion, with elaborate formal gardens. I made myself invisible, and went into the building through French windows that opened out onto a patio area. I walked along a corridor, with doors leading into several glass-walled meeting rooms. The first room had a dais at one end with a throne on it. Several men and women in costumes from the period of Louis XV were holding clipboards and check lists, busying themselves industriously.

In the next room, senior men like those I had seen on my last visit to the Near Earth, with silver hair, wearing silver suits edged with platinum, sat round a large meeting table. They were the brains of the terrorist empire referred to as "Our Group". I had seen them holding high level discussions in French. It occurred to me that they might originate in the French-speaking part of Canada, and later, I found out that they were based in Montreal. They had a huge undersea electromagnetic base there, that was reached via the East coast of North America, with hypersonic transport links to Toronto, Montreal and New York.

The "silver-suits" were working out Our Group's annual budget, based on contributions from the International Unity Guild. Representatives from different parts of their empire were assembled in other meeting rooms along the corridor. Once the budgets had been worked out, the Louis XV aristocrats communicated the details to senior representatives of each terrorist area, in nearby meeting rooms.

I went into the first of these meeting rooms. An oval table was laid for a modern business meeting, with water bottles, glasses and writing materials. Seated round it were representatives of the USA and South America. There were white Caucasians, American blacks and people of Hispanic origin. They had been waiting for some time and were getting restless. At that moment, a woman dressed as a Louis XV aristocrat came in.

'Sorry for the delay,' she said. 'We will of course be giving a full world picture of budget funding at this evening's conference, but I thought you would like to have the high-level picture now.'

'We've waited long enough,' said one of the black American delegates. 'We can't afford the time to attend the evening conference. Just give us our budgets and we can go.'

'OK,' said the lady. 'Here goes. All our outlets in South America have performed satisfactorily during the last year, and there will be no change to last year's budget.'

As she said that, there was a low murmuring among the South American delegates, who stood up, thanked her politely, packed their bags and left.

'Now, here are the budgets for the States,' continued the lady. 'We consider that black American representation has been concentrated too much in the South. In future, while the overall US budget will remain the same, the funding for black American outlets will be altered. We have re-apportioned the black American budget to achieve equal representation across all US states. This will mean that if you want to continue with Our Group, some of you will have to move to other states, and start new units. States with proportionately too much black American representation will have their budgets cut correspondingly.'

There were gasps and muttered protests at this announcement, from representatives of both black and white ethnic groups around the table. I had not realised that there were separate units for white and black terrorists. The approach seemed to reflect an earlier time in North American history.

The aristocratic lady made her apologies and moved to the next meeting room, where African representatives were waiting to hear from her, and I followed. There were a number of African delegates around the meeting room table, some in business suits, some in causal gear.

'I have to announce some changes to budget organisation,' the lady began. 'Some country representatives have been conscientious in submitting monthly activity and cost reports, and others have not. Those that failed to submit regular reports have lost their country status, and will now be managed from neighbouring countries.'

Countries singled out for poor performance included Nigeria, the Sudan and the Democratic Republic of Congo. At this point, several African representatives, presumably from poorly performing countries, got up and walked out in disgust. I sneaked out with them and moved to the next meeting room.

Compared to the other meeting rooms, the next one was by far the most colourful. The delegates around the table were not human. They all looked like artificial intelligence creatures.

'Why would they have any reason to be here?' I wondered. 'Surely, they have no self-determination, and therefore no interest in budget arrangements.'

Another aristocratic lady had just begun her speech to the creatures, when one of them, a yellow lizard, interrupted her.

'Excuse me, madam, my wife here,' he said, pointing to a rotund yellow lizard sitting next to him. 'Is about to give birth, so I'm afraid we will have to leave the meeting room.'

'Oh! Please do not let us detain you!' cried the lady, looking hopefully towards a liveried steward standing against the wall.

The two yellow lizards got up and left the room, the pregnant one, waddling clumsily, with difficulty. It looked as if the birth could happen any minute. I completely forgot the budgeting process, and went after them to see what would happen. The liveried steward led them towards a barn area. Inside, an attendant was laying out hay on the ground.

'That's all right then,' I thought, and withdrawing my attention from the electromagnetic environment, I went to make a cup of tea.

When I came back, I peeped into the barn. The female yellow lizard had laid six enormous eggs, and was now manoeuvring herself to sit on them, with her tail curled round the ones on the outside. The male lizard was hovering anxiously.

'They can't just be artificial intelligence creatures, can they?' I thought to myself. 'There has to be genetic modification of real animals going on here?'

A short time later, I checked back to see how things were going in the barn. Three of the eggs had hatched into green baby lizards! They looked like tiny green T Rex dinosaurs.

There were egg shell halves lying open on the floor. The attendant was leaning on his pitchfork, watching contentedly, as if he had done the whole thing himself. Daddy lizard had picked up one of the babies, and was cuddling it on his shoulder, his face full of happiness. Mother lizard was looking approvingly at the two other babies toddling around her feet, while she continued keeping the other eggs warm.

I never found out what the budget arrangements were for other parts of the Our Group terrorist world, but it did not seem that I had got to the heart of the terrorists' financing, anyway. I should have been focusing on the mechanism for making and recording financial transactions.

Refocussing my concentration, I went back into the electromagnetic environment, and viewed the Earth from above, tuning into frequencies to give me a steer for where to go. Immediately, I picked up a place in New York. It was the terrorists' equivalent of the United Nations, the International Unity Guild. The modern skyscraper had a row of flagpoles outside the building, each flying a terrorist flag. I had visited this place before. It seemed to be yet another talking shop. But what if it housed the Our Group payments computer system? It did.

I went down to the computer payments system offices, on the mezzanine floor, where rows of staff worked at desktops, inputting terrorist activity records, submitted from all over the world. The activity records were used by the computer to calculate entitlement to payments for services rendered. Payments were then sent to specified bank accounts for nominated international operational heads.

I was looking for a security back-up payments disk, which would record the payments made to bank accounts in the last week, and which ought also to contain a list of all the bank accounts into which payments were made. The disks were likely to be kept in a security cabinet, ready for transportation off-site, so that in the event of emergencies, payments could be made from another location. In this case, the sister site was a large data centre in Utah.

It was not difficult for me to gain access to the cabinets containing the latest payments disks, and earlier ones already deposited at the sister site. I decided to hand the disks in to the reception desk at the Canadian Military base at Calgary. I suggested that they might look for the bank accounts used by the Toronto mafia, details of which had recently been provided to them by their VIP prisoners.

The man on the reception desk called someone from IT division to come up and take delivery of the computer payment disks. I explained what they were, and he called another technical specialist to assist him. They went into a room which had technology that could read disks, and started examining them.

'Hey!' called one of the technicians. 'I know the code for that banking location, it's about sixty miles from here. And look at the amounts going through!'

Turning to me he said, 'Don't worry, we will liaise with our contacts in the United States and have all these bank accounts stopped. And then we will get the addresses for each of the bank accounts in Canada, and visit them.'

I returned home, hopeful that these developments would have some impact on terrorist funding arrangements, but not expecting too much. However, in the days that followed, the International Unity Guild expelled Our Group from their membership, which meant they did not get any more money.

This left local terrorists relying temporarily on Irish mafia family heads for continued support.

The IRA, who are separate from the Irish mafia, also severed communications with Our Group. All that was left of the collaborators were various mafia clans in Canada, the Irish Republic and Northern Ireland, and some minor potentates in the Middle and Far East. I was pleased to discover that the United States government had alerted Singapore, Malaysia and Indonesia, and notified them of suspect bank accounts in their countries. Terrorists were traced from the bank accounts in those countries, and were arrested.

LOUIS XV MOON PALACE

One day, I had been to visit people living in the Moon villages. Most of the folks living there had worked out how to make what they needed just by thinking about it, so they were doing well. You need to be in an electromagnetic environment to do this. As all the people who went to the Moon lived in that environment, they had no problem.

The Moon is a place of great beauty, especially at dawn and dusk. The light from the rocks shines and sparkles, creating an atmosphere of peace and aliveness. Looking out at the stars and planets, you feel the wonder of it all. I was floating above ground, taking in the landscape, when I saw a large hole, like a cave entrance, partly in shadow. I went in to explore it, and found an enormous underground space. It was as if the ground had once been a molten substance filled with gas, creating a huge bubble, which popped at the top, and cooled like that.

There were people in there. They looked like African tribesmen. I knew that I had not brought them there, so I went over to meet them and find out how they got there. The tribesmen were simple, friendly people, wearing loincloths, and not much else. They had a lot of hair, which stood out from their head in corkscrews, like sunrays. They smiled a lot and said they liked living on the Moon.

They told me that some North Americans had brought them there from Mali to work as labourers on a building site, because of their ability to breath without assistance on the Moon. I knew there was a terrorist base on the border between Mali and Algeria, run by North Americans. I had learned more about the development of that base on my previous mission — which was consistent with their account.

At one end of the cave there was a man-made opening, like a doorway. I went through, into an area surrounded by high rocks. At the base of the rocks there was a camp site, contained in a large plastic dome. There was a sleeping bay, with camp beds, and makeshift clothes storage, leading to wash rooms and a kitchen. A few men were asleep in bed. Others, wearing a uniform of red and blue check shirts and blue jeans, were making hot drinks in the kitchen. Outside the plastic dome, men with breathing apparatus and protective clothing, were working inside the high rocks. They operated electric drilling equipment to create a hollowed-out building, accessed through a doorway cut out of the rock at ground level.

The ground floor was nearly complete, with spaces for windows cut in the rock, and a staircase cut in stone, leading to the floor above. This is where work was underway. The window spaces were in place, and the floor had been sanded to a smooth finish. Men on ladders were smoothing the outside of the building, to give it a polished look. On the first floor, two of the African tribesmen were carrying furniture into one of the rooms.

I recognised the furniture. It was in the style of Louis XV, and quite ornate, just like ones I had seen in the electromagnetic castle constructed by Our Group scientists in Toronto. One of the Africans brought in an important chair, like a throne, and placed it behind a carved, wooden office desk. There was no doubt about it, Our Group were on the Moon, and that was not good news for the people who had chosen to live there.

Making myself invisible to human eyes, I went into the North American builders' camp, to try and find out how the men were getting up here from Earth. I passed through a leisure area, with a large, incongruous fridge that delivered ice cubes and fizzy drinks, and went along a corridor. There was an unfurnished room, with a projector screen set up along one wall, and a large square dais in front of it. About ten feet away, was a tripod, supporting what looked like photographic equipment of some kind. I waited there for a while.

Suddenly, a light came on in the lens of the equipment, and machinery started whirring in the background. I moved into the shadows and watched. The light from the lens grew brighter, shining onto the projection screen. Then, the shadow of a man in a cowboy hat was visible. The shadow took on depth and became three dimensional. Colours appeared — brown leather boots, blue jeans and a red and blue checked shirt. The man stepped off the dais and walked slowly into the leisure area, where he lay back on a sofa, with his feet up on a foot rest. Another man dressed in the same gear but without the hat, came into the room, and seeing him, produced a drink from the cold-drinks dispenser. There was some murmured conversation, and then both men went into the kitchen.

I decided to try and find where the men were coming from on Earth, so I went into the room with the projector, and tuned into the equipment on the tripod, trying to "back-engineer" the arrival process. Next moment, I was in a larger room, on a dais with a projection screen behind it, and similar equipment to what I had seen on the Moon, facing me. There was no one there, but through an internal glass partition, I could see men walking down a set of stairs, as if they were going home at the end of their work shift.

Then a man dressed in the same cowboy uniform as the builders on the Moon appeared, walking up the stairs. He came into the room, closed the door, and switched the tripod equipment on. After two minutes, a green light showed on the equipment, and the door to the room automatically locked. A red light went on outside the door. Then a panel in the back wall, near the ceiling, opened, and two bright light beams shone down onto the projector screen. The man stepped up onto the dais, in front of the projector screen. As he stood there, he started to shimmer, like a mirage. Then all I could see was a brilliant blinding light. He had gone.

Outside, the late afternoon sun was blazing down on a modern town with industrial buildings, shops and offices. I had no idea where I was. I needed to tell the authorities what was going on, but which authorities? The only ones I had been in contact with were in Canada, but it looked as if this town might be in the United States. I went back to Calgary to the military base, and spoke to the reception desk.

'The same people that you've got in custody here seem to be doing some secret construction work off planet. Is there anyone I can talk to about that?' I asked.

The man at reception recognised me, and smiled.

'Just a moment, please, I'll get someone for you,' he said.

One of the military staff, a manager called Oliver, who I had met previously, came out, and invited me to join him in one of the lounge coffee table areas. I explained what had happened on the Moon, and how the terrorists were operating from a building somewhere in North America.

'Can you go back to that building?' he asked. 'That way, we can find out whether it is in Canada or the States. Whichever country it is, we or they, can check if there are any suspicious activities, and if there are, we'll get the people running this racket.'

'OK,' I said.

Oliver led me through some glass doors at the end of the corridor into a technical specialist work area. The technicians put a tracker on me, so that they could follow my progress, and I took off again for the building where the "cowboys" were running their private Moon travel business. The Canadians were in voice contact with me as well.

'Hold it right there,' said a technician, as I entered the room with the projector screen. 'OK, great, we've got a fix on you.'

Then I heard him talking to another technician.

'Look what we've got here. Just look where we are.'

'Can I come back now?' I asked.

'Oh, sure,' came the reply.

I returned to the Canadian military room. The two technicians were leaning back in their chairs, smiling.

'Do you know where I was?' I asked.

'That's Texas,' said the Canadian. 'Don't worry. We've got the GPS coordinates for that place. We'll pass them on to the US military, so they can take a look.'

I went home, there being nothing more I could do to help, but I was curious to see what, if anything, would happen as a result of all this.

Making myself invisible to the human eye, I discreetly entered the Texas first floor room with the projector screen. It was dark and empty. On the landing outside, I could see a soldier in uniform, carrying a semi-automatic weapon. Outside at the back of the building, men in cowboy gear were climbing into the back of a large van, supervised by more soldiers. I could hear people talking, downstairs on the ground floor. Several men in military uniform were searching the building. They came up the stairs, opened the door to the projector room, and looked in. Then one of them made a call on his cellphone. Some technicians appeared, wearing protective clothing. They systematically stripped the room, including the wiring, and took away the lights that directed beams from the wall.

On the floor above, the technicians found and removed satellite WIFI communications technology, surveillance and recording equipment, and the consul that operated the teleportation equipment in the projection room below. It seems that Our Group's operations were not limited to teleportation. They had a keen interest in the activities of NASA. The building was located in a small dormitory town on the outskirts of Houston.

After the terrorists' Moon building work was permanently halted, I went back to see what had happened to the people working up there. There were no North Americans to be seen. Their camp was still there, but it was deserted. They would not have fled into hiding, as they could not breath on the Moon, unaided. The African tribesmen were now using the rock palace as part of their territory. They were sitting on the first floor, the outside of which was unfinished, their legs swinging from what had been destined to be Perspex window panels, enjoying the sunset. When they saw me, they greeted me in a friendly way.

'What happened to the North Americans?' I asked.

'Big men came and took them away,' said one of them. 'But one was hiding and escaped.'

I went and looked in the cowboys' camp. I could see someone lying on the sofa in the leisure area. He saw me and raised himself painfully into a sitting position.

'Are you all right?' I said. 'Do you have enough oxygen?'

'I have enough for now,' he said, haltingly. 'But there is not much left. These guys — pointing to the Africans — think I can learn to breath outside like them, but I can't. They mean well, but I think they will take me outside and kill me soon.'

Three Africans marched confidently into the camp kitchen and helped themselves to fizzy drinks from the fridge dispenser. Then they sat round the cowboy, smiling.

'Don't worry,' said one of them. 'You can stay here with us and you will be all right.'

'Do you want me to take you back to Earth?' I asked.

The man was undecided.

'I don't want you to hand me over to the authorities,' he said.

'Well is there somewhere you can go, then?' I asked.

'I can't think of anywhere safe now,' he said.

'Come with us,' said the Africans, and they began pushing and pulling him up on to his feet.

'Help me for God's sake!' shouted the man.

I picked him up, and took him back to the military base at Calgary, depositing him on the helipad outside the building. He lay back, unable to lift himself up, owing to the heavier gravity. I produced a high energy water drink to help him ground himself.

Oliver came out and asked what had happened. I explained, and he called for the medical team. Two men brought a stretcher, and lifted the cowboy onto it.

'I'm sorry I had to bring you here,' I said to the cowboy. 'But I really couldn't think where else to take you. At least you will be well looked after here.'

'Oh, I guess it's for the best,' the cowboy replied. 'Thanks anyway.'

He gave a wave of his hand, as the men carried him away.

DUTCH AND RUSSIAN PRISON VISITS

One afternoon, forty large, tall Caucasians arrived in the unit near where I lived. They had been summoned by the local terrorists, under the terms of the International Unity Guild treaty, which requires its members to provide troops to assist other members, for a fee, on request. The visitors were mainly fair haired or red headed, and strongly built. They had come from Zeeland, which is on the coast of the Netherlands, and had been travelling most of the day. They looked tired and hungry. Our local terrorists eyed them with suspicion. These guys might turn out to be better than they were, and their jobs could be at risk. The locals decided to put the Zeelanders in to bat as soon as they arrived, knowing they were already tired. They were to work from six p.m. to six in the morning, and their mission was to attack me.

But the Zeelanders had other ideas. They invaded the terrorists' common room, and staged a sit-down strike, demanding food and beds for the night. The local terrorists withdrew to commune amongst themselves. Physically, they were no match for these big Europeans. They started phoning round to other units for reinforcements, but none could be found at short notice.

Things didn't look good from my point of view either. We hardly ever had terrorist visitors from the European continent. I could hand them over to our prison service, but why should our under-staffed, hard-working prison officers have to put up with them? And why should these Europeans be given board and lodging at the taxpayers' expense?

Still, it was good that they didn't want to attack me. I thought I ought to make the effort to contact the Netherlands Prison Service, to see if they would be willing to take their own lot back. With that in mind, I looked up the Netherlands Prison Service on the internet. I was amazed to read that most Netherlands prisons are empty, because there is hardly any crime there.

'Great,' I thought. 'Then there will be plenty of room for these guys.'

So, I borrowed one of the Zeelanders, a man called Cas, who was looking rather disconsolate, and set off for the Netherlands. I selected a small Dutch prison from the internet, studied a photo of the building, and tuned into its frequency. I hoped that security there would be sufficient to enable me to communicate easily within an electromagnetic environment. I arrived on the first floor of the building, and leaving Cas there, made my way down towards the foyer. As I did so, I passed an office with an open door. A man was sitting at a desk. Pictures of his family were on the bookcase behind him. He looked up as I passed, and said, 'Hello, would you like to come in for a cup of tea?'

Then, spotting Cas standing rather uncomfortably at the top of the stairs, he added, 'Would you like a cup of tea as well?'

We both sat on the sofa, in what turned out to be the prison governor's office, and I explained why I had come. The prison governor, whose name was Adriaan, looked a little perplexed.

'The trouble is,' he said. 'I only have accommodation for eight prisoners here. We have a large new prison, that has plenty of room. I'm afraid it is a long way from here though.'

'Do you have a photograph of it?' I asked.

Adriaan left the office, while we sipped our tea, and came back with a publication detailing the benefits of the brand-new establishment. I looked at the photograph, and saved a copy in my mind.

'I can go now, and be there in a few minutes,' I said.

'Fine,' said Adriaan. 'Let me ring through first and see if it is all right.'

He phoned up the prison governor of the state-of-the-art prison, and got the go-ahead for all forty Zeelanders to go there. Cas was feeling exhausted, and didn't want to do any more teleporting. Turning to Adriaan, he said, 'Would it be OK if I stayed here tonight — if it's not inconvenient?'

'Of course,' said Adriaan. 'We have some free cells. I'll arrange for you to be taken to one right away.'

I left them to it and headed off to the modern prison. The prison governor was waiting for me in the foyer. He greeted me warmly, and took me into his office.

'This will be a special day for us,' he announced. 'We have no prisoners here at the moment, and we want to test out our ability to respond to emergencies. It will be an excellent opportunity. Just give us half an hour to prepare a light meal, and then bring the men in.'

I returned home to find the local terrorists and the Zeelanders just coming to the boil. The Zeelanders were not willing to leave the locals' common room, and the locals were arming themselves outside the house, in preparation for a confrontation. I called the Zeelanders together and explained that they were about to be escorted back to prison in their own country. The men brightened up immediately, especially when they heard it would be "door to door". They got all their belongings together and off we went, leaving the locals peering in through the windows, like animals that had been put out for the night.

As we arrived, the prison governor and his deputy were at the door to greet each prisoner personally. The men were led into the main hall, where a finger buffet had been laid out. At the other end of the hall, there was a long row of doors, leading to spacious cells, each with ensuite facilities. The prison governor and his deputy mingled with their "guests", but very soon the exhausted Zeelanders politely excused themselves, and headed for the cells. I thanked the governor for his hospitality and left. I was also looking forward to an early night.

Not long afterwards, I was looking for places to dump terrorists again, this time as a deterrent. The Irish mafia continued to bombard me with waves of low-level Irish criminals, who had all been promised a small fortune, if they could get me under their control. Their methods typically involved directing disorientating microwave beams at my head, and electromagnetic oscillator attacks. I could, and did, regularly wipe out senior terrorists who authorised such attacks, but I wanted a place to put low-level terrorists, that would be sufficiently unpleasant to discourage others from trying.

I decided that a prison in Siberia would not be a bad place to leave the criminals. So I looked up a prison on the internet, and using the frequency of a photograph to guide me, I arrived there with about thirty terrorists in tow. I placed them in the exercise yard outside the prison, and watched to see what would happen. There was high security cordon around the prison, including a great deal of electromagnetic technology.

Several Russian prison officers came out and rounded up the terrorists, dividing them into two groups, young people and the rest. A senior officer came out and phoned head office in Moscow. Apparently, they had captured my image on CCTV footage — not possible with standard technology, but despite that, they had got an image of me in my black puffa coat and hood. Their Head Office already knew all about me, and about my previous visits to prisons in Iran, from my past mission, and they directed the prison to accept the terrorists, and to do with them as they saw fit.

This tells you something about the state of readiness and investment in advanced technologies that we can expect from the Russians. Like most countries, the Russians are opposed to all forms of terrorism. In the past, I had quite a sympathetic response from Russia, partly because they were aware that the majority of my persecutors came from North America.

On an earlier occasion, I was attacked by black-clad weapons-group Canadian terrorists, who were transported along an electromagnetic pathway, a long airborne tunnel that extended from Toronto to my home. I picked up the end of the tunnel, towed it all the way to the suburbs of Moscow, and left it there. A few minutes later, the Russians produced an electromagnetic architecture of their own, which projected like a motorway flyover towards the Canadian tunnel. The Russians boarded the Canadian pathway, arrested all the Canadian terrorists, and took them away in unmarked vans.

But that was not the end of the story. That night, I was lying in bed, being attacked by yet more of these guys, when suddenly, the Russians arrived. They had tracked the Canadians back to my place. They gave the Canadians a hard time, removed them all, and waved a friendly goodbye as they left. Do not underestimate the Russians, that is my advice.

So, to return to Siberia, the prison officers sent all the older criminals off to a poor-quality building in a different part of town. They used the young men as male prostitutes and unpaid servants to help around the prison. The young men had no problem with this, as it was exactly the same treatment they got at home, and they settled in well. There was one young woman terrorist in the group, and she was sent to an austere woman's prison nearby. From what I could tell, the regime in Siberia was hard, but no worse than other prisons I had visited. Conditions in the prisons reflected the general lack of investment in that part of Russia.

All this happened before I invented the magick table restaurants. Once providing magick table restaurants was an option, I started revisiting places that might benefit from them. Siberia was high on my list of places, and I returned to the prison, and started by placing large baskets of biscuits which refilled themselves automatically, at the end of each corridor. Then I went to the prison kitchens and turned their tables into magick restaurant tables. I did the same for the women's prison as well.

The Siberia prison officers were pleased with the results. Their senior officers also approved, as requests for better pay and conditions were routinely ignored by their head office. Three prison officers came out and met me in the exercise yard. They were big, heavy men, who could, no doubt, turn ugly if you got on the wrong side of them. But they smiled warmly.

'Thanks for the food supply, it will help us a lot,' said one of the men, whose name was Sergei. 'But if you could see your way to helping us a bit more, that would be very good.'

'What did you have in mind?' I asked.

'Well,' said Sergei. ''What we really want is a brand-new, modern sports complex, over there by those trees, with an Olympic size pool, full gym and exercise equipment in a large hall, and several smaller halls for basketball and other sports, plus modern shower and toilet facilities. Oh, and we need to be able to maintain a comfortable room temperature indoors whatever the weather outside.'

'Hmm,' I thought. 'This could be tricky. There is no way I could picture what they want. The only way I could do it is to have them picture it all themselves, and use their blueprint to create the architecture.'

So I asked them to spend some time thinking in detail about what they wanted, and when they were ready, I would transfer what was in their mind into reality.

'No thinking necessary,' laughed another prison officer called Dmitri. 'I have all the details in my head.'

'Do you go along with that?' I asked the others.

They all nodded.

'Yes, yes, he is the best for that. He knows what we want.'

'OK, here goes then,' I said.

I selected the image in Dmitri's brain, and willed it to turn into the construction that the men wanted. Immediately, a long, one-storey building, with a lot of Perspex window space along the sides and on the roof appeared. The modern foyer was taller than the rest of the building, and the roof sloped with an artistic sweep across the whole construction. There were two sets of double doors at the back of the foyer, with Perspex panels. Through one of them, I could see the glint of water from an enormous pool.

'Maintenance of all this is going to cost a lot of time and money,' I thought. 'Let's make it that the sports complex reboots itself to be brand new and clean at the beginning of every day, and to be self-sufficient in the use of water, waste pipes and electricity, so that it doesn't need to be connected to local utilities.'

So, I did that, and Sergei, Dmitri and the others went in to inspect the result. After a while they came out, looking greatly heartened.

'Everything OK?' I asked.

'This is very good,' said Sergei. 'We need this to relax after our work.'

Since there appeared to be no problems, I said goodbye and went to the women's prison. I had already visited it earlier to provide food. Following the introduction of the magick restaurant tables, the atmosphere was much more humane, and both prison officers and prisoners looked in better health and less stressed. I asked to speak to the prison governor. The prison governor was a tall smartly dressed woman, with an efficient air about her. She came out and shook my hand.

'We are always pleased to see you,' she said politely. 'What is the reason for your visit?'

I explained that the prison officers in the men's prison had asked for a sports hall, and it seemed only fair that I should offer the women's prison one as well.

'Oh dear,' said the prison governor. 'We only have a small amount of land at the back of the prison, and there just isn't room. What a pity. It's just what we want.'

A thought occurred to me. The hall could be smaller on the outside than on the inside, like the Tardis in the famous science fiction television series 'Dr Who.'

'Would it be OK if the building looked small on the outside, but turned out to be larger when you went in?' I asked.

'Well, anything you can do would be appreciated, if you would like to try,' said the prison governor.

She called in one of her administrative assistants, and asked her to take me into the prison back garden. It was pretty grim, being mainly concrete paving, and about the size of three garages.

'Let's make the entrance to the foyer look like a small conservatory,' I thought.

So, I tried that, and we went in through the conservatory door. Immediately, we were inside the same large foyer that was at the front of the men's prison. It had worked.

Shortly after I got back home, I became aware of two familiar faces looking in on me from the ceiling in the electromagnetic environment. It was Mike and Tanya, from H.M. Special Prison Services. They had a part wistful, part indignant look on their faces.

'Is it possible, I mean…' began Mike.

'What we mean is,' said Tanya. 'If *Russian* prison officers can have a new sports complex, can we have one too?'

'Of course,' I said. 'Show me where you want it built.'

It was an absolutely baking day. Mike led me round to the back of the Special Prison Services building. Several other prison officers followed him.

'Over there would be best,' said one of them.

The site he chose was an unused area of grass. It wasn't going to be big enough, but we could work round that by making it larger inside than out.

'Are you all agreed on this as the best place?' I asked the men, and they nodded.

'Let's go then!' I said, and willed the creation of a state-of-the-art sports centre along the lines of the one in Siberia.

I must admit it looked rather good, and a great deal better than what had been there before. While I was admiring the outside architecture, designed by our Russian friends, the prison officers had all disappeared inside. I found them all in the Olympic pool hall. Some of them had stripped off to their trunks, and others wore even less. They just dived in and started swimming away. I watched one of them on the turn, up the other end. His arms cut through the water, and his face was spattered with water droplets. He was like a thirsty man, who had just been given a cooling drink. I had no idea how badly the prison officers needed a place to refresh and get rid of the stresses of their exceptionally challenging jobs.

Tanya was waiting for me outside.

'If I could make a suggestion,' she said. 'We would like a separate women's sports complex over here, but we don't want the same as the men. We want a large kitchen, and a small babies' paddling pool. As well as the Olympic pool, we want a shorter one, that women can use if they don't want to train for competitions, but just want to enjoy a relaxing swim.'

'OK,' I said.

Using what was in Tanya's mind, I made a separate women's sports hall. It blended into the background in the garden, and was larger inside than out. Tanya and two other women prison officers went in to check it out. They spent a long time in there, so I went to look for them. They were in the kitchen, busying themselves. There was a large fridge freezer, a dishwasher, a cooker and other kitchen equipment. Several other women came in with provisions, and started stocking the cupboards with food.

A woman with a baby buggy and a toddler came in through the automatic double doors. I saw them heading for the children's paddling pool. Then there was a ring at the door. Mike was standing outside, his hair still wet after a swim.

'The women's sports team from our main centre want to use the big pool,' he said.

'That was quick work,' I thought. 'The place has only been open half an hour.'

At that moment, several tall, fit women pushed past me, carrying a lot of kit, and went off towards the changing rooms.

I went outside, and left them to get on with it. I was about to go, when I recognised the white-coated senior government scientist, Elliot approaching.

'Could you spare me a minute?' he asked.

'Sure,' I said.

'Could you tell me how the sports halls are powered?' he asked. 'Is it solar power?'

'I can put some solar panels on the roof if you think it would look better,' I said. 'But it isn't solar powered. I think it works by extracting electricity from plasma. I know that plasma isn't normally available on the Earth, but perhaps it is possible to derive it within an electromagnetic environment such as the one we are in.'

What made me say that, and was it true? It was only a hunch, based on what I had observed when travelling to and from the Milky Way on errands for Lars. I have no scientific training and am just an old pensioner, so I might not have got it quite right.

'Could you print out a flow diagram that shows how that works?' asked Elliot.

We were walking towards his building now, and into his office.

'OK,' I said.

I willed a flow diagram to be produced that would answer the question that Elliot was asking, even if I hadn't grasped it myself. The flow diagram splurged out of nowhere and began to unfold all over the room. Then it had to fold itself back, in order to go out of the door into the garden.

'I'll make a short summary diagram as well,' I said, producing something the size of two A3 pages.

'Thanks, Martha,' said Elliot. 'That's very thoughtful of you.'

I could see two of his research staff helping to fold the giant flow diagram into manageable proportions. That was the last I saw of him for some time, and he never referred to the subject again.

LIFE IN OTHER WORLDS

It had been several months since Lars asked me to help him with his research. During that time, he had been writing a report about all the rock samples he had studied. Presumably, it was for restricted circulation. Then after that, he went on holiday. But now I received an invitation to go and visit him in his new building.

Before he went on holiday, Lars told me that he was leaving the Surrey science laboratory and moving somewhere else. He seemed to be saying that I could find him at a particular place, which he wrote in large letters, so that I could read it. The words he wrote spelt "LEIDEN ASTROPHYSICS". I looked them up on the internet, and found that there is an astronomical institute of the Faculty of Science at Leiden University in the Netherlands.

English is not Lars's first language, and communication with him is sometimes a challenge. It seemed that he was saying he was going to work in Leiden University. But when I checked the list of professors, he was not there. So I used my usual method of locating people, and tuned into his frequency.

It turned out that he was now working at London University, with a vast room all to himself, which was attached to a large laboratory. Perhaps Lars meant to say that Leiden

University had sponsored his work in London. Or perhaps Lars was due to move to Leiden University, but his plans changed in the light of exciting results from NASA's work on identifying planets with signs of life in the Milky Way. Maybe NASA invited London University to undertake a project on that, and they wanted Lars to join them.

When I arrived in Lars's room, he was in the lab with his new assistant, a rather dour PhD student called Philip. Philip was quizzing Lars about his background.

'You *are* Dutch, aren't you? I know you are,' said Philip.

'No, I am *not,*' said Lars indignantly.

'Well, Lars *is* a Dutch name,' retorted Philip.

I was fairly sure that Lars was from Norway, but Philip was obviously intrigued that Lars was connected to a university in the Netherlands, and wanted to get the explanation out of him. However, he was unsuccessful. Lars never wasted time on unnecessary talk.

Lars beckoned me into his personal office. Then, as usual, he showed me a photo of a planet he wanted me to get samples from. It was a tiny faint dot, and I did not think it likely I would find it, but off I went.

I found out I had landed when I hit the ground. There was no light. I dug with my fingers in the ground, and something like earth came out. It was fairly soft, and it felt damp. I put the earth in a plastic bag and was about to head back to the lab, when a light shone dimly through the clouds above. It looked like a moon. But wait... clouds! I had never seen clouds on my space errands before. I rose above the world and looked down. Yes, there were clouds, but only around the North Pole. Still, that was something out of the ordinary.

I deposited the earth on the weighing table in Lars's laboratory. A few bits fell off, and Philip frowned. He was clearly thinking, 'Now I'll have to clean that up.'

Philip took the results to Lars. I told Lars I had seen clouds like on Earth. Lars asked me to go back and check. So I made a second journey. By now, the planet was in daylight, somewhat overcast, as if it might rain. I hovered above the dark brown earth to check the North Pole area. The clouds were still there, but underneath, there was something which looked green.

'No, it couldn't be,' I thought.

I went down to investigate. What I saw was a large stretch of green vegetation, all the same type of plant, extending for miles. I took a leaf and brought it back for Lars to examine. It looked small on the weighing table, but massive when regurgitated through the technical ducting. Lars was standing there staring at it. Then he asked Philip to take a sample to someone in another part of the building. Soon a senior-looking lady appeared. Her name was Marion. No doubt she was a professor. She was in her late forties, with brown hair, and a beige skirt and jumper underneath her unbuttoned white coat. She and Lars talked for a while. Then she turned to me.

'Can you go and get a whole plant, please?' she said.

'I can,' I said. 'But it won't fit on the weighing table.'

'Oh, don't worry about that,' said Marion. 'Just go and get it. We'll sort out the rest.'

'Fine,' I thought, and I headed off towards the rather unprepossessing vegetation.

When I got there, I realised the plants were a lot taller than I had thought. Each one stood a good four feet above the ground. The stems were quite thick and had several leaves, all the way to the top. I tugged at a plant but the roots would not come up. In the end, I broke the stem off, at ground level and headed back, clutching the plant in a large plastic bag. As I left, I noticed the smell of warm, damp earth, similar to what we have here, after a heavy rain shower in Summer.

Philip was waiting. He looked a little less dour now. In fact, he was quite helpful.

'Just leave the plant in the bag next to the weighing table, and I'll sort it out,' he said.

Lars actually thanked me for my work.

'Please come back in a week,' he said.

During the week, I searched the internet for information about life on other worlds. According to some reports, NASA had been carrying out a search for Earth-sized planets that might be like ours for years, using its Kepler space telescope, and had found evidence of other worlds that might be inhabitable in the Milky Way galaxy. For more on NASA's Exoplanet exploration in the Milky Way, see www.exoplanets.nasa.gov.

When I returned to the science lab the next week, Lars had another planet for me to explore. He did not want samples at this stage. I headed off with a picture of a small dim light in my head, and arrived on bare ground, next to some hills with rocks and small cliffs emerging from them. There was nothing green to be seen. I could hear water running inside the rocks and went down to investigate. Inside was a very large, dark cave, lit only by light from the entrance at one end. Water poured out of the entrance and down a cliff into a deep pool below.

I could hear splashing, so I went into the cave to see what was making the noise. At first, I couldn't see anything in the darkness. Then I realised that there was something there, shining like a glow-worm in the dark. It looked like a horrific head with staring eye sockets and a strange tiara on top. In fact, it was the head of a large water serpent with horns on its head. Several parts of the serpent's face were luminous in the dark. Suddenly, it whizzed up onto the roof of the cave, and snapped at something, which it caught and swallowed whole. As it opened its mouth it displayed huge incisors like those of a sabre-toothed tiger. It seemed a good idea to make myself invisible.

I watched as the serpent hunted about on the ceiling, near where a large patch of lichen was growing. There were small brown animals nibbling the lichen. Then I saw one of them fly off. It was a bat. Despite my invisibility, the serpent seemed to detect my presence. It made a beeline for me. I raced for the exit and stood looking in from outside. Another serpent was floating near the exit. It did not have horns. The sabre-toothed serpent came chasing after me, but when it saw the other serpent, it stopped and seemed to be checking out how things were with it. Then it went shooting up onto the roof of the cave again to catch more bats. The other serpent looked back for a minute, and then shut its eyes, floating serenely on the water. I guessed it was a female, clearly unimpressed by its sabre-toothed companion's acrobatics.

I returned to the lab, and told Lars what I had seen.

'Can you check if there are any plants growing in the water?' he said. 'If there are, please could you bring me a sample?'

I went back and dived into the underground lake, as near to the exit as possible, so that I could get enough light to see what was there. The first things I saw were several large grey eels, and a smallish whale-shaped grey fish, not moving much. There were quite a few plants growing under the water, and the fish and eels seemed interested in them. At that moment, a thunderbolt hit the water. The sabre-toothed serpent came bombing towards me like a torpedo. I jumped sideways. I could see he was turning round to have another go. Quickly, I grabbed some bits of water plants and headed for home, stuffing the plants in a plastic bag as I went.

I arrived in the lab dripping wet, clutching the bag. As I did so, all the staff in that part of the building stood up and ran out covering their noses. There was a greasy oil on my clothes. I smelt appalling. Lars asked Philip to put on the air-conditioning and to clean the stuff off my clothes. I stood in a shower cubicle, as he directed the shower head all over me, retaining the dirty water for analysis. I willed my clothes to be fresh, clean and dry. Then I put the plastic bag, with the water plants in the glass cabinet.

I wondered what would happen if the plants came out of the stabilisation process smelling as bad as I had done. Lars was clearly wondering the same thing.

'No need to put the plants on the weighing table just yet,' said Lars. 'You go and freshen up. I'll see you same time next week.

Next week. Lars was waiting for me in his laboratory. He had his feet up on a leather footstool and was reading what looked like a novel.

'Ah, there you are,' he said, smiling. 'I have another planet for you to visit.'

Lars showed me another rather indistinct photograph, with a circle round the relevant light dot, and I did my best to memorise it, as I tuned into the frequency and went in search of whatever was out there.

This time, I landed on a desert floor in daylight. Then I heard Lars's voice, 'What can you see?'

'It's just a brown desert with mountains in the background,' I replied.

'Can you go and search the mountains, and look in any crevices,' said Lars. 'There might be some lichen in there.'

'OK,' I said.

The mountains were a sandy yellow colour. I looked down cracks in the rock, and saw some green moss. I scraped some off and was just putting it in a plastic bag, when something grabbed the bag and pulled it down a hole.

'Stop that! Give me back my bag!' I shouted, trying to get at it.

I heard a strange rattling noise. Then I saw a brown coppery coloured thing appear. It was like the leg of a cockroach. I stepped back. Then a beetle-like creature hauled itself out of the hole. How it got out, I couldn't say, as it was about ten feet long, and six feet high, when it finally emerged. I gave it a wide berth. It had a head with a long proboscis in the front, and several sets of legs. Its coppery wing cases opened up, showing brown metallic wings beneath. It could possibly be a member of the cockchafer family.

The giant insect began scouring the desert with its long feelers. It found what looked like pine needles, and began eating them. But there were no pine trees in sight. I looked around and saw a dark area, which might be a forest of spruce. The trees were so close together that there was no light under them. There was something moving, though. I went straight there. A group of giant, shiny black beetles, each about the size of a pig, was coming out of the forest. They came into a clearing and started burrowing in the earth with their mouths. They took the earth in their mouths, and seemed to add something to the earth before dropping it again. Then they burrowed deeper. Whatever they were doing, it softened and conditioned the earth. I could see thin white tendrils in the earth, like tiny roots. This was what the beetles were after. They grazed single-mindedly for some time.

Then I heard Marion's voice.

'Please can you try and bring back a biological sample from the mountain beetle.'

I realised that Marion could see what I was seeing. I suspected that the scientists had tuned into the cameras that the terrorists had put in my eyes.

I went back to the mountain area. By now, the ground at the base of the mountain was covered with giant cockchafer's apparently grazing on dust and pine needles. I willed myself to go into the hole through which the first beetle had emerged. It was not entirely dark inside, as there were plenty of holes and cracks in the mountain surface. The place was a sea of squirming and wriggling copper legs and wings. The young grubs of the beetles were in there too. I caught sight of a dead beetle and grabbed its leg. Hurrying back to the lab, I placed it on the weighing table.

'Well done!' said Marion.

'Now, could you go back and try and find the trees with the pine needles,' said Lars. 'If you can detect a breeze, look towards the direction that it is coming from.'

I returned to the planet and did as Lars had advised. This time, I spotted two very tall trees. They had no branches except near the top, and they were pine trees. They were standing on a bank near an estuary. The land around them was flat, and covered with puddles. It looked as if the water rose and fell at various times, like a tide.

I turned towards the mouth of the estuary and saw a wonderful blue sea, extending across the horizon. And then, inexplicably, walking across the sands by the water's edge, I saw an elephant! It was about ten feet tall, grey, and looked exactly like elephants on Earth. It had no tusks.

'Oh, it's got a baby!' cried Marion.

I checked the big elephant. At the back, was a small baby elephant, drinking from its mother's udder.

The mother elephant waded slowly into the sea, and began making its way to where a mass of algae was growing in the transparent seawater, close to some high rocks. I moved out into the sea, and round the other side of the rocks. There was an enormous underwater cavern, and I could see grey aquatic animals swimming in and out of it. I went into the cave. Part of the cave was above the water, and there was a waterfall at one end. Standing in the water was a marine creature that looked like the Loch Ness monster's younger cousin. Its neck was not as long as Nessie's but otherwise it was similar. Its mouth must have been very large, because it was crunching up the bodies of dead cockchafers as if they were popcorn, and each one of those was about ten feet long.

Marine mammals kept diving in and swimming out of the cave, apparently for fun. They were very large, with grey skin like a walrus, and faces a bit like a seal, without tusks. They had big feet, not flippers, with toes like an elephant, and teeny tails like dogs.

I was getting a bit tired now, so I moved back to the shore, and was preparing to leave, when I saw something moving in the sea, about half a mile out. I flew over to have a look. Two enormous grey creatures, like the one I saw in the cave but far larger, were leaping and cavorting together. They chased each other round and round, pulling each other's tails with their mouths, and rolling over, diving under the waves and shooting out above them again. They were really enjoying themselves. And why not? There did not seem to be any predators.

There were no fish in the sea. I wondered how the sea mammals, if they were mammals, found anything to eat, to make them get so big. I flew over the coast for a while. Then I came on several different sea mammals all pulling large swathes of algae and green goo out of a tangled mass which seemed to grow in the water near some tall cliffs. There were giant walrus or seal type animals, and some middle-sized Nessie type creatures all munching away on the seaweed. So *that* was what kept them all so fit and healthy.

I returned to the giant sea creatures. They were speeding under water. One of them, in the lead, had a tree trunk in its mouth, in spite of which it was clearly smiling. It dived enthusiastically into a deep cave, and came up for air. Several large marine mammals were lying above the water level on stone ledges that may have reflected a time when the sea was higher up than it was now. They waved a foot here, or a tail there, but ignored the enormous log-bearing retriever. With mounting excitement, the sea creature, still pursued by its friend, dived back out of the cave, and came up in a shallow, sandy bay. It headed for the shore, and deposited the log triumphantly on the beach. Then it started doing a lap of honour, as if it had scored a goal.

I returned to the science lab. There was a lot of talking going on in the next room, and I could see a large plasma screen on the wall, displaying what I had been looking at. A group of people were sitting watching and taking notes. Marion and Lars were resting on a comfortable brown leather sofa, looking relaxed.

'You can go and visit the planet anytime you like during the week,' said Lars. 'We will have a record of whatever you see. Can you come back in a week's time?'

'Sure,' I said.

I liked the idea of exploring the planet, but right then, all I wanted to do was rest. When I got home, I went straight to bed, and into a dreamless sleep.

During the following week, I went back to the planet and continued exploring. I flew up and looked down from far above, to get an overview of what was there. Inland, there were mountains with what looked like spruce trees. They were very tall and all their branches swept downwards. If you stood underneath it was like being in a tent, because the light could not come through directly, and the ground was covered with pine needles. The trees were covered with white stuff which glistened in the sun. At first, I thought it was snow, but later, I picked up some of it. It was thin pieces of silica that must have been blown there from a desert or salt flats.

Despite the prevalence of the trees, which monopolised the mountains for hundreds of miles, there were clearings with rich grass further down, and by the sea, there were tall grasses over six feet high, which curled over, creating tunnels beneath their shade.

'What was stopping the trees from growing further down the hills?' I wondered.

It soon became clear. Some of the tree branches were shaking. I looked to see what was causing it, and up on a branch I saw a large brown bear, eating the bark of the tree. That would finish off any tree. The bear was similar to ones on Earth. Then I saw what looked like a brown panda, eating the bark of another tree. The panda seemed to be smiling as it chomped through the bark on the branches.

As I continued my overview of the planet, I could see lush green grass, with a small river running through it. Large brown cows were sitting in the shade of the trees, apparently chewing the cud. Then I saw a bigger white cow with red spots. It had large horns set widely at the side of its head. And finally, I caught sight of a white horse grazing quietly by itself. It looked exactly like horses do on Earth.

I followed a stream that cascaded down the hills, creating shallow pools as it went. On the edge of one of these pools I saw small eels with fins like fish. The eels were using the fins to walk on the mud surrounding the pool. There were no fish in the sea, so the water in the river must have been more suitable for aquatic life. There were no birds in the air, no flowers and no insects.

It began to get dark, and I moved towards a flat, gravelled area, which might once have been under water, as there were a lot of small round stones. Suddenly I heard a noise like distant thunder, and the ground started shaking. Then the huge, shadowy figure of a bison, with rich, shaggy brown fur, galloped past me.

So far, all my exploration had been in the Northern Hemisphere. I decided to move from night to day, and from north to south. Again, there were spruce trees, but below them were what looked like deciduous trees with large green leaves, stronger in construction than ours. They had the consistency of textiles. I stood under one of these trees, whose branches brushed towards the ground. It seemed as if the wind was blowing the branches, then I realised that some animals were under the branches, rubbing their heads on the ground. They were a dark tan colour with cloven hooves, and the reason they were rubbing their heads on the ground was because they had antlers, which they were trying to get rid of. I saw one that had already shifted its antlers. It looked exactly like deer in our country.

Next day, I explored some cliffs by the sea. There, I found more elephants, several cows, and another bison. They sheltered from the sun underneath the enormously tall grass. Then one of the red and white spotted cows came out and walked towards a stream leading into the sea. The sides of the stream were muddy, and the cow waded into the mud and lay down, rubbing the front of its neck on the muddy side of the river bank.

Having got completely covered with mud, the cow began walking into the sea, and started swimming in the direction of a large mass of green algae and plankton, which had gathered in the sea, around the side of the cliffs. Further on, I found several more animals wading in an estuary and eating the algae which coated the surface of the water. As I left, I caught sight of a large white goat, with a long coat, large ears at right angles to its head, and vertical horns. The goat was munching contentedly on what looked like elephant grass.

At the end of the week, I returned to the science lab, where Marion and Lars were waiting.

Lars said, 'Can you go back to the planet with the animals?'

As he spoke, his eyes lit up like a child's. I realised that even he was excited by the mysterious planet, so far away in space, and yet so similar to Earth.

Marion asked me to get her some of the algae and plankton. This was not going to be as easy as bringing a rock or a plant. I filled a plastic bag with the watery stuff and sealed the top. Then I placed it in the glass cupboard. But how would the water and its contents be analysed? Could it be poured onto the weighing table, or would it have to be left to set into crystalline form? I left Philip to sort that out.

Then Marion asked me to get a sample of grass of the type that the cows had been eating. That was easier, and I brought a handful in a plastic bag, placing one blade on the weighing table. Philip operated the equipment that transformed the grass into something that could survive in our gravity and air pressure. When it came out the other end of the ducting it looked a healthy green colour, and succulent. Marion asked one of her staff to analyse the grass under a microscope. The white-coated assistant soon returned with the results.

'It is like our grass, but the structure is more complex,' she said. 'Also, the grass contains a special type of lipid that we have not seen before.'

I looked up "lipid" on the internet and from what I read, it seems that lipids are molecules that can contain fats and oils, amongst other things, and which, when digested, release a lot of energy. That sounded more nutritious than our ordinary grass, which apparently, contains mainly water-soluble carbohydrates such as glucose and fructose.

I left the scientists to their work, and did not check in to the lab for a week. When I did return, only Philip was in, and he did not conceal his irritation on seeing me.

'They've gone off to write their report now,' he said. 'And after that it will be the Summer holidays. I haven't time to talk to you. I've got my own PhD work to do, and now that Lars has gone, I will finally get time to do it.'

'Good,' I thought. 'That lets me off. Now I can get on with my gardening.'

But two weeks later, I had been rescuing some Irish children brought onto the battle field by the terrorists, when Elliot, the senior military scientist who worked in the Special Research operations area that backed onto HM Special Prison Service, asked me to come into the building. He held up a transparent plastic block about one inch by two inches, containing what looked like pale green dried seaweed, and faded orange organic material.

'Can you go and find where that comes from?' he asked.

'OK,' I said.

'Would you mind wearing these?' said Elliot.

He leant forward and placed a pair of mini glasses on my nose. He adjusted them so that they fitted firmly.

'That way we can see what you see,' he explained.

Previously, Lars and Marion had tuned into the cameras in my eyes, but since then I had learned how to wipe them from my head, and from the heads of other victims, using mental intention combined with self-generated electromagnetic energy. That was why Elliot wanted me to wear the glasses.

'Off you go then,' said Elliot.

I tuned into the plastic slide and focussed hard on aligning my frequency with it. I did not have a clue where I was going. In a minute, I was on a new planet. It looked even more like Earth than the last one I visited. I was standing on top of a white cliff, looking down at white pebbles, and sand, and out to a grey-blue sea. The sky was pale blue, with quite a lot of thin cloud in strands across it.

There was grass where I was standing, but it was sparse and harsh, growing in gravel. I looked up to a higher cliff on my left. There was something moving. It was a large, black flightless bird. The beak reminded me of a small dinosaur in profile. Then a larger version of the same bird, about five feet high came into view. The first bird must have been a chick. I searched the ground up there, and found egg shells lying all over the gravel. There were several other small black chicks, struggling to walk.

There was quite a breeze, and though I could not feel hot or cold temperatures in my electromagnetic form, I could tell that the weather was chilly, like Scotland in Spring. I moved up the rocks and inland. There were a few trees like silver birch, but taller and with stronger branches. One of them was shaking vigorously. A black and white animal about four feet high, a bit like a skunk, was climbing up the branches, to get at the best leaves on the top. The skunk had a huge feathery tail, streaked black and white.

Nearby, a strange animal was grazing. It was a cross between an okapi and sheep. It was coffee-coloured, with white horizontal stripes at the top of its back legs, and short, grey fleece growing on parts of its body, like a waistcoat. It had the same grey fleece on the outside of its long, floppy ears.

Turning back to the top of the cliff, I noticed a large, red cow, sitting on the ground near me. It had a magnificent coat of thick, red fleece. As I turned to look at it, it lifted up its hooves and rolled on its back. Further on, there was a white horse grazing. Then I saw several more. Again, as I looked at them, they all started to roll on the ground, before getting up again and giving themselves a good shake. The horses made their way up a steep hill, following a winding track with shrubs, grasses and trees on either side. At the top, they turned left along the cliff path, their coats shining in the sun.

I turned to the right, and saw what looked like an enormous nest of grass, on the very top of a black granite cliff, with six large chicks bobbing up and down on it. The chicks had bright orange fleece, with streaks of red on their heads, that would one day become fully developed combs. Each chick stayed put in one place, while attempting to move in all directions. They had fans of feathers on their tails, like a capercaillie, and they leaned back on these, giving a push to try and shoot themselves into the air. They carried on like this, with accompanying chirrups and cheeps.

I began to wonder whether they had been given enough to eat, as there was nothing around they could peck. Their bills were slightly curved, which did not help. The chick nearest the edge of the granite cliff started leaning forward to look over. I could see the crumpled body of a dead chick at the bottom. This did not look good. I tried to shoo the chick back a bit. It just looked at me without comprehension.

'Perhaps the mother hen is dead,' I thought. 'Maybe the chicks will die of hunger.'

The chicks redoubled their cheeping and bobbing up and down, in a desperate manner. At that moment, the silhouettes of six huge hens about five feet high could be seen making their way up the cliff path. They carried slimy things in their beaks, which they transferred into the mouths of the chicks. Then they disappeared down the hill again. I stayed watching to see when they would come back, but they never did. So that was it for the day. The chicks became very distressed, and carried on cheeping till they collapsed with exhaustion on their fronts.

Next day, I went to see how the chicks were doing. They were still cheeping and jumping up and down a lot. I didn't know if they had been given any more food. Then the hens reappeared and fed them once again. After they left, I decided to try and lend a hand. Using "evoked potentials", or communication at gut reaction level, I implied to the chicks that they should stop trying to walk on their tails and stick their legs out in front of them, as that was what they were supposed to be walking on. Then they should exercise their muscles by trying to get up on their feet. At this, the chick nearest the edge lurched dangerously forward, and I immediately created a safety fence around the nest to prevent any further chick deaths.

After a short time, the chicks stopped their desperate cheeping, and started to focus on their legs. Then one of them stood up and took a few shaky steps. Soon, all but one of the chicks were on their feet, starting to explore their environment. At this point, possibly alerted by the absence of cheeping, the six hens appeared.

When they saw the chicks walking about, five of the hens ushered their chicks down the long, winding path. The sixth hen gave its chick, still struggling to walk, a stern look. Then it turned to me and gave me a disapproving shake of its head. It stared at the little fence I had constructed, and intimated via non-verbal silent communication, that I should remove it immediately. Then it turned and walked off down the hill, leaving the poor chick desperately trying to get to its feet.

This was too much for me. I lifted the chick to its feet, and helped it to walk about. Then I supported it on one side, as I encouraged it down the hill. But the other chicks were a long way ahead, and I didn't think the chick would make it, so I gave it a lift, and brought it down just behind the others.

At the bottom of the hill was a shallow marsh. As soon as the chicks reached the water they all plunged in, taking the weight off their legs, and splashing about. They were soon diving under the water, and discovering for themselves, that there were water worms, and tiny freshwater fish like minnows, which the hens had been bringing to the chicks twice a day. Now the chicks could feed themselves.

Meanwhile, the hens had moved off across a pebbled beach towards a shallow cave, which was their home, and settled down in the sun. The sixth hen stood by the marsh, watching her chick, which was now happily diving for worms. Then she stomped off after the other hens. Somewhat overprotectively, I stayed by the chicks, watching, as they showed off their new-found skills at backstroke and butterfly.

They wanted me to watch them. It had been a life-changing event for them, to escape from the cliff top and into such an exciting new water world. They felt secure when I was there, and soon developed their confidence to the point where they could make their own explorations. They climbed up out of the pond, staggered over the pebbles, and settled down with the adults in the hen cave.

At last I left the beach scene. I had broken all the rules about leaving nature to take its course. I had intervened unnecessarily, got emotionally involved, and annoyed one of the hens. Still, there was much more to see. I went inland, across hills and fields, with a variety of hedges and grasses. There were no flowers, no insects, no fish in the sea, though there were small freshwater fish, and no birds in the air. But there was a wide variety of green and yellow plants growing everywhere, with trees of many types I had not seen before.

I came over a hill to a sheltered area, with high banks and a pebble beach below it, extending into a lake. It was as if at one time the sea level had been much higher, and this was all that was left after the water level receded. Looking up one side of the bank I saw three large tan-coloured animals with large snouts.

'They must be pigs,' I thought.

The pigs descended the bank round the corner from where I was, and I lost sight of them. Then, as I looked out across the lake, a huge animal with tusks emerged from the water, and came towards me. At first, I thought it was a rhino, but the tusks looked more like those of a wild boar. I went round the corner of the bank and found six more pigs, some large ones with tusks, and some smaller ones without them.

I moved back towards the sea, looking for a way down onto the beach. After a few miles, I found a sheltered bay, with a wide beach and much smaller pebbles. The sea was completely transparent. I looked into the water, and could see the rocks drop away into deeper levels quite quickly. There was something swimming down there. It looked like a flat beige shadow with brown flecks, moving mysteriously under its own volition. Then it turned ninety degrees, and swam sideways. But what was it? I could not make it out.

A few minutes later, the thing crawled out of the water. It had four legs and a tail, was about seven feet long and stood about four feet high. It looked like some kind of lizard. It was the same colours as the beach and merged into it. But its head was covered in a mass of strange extrusions that hid its eyes. A moment later, it gave itself a shake, and the stuff on its head flew backwards and rested on its shoulders. It was a frilled lizard. It moved slowly away from the beach, under a stone archway carved by the wind, and into a field of long grass, where it crouched, concealed, with several other lizards.

Wanting to get a better idea of the terrain, I decided to explore the Southern Hemisphere. It turned out to be much the same as what I had already seen, with gentle hills, downs, lakes and valleys. Here and there a few animals were eating the grass, but there were vast expanses with no apparent animal life. Then I went down to the beaches. What a difference. On every beach there was an enormous sea mammal, like a seal, each with three pups. The pups played in the sea, and suckled from the supine mothers. The mothers were so huge, it seemed impossible they could ever make their way back to the sea unaided, but they must have done, because from time to time, I found them feeding from the masses of green algae that gathered round the bases of cliffs, extending for miles.

Those glasses that Elliot had given me must have been sending back everything I saw, transmitting to the plasma screens in London University, because all of a sudden, I could hear Marion's voice.

'Martha, please can you try and get some samples from the body of the chick that died.'

'OK,' I said, turning back to the northern lands where the great hens lived.

When I arrived, the hens were out in a nearby field, eating grass. They shredded each blade of grass into bits with their beaks, before swallowing them. Some of the chicks were now eating grass as well. I went to look for the body of the dead chick and found a wing. It had dried hard, and was blackened in colour. As I approached the bottom of the high cliff, where the chicks were splashing and playing in the marsh, they started cheeping as if they recognised me. I sat for a moment, watching them, the wing of the dead chick on my lap. Then suddenly, the chicks were all round me, snuggling up to me, as if I was their mother hen. Each one had brought me another bit of the dead chick. They did not know why I wanted it, but if it made me happy, they wanted to bring it to me.

This was all a bit too much for me. I knew I should not have got emotionally involved, but it was too late. The chicks had experienced something from me that they would not get from their own kind. They had felt my appreciation of their beautiful colours, their indomitable spirit and their joyous participation in life. They had registered my concern for their welfare, and responded. Then I understood what made the animals roll on their backs when I looked at them. They could pick up my happiness at their existence, and they in turn felt happiness too.

I took the carcass of the dead chick back to the London lab, and left it with Philip. Then I remembered what Elliot had asked me to do. He had given me a slide of pale green, dried seaweed, and faded orange organic material, and said, 'Can you go and find where that comes from?'

I returned to the planet which had so many marvels in it, and tuned into the green and orange frequency on the slide. I found a cave, inaccessible from land, carved out by the sea. On the entrance to the cave, at the top, there was green lichen growing, and mixed in with it, an orange fungus. I gathered some in a plastic bag, and returned to the Special Science Research lab. Elliot appeared, and I gave him the bag.

'Thanks,' I said. 'That was the best trip so far.'

A question I am unable to answer is how Elliot got hold of the plastic slide containing actual samples of seaweed and fungi from the planet. Did NASA give it to him? If so, that suggests that there are already technologies sufficiently advanced to visit distant planets and take samples. Perhaps that could be done by an unmanned space craft.

Another unresolved question in my mind was how the animals reproduced. I never saw any specifically male animals. All the animals I saw on this planet were either gender neutral or one parent families, where the parent might be considered female. But how could the baby animals arrive without males? One possible explanation might be parthenogenesis, which is the naturally occurring development of an egg without fertilisation.

WHAT YOU PUT OUT IS WHAT YOU GET BACK

This chapter includes disturbing content about terrorist child abuse.

All the terrorists that I met, wherever they came from, considered abuse of children to be perfectly normal. The reason it was so prevalent within the electromagnetic environment was that perpetrators were sure that they would never be discovered by the authorities. They were so out of touch with the real world that they had no idea how shocking such behaviour would be to normal people.

It was easy for mafia and terrorist bosses in North America and parts of the Irish Republic to recruit paedophiles into their employment, with the promise of free access to young children. It was also easy to blackmail known paedophiles into working for them. From their earliest years, children were brought up as sex slaves, and North American terrorists considered that enslavement and torture of children at an early age made them compliant and suitable for training as child soldiers. Human values simply went out of the window.

It was something you could never get away from. The terrorists revealed their paedophile predilections when least expected. One day I was listening to a well-known group of young UK choristers called Libera. They were singing a carol, which I had downloaded onto my iPad. There was a picture of the boys in my music file, looking like little angels. This picture had an unexpected effect on some elderly Irish terrorists who were spying on me through the cameras which, at that time, were implanted in my eyes. I heard the voice of an elderly Irish terrorist over the synthetic telepathy system saying, 'Hey, mate, come over here. You've gotta see this junket stuff.'

I looked up to see what the fuss was about. The paedophile had gone on the internet, found the picture of the kids on the Libera CD and printed it out.

In everyday life we hear of such things, but it is different to being thrown into an environment where all this is going on wherever you look. Nothing prepared me for what I was obliged to witness when it came to certain groups of Asian terrorists. Even the North American terrorists were horrified by some of their practices. I remember a stand-off between the two groups on one occasion, when an Irish terrorist shouted in indignation at some Asians, 'At least we leave the kids alone till they are six years old.'

The Irish and North Americans were outraged by the behaviour of the Asians. But it was written into the Al-Qaida contract, under which the Asians were employed in the European Theatre of War, that part of their wages should be paid in the form of access to very young, white children, for the refreshment of their warriors. You have to ask yourself why this contractual clause should be so important to the Asian terrorists. But it was.

The Asians took on high risk work that Irish and North Americans were unwilling to undertake, in conditions where they were likely to be caught by the authorities. They demanded to be paid in advance, in case they were killed while carrying out their duties. That meant that children had to be made available to them before they started work.

One night, about midnight, I was woken from sleep by the sound of Irish Mafia managers handing over at the end of a shift to a group of forty Asians. The Asians had been brought in at the last minute from underground hideouts near the Caspian Sea. I had removed a large number of terrorists from the planet earlier that day, and there were no North American or Irish troops left in the right place.

The Asians were transported via an electromagnetic pathway, leading up to an embarkment portal, where troops were transferred to a flying transport vehicle, which looked like a giant potato crisp, or Pringle. These electromagnetic contraptions could carry people quickly across the world, at high speed, and deliver them, via another electromagnetic pathway, to wherever they were required.

On this occasion, the forty Asians had come all the way from Azerbaijan, where they had been waiting for over a day in an underground hideout known to terrorists as a "depth charge". Depth charges are hollowed out of the earth using electromagnetic processes to create a spherical underground hideout. On arrival, the Asians were adamant that they were not going anywhere until they had been given their kids. A large van arrived outside the local electromagnetic area. It contained rows of baby car seats, suspended from wooden slats inside the van, and inside each car seat was a baby about one year old.

The woman who managed the child brothel, and her assistant brought the children out, still strapped in their car seats, and put them in a locked room. Then the Asians lined up, as if queuing to buy coffee, and were each given one of these babes in arms. They took the babies into two adjoining rooms and obtained physical gratification from sexual attacks them. It looked to me as if some of the babies would not survive these attacks. This was also a concern of the dreadful brothel managers. They had a group of children aged from two to ten years old, as backup.

Some of the Asians arrived later than the rest. One of them was angered that he had missed the distribution of younger babies.

'If I can't have what I want, I'm not staying,' he shouted, and he knocked over a three-year-old child and hit a nine-year-old girl who was standing nearby, breaking her arm, before storming out in a temper. When I saw all this, I knew I must step in. Finishing the Asians off was not enough. I needed a deterrent to make the Asians think twice before turning up again.

'If this is how they behave every day, they must have accumulated an appalling amount of atrocities in their life experience,' I thought, 'So an appropriate deterrent would be to let them experience what they had done to others.'

I decided to use the decree, 'What you put out is what you get back,' and see what happened.

I went looking for the man who had hit the children, and pointing at him in my mind, I sent out an electronic beam, while thinking, 'What you put out is what you get back.'

The effect was unexpected and hair-raising. The man fell to the ground screaming in agony, and began to experience in reverse, all the sensations that he had caused his victims to suffer. He died soon afterwards. Then I mentally selected all the babies and children at once, and decreed, 'Let anyone who touches these children get "What you put out is what you get back!".'

Soon, the whole area was full of men and child brothel women writhing on the floor in agony. The babies had become untouchable. The terrorists had to bring in a childminder who had never been connected to their computer systems, to collect all the surviving babies. The woman loaded them back into the van in their car seats, before driving them out of the electromagnetic environment. I could not guarantee the safety of the babies in the real world outside, but they would never be brought back into the electromagnetic environment again.

I took the girl with the broken arm to the Special Prison Services building, where she received hospital treatment. She was admitted into the care of H.M. Special Prison Services, because she was broadly old enough for them to take her in.

Next time I saw a troop of Asians arriving, I went looking for the children. This time they were toddlers about eighteen months old. I found them being unloaded by their brothel managers. I selected all the children and decreed, 'Let anyone who touches these children get "What you get out is what you put back".'

All the brothel managers got it at once. When the Asians arrived, as soon as they touched the children, they were in their death throws. When the children saw this, they very quickly realised the new power that they had been given. They started toddling towards the nearest perpetrators, and putting their hands on their legs. When the paedophiles went down, the kids burst into peals of laughter, and started kicking them. Then they began to communicate at the sub-vocal level with me. They knew I had given them the power, and they wanted me to do more for them.

I was busy doing housework that afternoon. The kids could contact me via the terrorists' ultrasound communications system, using what is termed "evoked potentials" to deliver nonverbal messages to me.

'Come over here, now!' demanded one of the children.

I turned my attention to it. The child had just delivered a terminal blow to its perpetrator, but it wanted to do a lot more to the man before he died. There was no mistaking what the child wanted. It wanted me to pull down the man's trousers. In a misguided wish to make things right for the child, I did so. The child immediately attacked the man's genitals with its bare hands. I realised that it was replicating the behaviour that it had learned from men who had abused it in the past.

Another child called me over to assist it in finishing off another paedophile. This time, it not only wanted the man's trousers removed, but it demanded that I give it a stick. Then to my horror, it began to hit the man's genitals, while going through the motions of masturbating itself. That told you exactly what the child had been forced to endure in the past.

After that, there was a reduction in Asian terrorists' visits. If they were deployed in the UK, they kept as far away from my area as possible, and if they saw me, they ran for it. For my part, if I saw them, I removed them from the planet immediately. But if the children got them, the Asians certainly learned their lesson the hard way.

Sadly, I could not protect these very young children once they left the electromagnetic environment. On one occasion, a toddler had despatched several men who had foolishly tried to approach it. The local terrorists quickly called in the girl who was not registered on their computer system, to remove him. He confidently toddled towards her, and reached out his arm to touch her leg, seeking to give her the same treatment. When he found that nothing happened, he turned and gave me a dreadful look.

'You promised to protect me, and you failed,' was what he was saying.

I tried to explain to him that the power only operated within the electromagnetic environment, but you try explaining that to a toddler. I felt awful about it.

Until then, I had thought that children's limited verbal communication was a reflection of their developing brain. Now I think differently. The children I met were not that different from adults in the way they thought. What held them back was their inability to speak their native tongue, which was something they had to learn. We have all seen mothers hurrying out of the supermarket, bearing in their arms a child that has just gone ballistic. Children already have a clear idea about their human rights, and if they think you have not respected them, they will let you know it.

Next day, I saw a tall rough-looking man in the terrorists' amphitheatre. His name was Joe. He did not belong to the psychological warfare group or the electronic weapons group. He was sitting on a bank, a cigarette hanging out of his mouth, reading my book 'Terror in Britain.' The local terrorists had bought a copy, as a training aid for junior staff, because it described how their systems worked. But their managers had second thoughts after they read more of the book.

'I don't think people ought to know about that sort of thing,' said one manager.

'What do you want me to do about it then?' asked his assistant.

'Better pull out all the pages that tell you anything useful,' said his manager.

Joe was now reading this mangled copy of the book.

I asked a henchman what Joe was doing in the amphitheatre.

'He's a people trafficker,' said the henchman. 'He brings in all the children whenever the Asians are on duty.'

Michael, the prison officer from H.M. Special Prison Services, put his head through the ceiling of the terrorists' electromagnetic environment.

'That one's mine. Can you bring him in please?' he said.

I lifted Joe into the back garden of the Prison Service building. Michael was waiting to take him into custody. Two other prison officers were standing there with him.

'What nationality are you?' asked Michael.

'British,' said Joe, the cigarette, still hanging from his mouth.

Tanya appeared. 'You monster!' she said. 'How could you do that to kids?'

Joe shrugged his shoulders.

'At least I'm in gainful employment,' he said. 'And I have to bear all the up-front costs. My kids have to be fed, clothed and kept healthy. There's a man over the road from me, in the same line of business. He says he's not making a penny out of it these days.'

Joe took a drag on his cigarette.

'You know, not everyone cares for their kids the way I do,' he added.

'Come with me,' said Michael.

The two other prison officers closed round Joe, and he reluctantly got to his feet. Then suddenly he ducked sideways and ran back, giving the prison officers the slip. He picked something up from the ground and turned round, nearly crashing into the two prison officers, who were in hot pursuit.

'My book,' said Joe. 'Nearly forgot it.'

The prison officers firmly put the cuffs on him, and he was led away.

The sexual exploitation of kids in the electromagnetic environment is the start of a cycle of terror for them, leading on to the slavery of child soldiers and ending with the systematic murder of youths on the front line as cannon fodder. There are no young volunteers, only conscripts.

Towards the end of the electromagnetic war, the North American terrorists and Irish mafia were having a hard time motivating anyone to come and join them. They let it be known that instant promotion to real jobs outside was there for men of the right type. The prospect of leaving the electromagnetic environment was sufficient motivation in itself, but what was meant by "men of the right type". The steer from the top was that men who did not compromise on staff discipline were what was wanted.

A group of mafia bosses from the Bosnia-Herzegovina region chose to interpret "men of the right type" as those who were willing to torture to death at least one junior staff member every night. When these men arrived in my area to respond to the call of their fellow terrorist unit, the local North American terrorists had no idea what they were like.

The behaviour of their junior staff aroused comment. They were terrified all the time, looking for a way to escape. I rescued most of them by disconnecting them from the terrorists' computer systems. They now had a transparent cross on their foreheads, which prevented them from ever being used by the terrorists again. I took them to the magick table restaurants and created an invisible house which they could live in there. Later they went to the Irish Republic, before being repatriated and rehabilitated by their own government.

The mafia bosses and their henchmen thought that getting rid of an old biddy was going to be a piece of cake, and they strutted arrogantly around making insulting comments about me, while ordering people in to attack me. There was something particularly repellent about these Eastern Europeans. I selected all of them at once, saying, 'What you put out is what you get back.'

What happened after that shocked even the North American terrorists. We could see what the Bosnians had been doing recently. They died screaming.

'Who have they been doing it too?' I wondered.

I hoped desperately that they had not been doing it to kids. Then a North American told me that their top boss, who was hiding in a "Near Earth" contraption high up in the Earth's atmosphere, was looking to fill a vacancy up there, for a hardened leader. The hardened leader was one who would not be soft on his staff. This was driving the atrocities that the Eastern European mafia were committing on young men in their early twenties.

I had seen "Near Earth" constructions flying around in the Earth's atmosphere before. Some of them were used by the IRA. They looked like enormous circular conservatories, built with pine wood timbers, stained a tan colour. They had several decks, including dedicated areas for communicating by WIFI with terrorists on the ground below. The living accommodation was extremely comfortable. There were conference facilities for senior men to discuss terrorist strategy, and, of course, excellent waitress service dining facilities.

I knew that the British Military and other NATO groups could look in on flying conservatories, so up to now, I had not paid much attention to them. But one day, I made up a new rule:

'Whenever any terrorists on the ground gets hit by me, let those authorising or funding associated terrorist activities get the same thing.'

In the case of "What you put out is what you get back", this worked better than expected. The senior terrorists who authorised the atrocities got it all right, even if they were hiding in flying conservatories. When these guys got hit, their colleagues did not want to watch them die, so they chucked them out. The monsters came hurtling down through the Earth's atmosphere screaming horribly, and went crashing to the ground like meteorites. As they landed, their uniforms cracked open, revealing the identity of the terrorists inside.

RITES OF PASSAGE

As the fortunes of our local terrorists began to decline, they searched around for other opportunities to make money. Provision of terrorist training courses had been tried, and had failed, mainly because it involved practising prison camp control techniques on local British people. If they tried that, they were usually killed by me or by the Special Prison Services. Also, the British Military regularly flew over the terrorists' technical support sections disconnecting their industrial WIFI and satellite links.

The Irish mafia, in cooperation with the IRA, hit on another option. There was a demand from Arab terrorists for provision of facilities in which they could hold sex education courses for young boys and girls reaching puberty, and sexual initiations for teenage boys. Why they would want to come to the UK for this is hard to understand, except that Al-Qaida was willing to provide money for "Summer Schools", and the prospect of a holiday in the UK for the adult chaperones was appealing.

Throughout the Summer months, I would see parties of teenage youths, escorted by an official mother figure and several men from the Middle East, walking down the road next to ours, to an IRA safehouse which offered suitable accommodation. These parties described themselves as "Friends of Daesh", The visits were partly social, partly tourism and partly terrorist Summer school training. There were days in London organised by the locals, visits to places of interest to Muslims around the British Isles, and youth education events.

The youths received training in martial arts, woodcraft, assault courses and the biology of the female body. Towards the end of the visits, the local IRA would arrange for a European female prostitute to spend an afternoon with each youth. The idea was that the boys would have a chance to put into practice the skills that would be expected of them when the time came for them to be married. The mother would preside over these afternoon sessions, to ensure that the boys made the most of the opportunities. Whether this helped the youths to form appropriate relationships with women, I never found out. The main thing, from the local terrorists' point of view was that they ensured a modest regular income throughout the Summer.

One day, I was hunting for terrorists in an electromagnetic amphitheatre in the next village. The amphitheatre included a smart modern Perspex building known as "The Atrium", because of its large glass dome in the foyer. The building was invisible, except to those registered and set up on the electromagnetic computer system, so it was a safe place for terrorists to carry out their operations without fear of discovery.

In invisibility mode, I went through the foyer of the Atrium, looking for a group of perpetrators, and checking in every room on the ground floor. I went into the main classroom used for training courses, and was astonished to see rows of naked seven-year-old Arab boys, sitting at desks, supervised by a naked black woman in her forties. The woman, whose name was Karenna, sat at the teacher's desk. Behind her, on the black board were drawings of female genitalia.

Karenna called a young boy out of his desk and invited him to come up to her and examine her for himself. She spread her legs and guided the young boy's hands around her genitalia.

'Mm, that feels nice,' she said encouragingly.

The young lad looked both intimidated, and a little chuffed that he had had the guts to do such a scary thing. Karenna had a kind supportive manner, and made each boy feel accepted and successful, which was all that could be expected. I wondered which country the boys had come from. It looked like somewhere in the Levant. The boys were not poor, and their parents had paid good money to the terrorists, to cover the costs of their training course.

I found the terrorists I was looking for in the room opposite the training room, and removed them. The next day, I decided to visit the room again, in case there were any more of them. The room was empty, so I checked the training room opposite. This time, there were twenty girls aged eleven, sitting in the desks, completely naked. They had brown skin, and looked as if they had come from Africa. They were Tuareg people, part Berber and part black African. They were chatting excitedly amongst themselves, laughing and playing around, as kids do, I was somewhat concerned for their welfare. Perhaps they were about to be turned into prostitutes in one of the terrorist mafia brothels. Seeing that they were African, it occurred to me that they would be able to breathe on the Moon. I thought they would be a lot better off there than they would here, so I created clothes for them, grouped them all in an electromagnetic envelope, and took them straight over to the lunar crater where Wayne and some of the black families had made their homes. They were welcomed by David and Jesalynn, whose sons I had brought to them, and soon settled in with the rest.

Then, in invisible mode, I returned to the training room where the girls had been, to see what fate had been planned for them. The room was empty now, except for the teacher's desk, where a black man in his forties was standing. His name was Raymond. He was wearing a mackintosh, but was otherwise completely naked. The board behind him was covered with biological diagrams of the male sex organ.

At that moment, one of the managers from the Atrium came in. Raymond looked rather uncomfortable.

'Excuse me,' he said. 'I was expecting a class of schoolgirls, but there is nobody here. Do you know where they are?'

The manager apologised, and went to look for them. He came back shortly afterwards, looking even more apologetic, and said that the training course would not be going ahead as planned. He said that Raymond would still be paid, as the absence of the schoolgirls was not his fault. I watched as Raymond, his mac now buttoned up, marched out of the building and got into his car.

That night, I was thinking about the twenty schoolgirls up on the Moon. They needed a dedicated mother and father, and it was expecting a lot of the community they had been brought into to adopt them all. I decided to go and look for Karenna, the black lady who had given the sex education to the seven-year-olds. Tuning into her frequency, I found her cooking in the kitchen. I was about to make myself visible to her, when Raymond, the man in the mac, walked in and gave her a hug.

'Darling,' he said, kissing her. 'Sorry I'm late. I hope there's still some food left.'

'Of course,' laughed Karenna. 'Do you think I would start without you? Anyway, I've only just finished cooking.'

They both sat down and started their food. I cautiously knocked at the door outside, not sure how things would work. Raymond came to the door. I was standing there in my black puffa coat and hood.

'Good evening,' I said. 'You won't know me, but I saw you and your wife at the Atrium this week, and I have a job to offer you, if you are interested.'

Raymond looked at me. Then he laughed.

'Oh yes, you're the lady who appeared in the classroom rather suddenly today!' he said. 'Come in, you're most welcome.'

'You mean you saw me?' I asked.

'Oh sure,' smiled Raymond. 'In fact, my wife told me she saw you the day before. We know a bit about you. It seems you are known for arriving unannounced within our community, and offering most unusual possibilities.'

We went into the kitchen, and Raymond introduced me to Karenna. I apologised for interrupting their meal, and asked them to carry on, if they were willing to hear what I had to say. Karenna and Raymond were smiling broadly at each other.

'I don't know if you have heard that it is possible for ethnic African and Chinese people to live on the Moon,' I began.

'Mm,' Karenna nodded. 'We have heard something about that. In fact, I know someone that you took up there. She and her family are doing fine. They love the lifestyle.'

'How do you keep in contact?' I asked.

Raymond smiled.

'It's part of our culture. We were brought up in the UK, and we are British, but there's a lot of things about our life that you whites miss completely.'

'OK,' I said. 'Would you consider joining your friends up there? The reason I ask is that I just took twenty eleven-year-old girls to stay with them. But the girls need family — mums and dads, to be there for them. There are parents with children living up there already. But we need more people the right age, who don't have kids. I know it's asking a lot, but I thought you two would make a good job of it, that is, if you are interested.'

Karenna and Raymond looked at each other.

'We are going to need time to think about this,' said Karenna. 'It's a big decision. But it's the sort of work we have done before. We always wanted kids, but it didn't happen for us. So, we've looked for opportunities to help kids who haven't had the best start in life.'

'I like the idea,' said Raymond. 'We have worked as carers for disabled children, with support from local councils. Sex education isn't really our thing, but if we are asked to do it, we take it seriously... and it brings in the money. Not having to work for someone else, or worry about money, would be a completely new situation. But it means saying goodbye to friends and family, unless they want to come too...'

'Would it be OK if I came back in a week?' I asked. 'You can let me know your decision then.'

The couple agreed that would be best.

A week later I was back. Karenna welcomed me at the front door, and led me into their living room. After we had all sat down, she said, 'We'd like to go, but we don't like the idea of cutting of completely from the British Isles. Is there some way you could arrange for us to go back home whenever we wanted to?'

'What do I do about that?' I thought.

Then I had an idea.

'I wonder if I could transfer my electromagnetic abilities to you?' I said. 'But would it work?'

'Let's try, shall we?' said Raymond.

I surrounded Raymond and Karenna in an electromagnetic field, and said, 'Let these two have the same abilities as I have.'

Raymond and Karenna looked at me. Nothing seemed to have changed. Then Karenna said, 'Would you like a cup of tea?'

A cup of tea came floating towards me, and landed on the table by my hand.

'Thanks,' I said. 'Why don't I try doing things like that?'

'Lack of imagination,' laughed Karenna.

After that, it was agreed that Raymond and Karenna would go to be foster parents for the twenty African girls. I let Wayne, David and Jesalynn know in advance that they were coming, so that they had time to talk to the girls about it. I had to allow time, in case the girls had reservations about the arrangement. But they were quite happy, at least, as happy as they could be, since they had not met Raymond and Karenna.

When Raymond and Karenna arrived in the lunar crater, the entire village came out to meet them. Wayne gave them a guided tour and introduced them to everyone. The girls had already started to make friends in the village, and did not want to be too far away from them, but they got on well with their new foster parents. I went up above the crater, and looked around for a place for them to live. There wasn't anywhere I could see that would be suitable, except a large cave up above in the hills.

'How would it be, if I could construct a building inside the rocks, like the terrorists did,' I thought.

I had constructed plenty of buildings before on my past mission, so I visualised the rocky hills, and said, 'Let a suitable house for the twenty girls and Raymond and Karenna be created inside the hills, with a wide stairway up from the lunar crater, and an entrance into the cave at the other end.'

That worked quite well, and the rock building blended in well with its surroundings. The wide staircase down to the ground looked particularly good.

Karenna said she would try making more rock houses, if anyone wanted one. She and Raymond had become confident in using their new-found powers. They were doing so well that I decided to transfer the same powers to everyone else on the Moon, knowing that those powers could only be used for good purposes. By now, half the people on the Moon had already discovered how to use their minds to create what they needed.

I thought everything on the Moon would work by itself from now on. But it wasn't too long before I got a call from Karenna, asking if I could come and visit her. I turned up in their lunar crater, where Karenna was sitting on a stone bench, admiring the spectacular view of the lunar landscape.

'Hi there, Karenna,' I said. 'How are things with you and Raymond?'

I sat down on the seat beside her.

'Oh, we're just fine,' said Karenna. 'And thank you for coming. I would not have bothered you, but there is something I think you ought to know.'

'Oh yes?' I said, wondering if I should prepare myself for some earth-shattering revelation.

'Yes,' said Karenna. 'There is a Japanese man on Earth, who has been doing the same as you.'

'What do you mean?' I asked.

Karenna leaned closer and said in a lowered voice, 'He's been putting people up here — Japanese people. There are three teenage boys and they are drug addicts.'

'I guess they've stopped being drug addicts by now,' I said. 'As there are no drugs up here.'

'That's right,' said Karenna. 'Apparently, he put them up here to come off drugs.'

'OK, so that's good then, isn't it?' I asked.

'They haven't integrated with the rest of us,' said Karenna. 'And at night, they go round the lunar craters, looking at women and openly masturbating.'

'Have any of the men spoken to them about it?' I asked.

'Oh sure, they've spoken to them all right,' laughed Karenna. 'But we do have a problem, because there aren't any teenage girls the right age that they could get to know. And I'm not letting my little princesses anywhere near them.'

I sighed. I was getting fed up with finding partners for men on the Moon. It was unreasonable to expect these boys to return to their Earth home, unassisted, and rebuild social contacts, especially if they were drug addicts. But there again… it was amazing what people could learn to do within the electromagnetic environment.

My mind went back to a black couple, Craig and Dina, who arrived on the Moon with a group of people. Their relationship was already in trouble, and the man was starting to chat up other women. The couple asked me to take them back to their former home on Earth, which I did. There were other people living in their old house now, but they willingly gave it back. Soon, however, Dina asked for a divorce, and went to live with her sister. Craig started to get depressed, he took to drinking, and got into fights, after which, he was warned to get a grip by the police. He developed an obsessive interest in a woman who already had a partner, who was living on the Moon.

One night, he found a way to take himself back up there, simply by wanting to enough. He was familiar with the frequency of the place he wanted to be, and focussing on it, he got there. I happened to see him doing it. It was a shock, but I picked up on him, and managed to catch him, just as he arrived on the Moon. He was shouting and swearing and hitting out at people, so I handed him over to Michael in the Special Prison Service, and they took him into prison, where he was diagnosed with mental health problems.

Now, hearing about these Japanese teenagers, I wondered if we were going to have more trouble. Karenna told me where they were living, and I went to see them. They were wandering about in a rocky area, exploring. They looked a bit bored.

'Hello,' I said. 'I hear you have joined the local community here. I'm from Earth, and I wondered how you were settling in, and if there was anything you needed from home.'

The young men stared at me. Their names were Ryota, Tomio and Arata, and to judge by their appearance they were aged between seventeen and eighteen.

'It's not much of a life here,' said Arata, the eighteen-year-old.

'Would you like to return to Earth?' I asked.

Arata shook his head.

'It wasn't much of a life on Earth either,' said Ryota.

'We don't really have a home anywhere,' said Tomio.

'How would things need to be different, to make it feel more like home here?' I asked.

'Well,' said Ryota, nervously. 'I had five brothers and sisters. There was always work to do, we spent our time labouring in the fields, and when we got home there was cleaning, and cooking. Our mother expected us all to do our share.'

'I don't want to go back to all that,' said Tomio. 'But its lonely up here.'

'I always wanted to become an artist,' said Arata. 'But my parents could not afford the fees.'

'Hmm,' I thought. 'This is going to be tricky, I can't provide them with a ready-made community, although I might be able to help Arata to get started as an artist.'

'How good are you at creating things that you need?' I asked.

The three boys looked despairing.

'We don't know about that' said Arata.

'Right,' I said. 'We'd better start there then. Are there any sports you like to play — football, tennis, baseball?'

'Yeah, we like all of those,' said Ryota.

'Can you picture a baseball or a football in your mind?' I said.

The boys nodded.

'Now, imagine you are going to throw the ball over there,' I said, pointing to the side of the mountain. 'And then actually throw it.'

A tennis ball appeared and hurtled against the mountain wall, bouncing back with huge velocity, owing to the Moon's lighter gravity.

'Well, somebody had the right idea,' I said, 'Who threw the tennis ball?'

'I did,' laughed Ryota.

At that moment, a football appeared at Tomio's feet, and he gave it a kick. It behaved rather like the tennis ball had done.

Soon the boys were making themselves tennis rackets, football boots, and then, a large wooden hut appeared. The boys made themselves three large huts, and furnished them. Then Arata started to design a stone garden, with statues of buddhas. He coloured some of the stones green, so they looked more like plants.

'Now, you can make yourself whatever art materials you like,' I said. 'Whether it's painting, sculpture or even textiles.'

The sun was getting too bright now, and the boys created a shaded area, which looked like trees, but was made of artificial materials, giving the effect of an oasis in the desert. Ryota put on some sunglasses.

'OK, now you've got the idea,' I said. 'Shall we talk about bringing you some more friends from Earth? You can still go back there if you prefer.'

Arata sat cross-legged in the shade. He had made himself some comfortable loose clothes, and looked quite stylish.

'If I was on Earth, I would have a girlfriend by now,' he said. 'But how can I ask a girl to come and live here? There again, if I went back to Earth, I would have money worries, and the boys I went around with were no good for me.'

'What if you could visit on Earth for an hour, and then come back here?' I asked.

The three boys looked at me in disbelief.

'How would you do that?' said Tomio.

'First of all, create a photo of a place you would like to return to on Earth,' I suggested. 'Can you do that?'

The boys played around with this, producing photographs of the Statue of Liberty, Mount Fuji and, as a nod to me, Buckingham Palace. Then they made photos of places they knew in Japan. I explained how aligning yourself with the frequency of a photograph would alter your global positioning system locator to that of the photograph.

'But if you go there, can you get back here?' I asked. 'Better make yourself a photo of this place, if you want to return.'

The boys created a polaroid camera, and took photos of each other.

'Great!' I said. 'Now you need to practice visiting the place on Earth that you've picked, and returning here. Make sure you have the right clothes for the weather there.'

'If I start,' said Arata. 'Will you bring me back in five minutes, in case I get stuck?'

'OK,' I said.

In fact, I realised I would have to go over with him, invisibly, as anything could happen. Arata stared at his Earth photo, and disappeared. Ryota and Tomio immediately started to look anxious.

'Don't worry,' I said. 'I'm on my way.' And I headed off after Arata.

He was walking along a street, and seemed to have coped well with the heavier gravity on Earth. I changed my clothes to blend in, and joined him.

'Everything OK?' I asked.

'Look,' said Arata. 'I'm going to meet a certain girl, if I can find her, so can you please clear off.'

'I can find her for you,' I said. 'Think what she looks like, and I'll do it.'

Arata immediately pictured an attractive young girl in his mind, and I tuned into her frequency. She looked a bit older than Arata, perhaps twenty or twenty-one. She was at home, talking on her cellphone. I returned to Arata.

'She's at home,' I said. 'I can put you outside her door, if you like?'

'Well, I've nothing to lose, I suppose,' said Arata.

I set him down on the doorstep and withdrew. Arata rang the bell, and a woman in her fifties answered. She disappeared, and a moment later, Arata's friend was there. I could hear them talking in low voices. After a while, Arata called for me, and I appeared.

'This is Gina,' he said. 'She wants to come for a short visit, and then go home. Can you fix that, please?'

I could see that teleporting another person was a bit advanced for his first outing, so I took Arata and Gina back to the little home area that the boys had just created. As we arrived, Ryota and Tomio jumped up, 'Oh, there you are. We were so worried,' said Ryota. 'We thought you'd never come back.'

'Oh, it was no problem at all,' said Arata. 'I'd like you to meet my friend, Gina.'

The boys gave Gina a ceremonial drink of the special Moon liquid, and took her on a short walk, pointing out the scenery. Gina was totally taken aback, and delighted by everything she saw. Then it was time for her to return home. I explained to Arata how to take someone with you when teleporting, by holding onto their arm, and Arata offered to take Gina home and return on his own. He disappeared, and then reappeared, five minutes later, glowing with pride at his achievement.

I asked Arata if he felt able to accompany Ryota and Tomio on their trips, and he said he was fine about that. So I let them go, secretly following to make sure they were all right. The boys managed to arrive in the right place, and met up with a few friends. They talked for a while, and then returned.

'Well done!' I said. 'You have made great progress in a short time.'

The boys looked more confident now.

'It's too soon for us to think about inviting people back here yet,' said Ryota. 'But now we know how to do it, we don't feel so alone any more.'

For some weeks after that, I was busy, and left them to themselves. Then one day, I looked in on them, discretely, to see how they were doing. There were several boys and girls that I didn't recognise, laughing together, taking photos of the spectacular scenery and of each other. All that seemed very normal and natural. At one end of the garden, Arata had created an artist's studio, and several of his paintings were on display. They were Moonscapes, and one was a portrait of Gina against a background of Moonrocks. On the Moon, light and shadows are a lot different from on Earth, with some very strong contrasts. Arata's pictures were nothing like any I had seen before.

As of today, things are just starting for the three boys. I have no idea how their story will unfold, but things are a lot more hopeful now.

RETURN TO THE IRISH REPUBLIC

Back home, nothing much seemed to have changed. The terrorists were attacking me with an array of electromagnetic and microwave weapons, and I was dealing with them.

'Armless, legless,' I shouted.

The troops fell to the ground, unable to move. Their bosses would have to shoot them, as they could not get their arms and legs to work again. This was costly, and time-consuming. It deterred terrorists from further attacks for a while. I noticed a group of young Irish children standing at the side of the battlefield. I called out to H.M. Special Prison Services, 'There are young Irish children here.'

Michael's face appeared through the ceiling of the electromagnetic environment.

'Sorry, we cannot take them any more unless they are British. We've got different orders now.'

'Well, what shall I do with them,' I thought. 'They are the responsibility of the Irish Republic, but I have no contacts there.'

Then I remembered a time when I had seen Irish terrorist sympathisers trying to get the Irish Military to sponsor a disguised member of the IRA as an applicant for a job in a US military base in Yorkshire. The interview for that had taken place in an Irish Republic military barracks. I could go there.

I picked up the children and deposited them in the square inside the barracks. A few minutes later, some men in military uniform appeared. I materialised myself and explained about the children. The kids stood there, two by two, holding hands and looking disoriented.

'We'll take them,' said the officer in charge.

Two women soldiers arrived, and led the children into a building nearby.

'We will have to find where they come from, and return them to their homes,' said the officer.

He looked unsure how to go about this.

I said, 'Let the children have their home towns written on labels attached to their wrists.'

Then the officer in charge accompanied me into the building, to see what, if anything that had achieved. Every child now had a plastic wristband, with a label attached to it. I had a look at them. They all said the same thing — Tyrone.

'Ah,' said the officer. 'That's in Northern Ireland. We will have to hand them over to the Northern Ireland military.'

He looked relieved. I wondered how so many children could have gone missing from Tyrone without anyone noticing. Had they been kidnapped, and smuggled over the border by traffickers? There was much for the authorities to look into.

Considering how proactive the Canadians had been in rescuing their young and vulnerable people from a life of terrorism, as soon as they knew what was going on, I was surprised that the Irish Republic had not made similar arrangements. I decided that from now on, whenever Irish youths and low-level terrorists showed up to attack me, I would send them straight back to the Irish Republic. I set up a system under which all that a terrorist had to do was to think, 'I want to go to the Irish Republic.'

If they did that, they would arrive there, in a designated area, wearing presentable clothes, and with any microchips or other prostheses wiped from their bodies. The place they arrived in would have several large magick restaurant tables, and would have a large number of mini magick cupboards, lying around which could be used for any purpose the returnees wanted.

There would be invisible toilet cubicles, with doors that would become visible to the person wanting to use them. Once the person was inside, the doors would become invisible, until the user left. Inside, there were shower cubicles, mirrors and all modern conveniences. The toilets created themselves if anyone looked for them, and disintegrated after one use. There were also invisible beds which would appear to individuals if they wanted to sleep. On climbing into them, the bed and its contents would become invisible, until the person got up, after which, they too disintegrated.

On exiting the arrival area, there would be goody bags containing a mini magick restaurant table and mini-cupboard, for those starting a new life to take with them. Although the system was designed for those volunteering to escape from the terrorist life, it worked exactly the same if I sent terrorists there on an involuntary basis, and I did this on many occasions.

The first group of people who arrived were delivered by me. They were the dregs of the terrorist community. Their managers had sent into the front line as cannon fodder. I selected them all and said, 'Return to the Irish Republic.'

Twelve low-level terrorists came flying into the Irish Republic, in the arrival area. They immediately headed for the magick restaurant tables, and made themselves at home. The possibility of leaving the area had not occurred to them. I sat with them, and explained that they could use the mini-cupboard to make themselves clothes of any type they wanted. Seven of the first arrivals were transvestites, who had eked out a life as male prostitutes within the terrorist community. They were at various stages of wanting to have the operation to change gender. Some of them wanted to have the full operation, some just want to lose all body hair, and obtain a bit of cleavage, and some wanted all of the former.

I explained to them that they needed to put their fingers on the mini-cupboard if they wanted to make changes to their bodies, so that the devices could analyse their genes, and identify the person requesting the changes. Then they could be anything they wanted — taller, thinner, younger, bigger, whatever. The first transvestite asked me if I would come into the toilet cubicle with him, and help him to make the changes. I told him what to do, and the physical changes appeared immediately. When s/he saw what had happened, s/he sank to the floor, weeping with happiness.

'My dreams have come true,' S/he sobbed. 'Now I can start again as myself.'

When she finally emerged, with a new body, a new hairdo, wearing a smart dress with matching shoes and a Gucci handbag, she really was a new person.

After the transvestites had left, there were still five people sitting there looking bemused. Four of them turned out to be mentally disabled people, who did not know what their names were, or how they had become terrorists. It turned out later, that they had been kidnapped from a care home in the Irish Republic, by the Irish mafia, who got a fee for each individual they provided to the terrorist cause, whatever the quality of the recruit.

I sat down with the first man. He was in his forties, and he looked a wreck, with matted hair, and a downtrodden expression. If he was going to start a new life, things would have to change a lot. What could be done. Then I had an idea.

'Put your finger in this wooden box,' I said, presenting him with a mini-cupboard.

He did so, in an unthinking way.

'Now say, "I have the cleverest brain in the world",' I suggested to him.

The man repeated the words after me, with partial comprehension. But it was enough to do the trick. He fell backward onto the ground, and a big smile came over his face.

'I can think!' he said. 'Everything is becoming clear. It was all cloudy before. Now everything makes sense.'

Picking up the mini-cupboard, he asked, 'Is this what did it? Can I keep it? What else will it do?'

I explained everything to him, and he went into the toilet cubicle, had a shower, got himself new clothes, a haircut, and emerged smelling of aftershave. Then he went over to another of the mentally disabled men, and started helping him to use the mini-cupboard. What a relief it was to see the change in him. I knew he would be able to look after himself outside.

The mentally disabled men got themselves fixed up and left. There was one man in his twenties still sitting there. I went over to him.

'What's the problem? Do you need help?' I asked.

'I'm partially sighted,' he said. 'Can you help me to do what the others have done?'

'Sure,' I said.

We went into the toilet cubicle, to make him a new brain and get him some new clothes, then I asked him if he wanted to make any changes to his physical body, as all the others had done.

'Can you do anything about my sight?' he asked.

I took a breath. This was outside my experience.

'We can try with the mini-cupboard,' I said.

So, I picked up the mini-cupboard, and placed his fingers in it.

'Just a minute,' he said, and he removed his glass eye.

We started again. He put his fingers in the mini-cupboard.

'Repeat after me,' I said. 'I now have perfect sight.'

The young man murmured the words to himself. He looked down for a minute. Then he looked up. Then he looked in the mirror. I realised that he had two fully functioning eyes. He turned to me.

'I can see with both eyes,' he said.

'Yes,' I said. 'Now you can choose some clothes for yourself, and make any changes you want to your physical appearance.'

I waited outside, while the young man completed his transformation. What had happened was hard to take in. If the electromagnetic system could do that, then... My thoughts tailed off. I was not ready to process the implications of this.

After that, I started sending hundreds of men to the Irish Republic every day.

On the second day, two members of the Irish Constabulary set up camp in the arrival area. They sat at a table, watching what went on. On the third day, the authorities had built a covered way out of the area, leading to a coach park, where coaches pulled in as required throughout the day, taking the reconstructed terrorists to a reception centre.

At the centre, members of the Irish Constabulary took the finger prints of each person, and looked on the police computer, to see if there was a record of them, where they had come from, what their name was, and any next of kin. Then after discussion about what was best in each case, the terrorists were taken to different parts of the Irish Republic, where local authorities took responsibility for providing them with a place to live.

On the third day, one of the returning terrorists picked up a mini-cupboard lying on the ground and asked, 'Does it do drugs?'

My mind raced through the possibilities. Then I said, 'Yes, and they are the best you've ever tried.'

The man looked at the mini-cupboard and a large transparent plastic bag full of white powder appeared. The man took some of the powder and tasted it. Then he leaned back against a wall, his face lighting up with a happy look.

'Oh! That's the best stuff I've ever tasted. I'm never going to use anything else again,' he said.

All his friends immediately copied him, and they all agreed that there was nothing in the world that could equal the white powder. The Irish Constable looked at me inquiringly.

'If I'm right about this,' I said. 'It does not contain anything harmful, and will help people come off drugs. It will make them healthier, while giving them a happy feeling.'

The Irish Constable got on his mobile to his boss. There was some discussion, and after the phone call was over, I had the impression that the constable was waiting for someone to get back to him. Then Elliot, the senior scientist from the Special Service research centre suddenly appeared from nowhere, in his white coat.

'Hello,' he said, smiling.

Then he whispered confidentially in my ear, 'What's this stuff?'

I made some more in a transparent plastic bag and gave it to him.

'If I'm right, it ought to work like the "alcoholic" drinks that come from the magick table,' I said. 'And be completely safe for people to use.'

Elliot disappeared as mysteriously as he had arrived. I used to call him the Chief Scientist, because of his air of authority. That elevated status was not his official rank, but who knows what his official description was. The world of secret science and special technology was a mystery to me.

Five minutes later, Elliot was back. He had a word with the Irish Constable, who looked relieved. Then he came over to me.

'OK, its fine,' he said. 'Just a mixture of proteins, minerals and vitamins, as you said. But how does it work? What gives it the buzz that users are looking for?'

'Your analysis needs to be able to identify the interaction of subatomic particles and electrons,' I said, not really understanding what I was talking about. 'Does it do that?'

'No,' said Elliot. 'We've got equipment that can do that, but it's not portable.'

'Would you like a portable version?' I asked.

'No,' said Elliot, looking shocked for a moment.

Then he laughed. 'Oh, go on then, if you must.'

I produced something about the size of a photocopying machine. It could print out results. I did not know how it worked, but Elliot did. He switched it on, opened a small partition in the equipment, and dropped a bit of the white powder into it. Flashing lights appeared. The machine whirred a bit, and several sheets of A4 came out, with lots of numbers on them, and a graphic showing an X/Y axis, with values on them, and a lot of black dots indicating values or qualities.

Elliot studied the papers. Then he pointed to a page that was just rows of numbers. It could have been computer code, for all I knew.

'I think that's it,' he said. 'It's an ionization reaction. Anyway, it's nothing we need worry about. The stuff is perfectly safe, perfectly legal, and, as you said, quite good for you.'

He disappeared, taking the machine with him.

In the following days, word got around about how you could escape from the terrorist bosses, get a new brain, a new body and start a new life, with free drugs, all courtesy of the Irish Republic. I didn't have to send people there, they were queueing up to think, 'I want to go to the Irish Republic.' The rest was history.

The terrorists were not happy about this. They were losing staff, and they were losing control. So they devised a plan to try and subvert the process, by sending their people into the arrival area. They could do this simply by walking in through the covered way, or climbing over a fence. The idea was that they would tell escapees that the terrorists were watching them, and would come and get them later.

I upgraded the arrival routine. When refugees arrived, they all got a new brain automatically, which was the cleverest in the Universe, plus a goody bag with a magick table and mini-cupboard. But there was still something they nearly all wanted, and that was to seek the privacy of the invisible toilets, in order to increase the size of their male member. No longer lacking in confidence, they emerged reassured that they were now just as good as everyone else.

At night, not all men bothered to seek the privacy of the invisible toilets. One young man was standing in the shadows, and had just given himself the thing he had always wanted, when a rough rasping voice was heard from the bushes, 'Come here boy and let me see you. Goodness, what a good-looking young man it is, to be sure.'

The creepy voyeur had given himself away. He could be seen in the bushes, staring at the young man's new credentials. He had been sent to keep a record of all the men who arrived, but he could not resist making his presence felt. The dirty old man was caught. But after becoming "the cleverest person in the world" he was transformed into a regenerated human being with a brain. It is hard to believe, but it happened.

One day, I had sent forty weapons group terrorists to the Irish Republic, and they were all rushing about, getting their brains changed, collecting their goody bags, and moving towards the coach park, when a man in his thirties, called Peter, hurried through the walkway looking for me.

'Did you want something?' I asked.

'It's my mother, she is ill and I want to take a mini-cupboard to her,' he said. 'It's a long way and I need a taxi, but I've heard that the taxis here won't give lifts to us returnees.'

'OK,' I said. 'Can you picture your mother in your mind?'

He did that, and I picked up her frequency, and brought us both to where she was. She was lying in bed, in hospital, and it didn't look as if she was conscious. She looked very ill. Peter took out the mini-cupboard, but what use was that if she wasn't conscious. He turned to me with a look of desperation.

'Put your mother's finger in the mini-cupboard, and your finger as well,' I said. 'Now say, "My mother is perfectly well and in the prime of her life".'

That was the best that I could suggest, and it had worked in China. Peter did that, and waited, hardly daring to breathe, in case it didn't work. I wasn't sure if it would work either. For a moment, nothing happened. Then, the woman sat bolt upright in bed. She now looked about forty.

'What am I doing here,' she said.

Then she saw her son.

'Peter, what are *you* doing here?' she said.

Peter gave her a hug.

'You're better now, Mum, that's all that matters,' he said.

'Well, I'd better get dressed and come with you,' said his mum.

Peter's mum got dressed, and got ready to leave. She had previously been living in a care home. Peter was greatly reassured now that his mum was out of danger, but there were a lot of arrangements to make, and he was worried about how to get everything done. He wanted to take his mum back with him to the reception centre, so that they could both start again and live under the same roof.

I took them directly to the reception centre, and explained to the Irish Constabulary what had happened. It was the first time I had been there. There were several officials sitting at desks with computers, checking the records of the returnees, and phoning local authorities to arrange accommodation and transport for them.

Peter went to a desk, and registered himself and his mum with an official. The official fixed them up with a local authority, who could provide temporary sheltered accommodation for them, until a council house was available. Their transport wasn't due for an hour, so they were directed to a canteen where they could have a free meal. Peter was much more relaxed now. His mum was doing better by the hour. Things had started to look up. It seemed to me that the Irish Republic were taking their responsibilities to the returnees seriously, and doing the best they could for them.

So far, all the people I returned to the Irish Republic were either Irish or from the British Isles. There were arrangements in place to return North Americans to Canada and the US, but as the European War began to draw to a close, the terrorists started to draw on European members of the International Unity Guild.

One day, I saw a lot of small kids running around in the terrorists' garden. Tanya appeared and asked me to take them into H.M. Special Prison Services, because she thought they might be British. She asked me to put labels on their wrists, showing where they came from, which I did. To our surprise they all said Krakow.

'Do you want me to take them to the Irish Republic? I asked.

'Oh, that's all right, we can send them there ourselves,' she said.

H.M. Special Prison Services had for a long time had a good working relationship with the US NATO base in the Irish Republic, and had no difficulty in transporting people there.

It had been a hot, sunny day, and in the evening, I was watering the garden, when I looked up and saw about forty terrorist soldiers running in formation. They had just arrived by Pringle transport.

They were the best turned out set of terrorist soldier men I had ever seen. I couldn't believe my eyes when I saw these guys. They wore smart uniforms with long grey shorts and red combat tops, grey socks and boots. In their thirties, they looked a serious bunch of men who meant business. They had been brought in to replace some forty North American troops that I had just returned to the United States military in America.

I asked one of them where he was from. He told me that he was from the Irish Republic. This was not true, and I could see that the men had been told to say that. I couldn't work out where they were from. Anyway, it didn't matter. I decided to send them to the Irish Republic so that they could be freed and given the cleverest brains in the universe, as it seemed a waste for the men to be slaughtered unnecessarily.

Selecting the entire group, I sent them to the arrival area in the Irish Republic. As they landed, their feet had only touched the ground for a moment, before a huge wind suddenly took them up into the air with a strange rushing noise. I stood in the arrival hall and watched as they all flew past above my head, and off into the distance. They just had time to get the cleverest brain in the universe before taking off, and their faces showed shock, pleasure and disbelief, as they all suddenly rose up into the air.

I asked an Irish Intelligence Officer, who was on duty in the arrivals area, what was going on.

'Those are Polish soldiers,' he said. 'NATO decided they didn't like the look of them, and took them away just like that.'

'Where have they gone?' I asked.

'To the NATO Irish base, initially,' said the officer. 'Then they will go on to the NATO base in Poland.'

I went back home, and was getting on with watering the garden when I saw another twenty Polish soldiers just coming out of a large underground cavern, halfway up the hill. Again, I heard a loud noise like a rushing wind, and all the men flew up in the air about fifteen feet, and continued climbing as they soared off and disappeared.

'NATO really *don't* like the look of them,' I thought.

Later, I heard a terrorist manager whisper to his colleague that he had asked the Polish terrorists to send soldiers "with sticks and swords", forgetting to specify that the soldiers needed to work in the electromagnetic environment. So, the Polish terrorists had sent regular terrorist soldiers instead of electromagnetic warriors.

That night, a group of hardened North American terrorist henchmen launched yet another attack on me. All their junior staff had rescued themselves by thinking, 'I want to go to the Irish Republic,' and their supervisors were now having to do the dangerous work of taking me on, by themselves. They started firing laser weapons at me.

I selected them all in one group, shouting, 'Armless, legless,'

They fell to the ground, unable to move, having lost the ability to feel their arms and legs. One of their supervisors appeared with a rifle.

'I'm going to have to shoot you all,' he said. 'You're not going to be any use to us after this.'

As he was loading the gun, I spoke to the fallen men, 'You've got a choice now. You can either be dead or go to the

Irish Republic, and you all know how to do that. Which is it to be?'

They all jumped, arriving together in the Irish Republic. As they arrived, the policemen on duty spotted that they were villains rather than victims, and called in an armed soldier. In such cases, suspects were usually taken away in vans by the Irish Military. A soldier went to get a van, and while he was away, the villains discovered that they now had the cleverest brains in the universe.

What happened next was not as expected. The hardened men sat on the ground with their heads in their hands, in a shocked state, reliving their past lives in the light of their new-found intelligence. They were unable to cope with the memories that came flooding back.

The policeman on duty called in the medical team, and they examined the men.

'We think it is Post Traumatic Stress Disorder,' they announced.

Wheelchairs were brought for the men, who were still sitting on the ground, taking no notice of what was going on around them. Then the men were wheeled off to waiting vans. From there, they went to a military medical centre. They were kept under observation for twenty-four hours, and were a lot better a day later.

The Irish Military were very sharp. One day, I selected a flying Pringle, full of terrorists, and sent it to the Irish Republic. About forty men landed in the arrival area, and were milling about, getting help from the Irish police. In the midst of the turmoil, a large man with an air of command, emerged from the crowd. The soldiers instantly recognised him as a terrorist unit head. As he now had the cleverest brains in the universe, he went quietly. He was taken away, and I heard that he was being held in a military prison.

What happened to men taken away by the military? I don't know, as they were now under military jurisdiction. I guess it might make a difference that they now had new brains, and were no longer the same people who wanted to attack and kill people. But justice would have to be done. They would still have to face a Court Martial. If, however, they were no longer a danger to the public, and if they wanted to change, they were in the best place to do so.

By now it was getting dark. It was time to go home. As I left the arrival area, the street outside was already in shadow. The buildings belonged to an earlier time, and the cobbled streets in the pedestrian area had an ancient feel about them. Three elderly terrorist henchmen from the local IRA terrorist unit, were sitting on a bench, talking to each other in the secret code that the old guard used.

'I left my coat with the tortellini downstairs,' said the first. 'And I was just sitting down at the table when my boss genuflected me in to benedict *her* out of it.'

'Who do you mean?' said the second.

'Oh, you know, that friggate bird whose husband supplies the kindercrafts' replied the third.

'Oh *her*,' said the second man, lowering his voice. 'I heard she is about to make her first purchase.'

At that moment, a fashionable young girl wearing leggings and a tight sports top came jogging by. The three elderly terrorists watched in silence till she disappeared.

'What pulchritude,' said the first man, with sincere admiration.

To most people, the three henchmen might just as well have been speaking French, but to the terrorists, it was perfectly intelligible. When translated, the discussion between the three men reads:

'I left my coat with the little tart downstairs, and I was sitting down to eat, when my boss phoned me to say he had got me the job of removing that woman from the planet.'

'Who are you talking about?'

'Oh, you know, that fucking female whose husband provides children for the business.'

'Really, I heard she is expecting her first baby.'

'Did you see that young woman over there, what a smasher!'

I thought how removed from the real world the terrorist community had become. Leaving the electromagnetic environment and returning to the Irish Republic outside was like stepping from the 1950s into the 21st century.

TARGETED INDIVIDUALS IN NORTH AMERICA

Next day, I received an automated email from a well-known writer in the United States, who campaigned on behalf of individuals targeted by electromagnetic terrorists in North America. I'm not sure how she got my email address. The email stated that for a long time she had been inundated with attacks by terrorists. She had begged them to stop, but, unsurprisingly, they had no mercy. She was at the end of her endurance, and calling for help.

I tuned into the frequency of the email, and found myself in a pleasant airy house in North America. As soon as I arrived, I noticed terrorist technicians crawling about all over the ceiling. They had laid out invisible ceiling rails to enable them to snipe at people from above, using lasers and microwave beams. I removed them. The woman, whose name was Teresa, was sitting at a work table, reading a book. She looked tired and worn. I spoke to her.

'Hi, I'm from the UK. You sent an email calling for help. I think I may be able to assist you.'

Teresa seemed to recognise my frequency.

'Are you the person who wrote that book 'Terror in Britain?' she asked.

'Yes,' I said. 'You need a place to be safe in your house. I will build you a place that only you can see, and only you can enter.'

I created a small apartment inside her house, with a front door, that only she could open. It had a living room, bedroom, bathroom and kitchen. Teresa chose what furniture and decorations she wanted, and I took them from her head and put them in the house. The house worked just as well as any normal house. Teresa could have the television on, but the terrorists could not use the radio waves as a route into her living room. The electricals worked properly, but terrorists could not use the house wiring as a route into the building.

I transferred my electromagnetic faculties to Teresa, and showed her how to point with her finger at a terrorist, and remove him from the planet. Then Teresa took the book she was reading, went inside her new house and shut the door after her. She was now invisible, and so was her house. The terrorists could not see or detect her.

A few days later, I checked to see if she was all right. She was just going into her inner house with some shopping, when a terrorist technician began climbing down the wall. She pointed her finger at him, and he disappeared. Then she was gone.

'That seems to be working all right,' I thought.

I went to look on Teresa's blog, to see if she had updated it since my visit. She hadn't, but while I was surfing the internet, I noticed that a group of people campaigning against electromagnetic terrorism had got together and started a website. They came from many different walks of life, and one of them, a woman called Astrid, caught my eye. A friend of mine knew her and had told me about her. She used to live in the UK in the same town as him, but had moved to the States. He now kept in regular contact with her. I decided to tune into Astrid's frequency, and see whether she needed any help.

When I arrived, she was in some kind of conference centre, sitting in a small work room.

'Hello,' I said. 'I've come from the UK, to see if I can offer any help.'

'Oh yes,' she said. 'Teresa told me about you.'

'Would you like me to transfer my electromagnetic faculties to you?' I asked.

'Yes, please,' said Astrid.

At that moment, a man whose picture I had seen on the same website suddenly arrived in his electromagnetic form. His name was Monty.

'Can I have the same thing too,' he said.

I transferred everything I had to both of them, which included the ability to pass on what they had received to other people.

After that, I did not see them for several weeks. Then one day, when I was walking down the road, it occurred to me that rather than transferring what I had got to individuals, I ought to make it available to all human beings who wished to use it, should the situation arise for them. Immediately, I selected the Earth and transferred whatever I had got into the airwaves, to be of assistance, if required.

Later that day, I went back to the conference centre, where I had met Astrid and Monty, and looked to see if they were there. The room I arrived in was a theatre hall, and I was standing backstage in the wings. Monty and several other people were on the stage, giving a talk, and about fifty people were sitting or standing in the auditorium.

One of the people in the audience was asking, 'What is the best way to deal with several terrorists at once if they are attacking you? It takes a long time to pick them off individually.'

'Yes, I have found that a problem too,' said someone else.

Monty turned and looked at me. With his enhanced abilities, he was able to tell, intuitively, that I was there.

'Well,' he said. 'What would you advise?'

I explained that I generally applied methods used in computer applications, such as "select all", and "group", after which whatever was needed could be done to all the terrorists at once.

Later that week, Teresa introduced me to two elderly friends of hers, Mia and Donald, who lived in a hostel for homeless people on welfare. Mia asked me to build her a safehouse like the one I had made for Teresa. I created one similar to Teresa's, including a magick restaurant table.

'Look at the table and think of some food,' I said.

Mia produced a rather plain sandwich, cut into quarters. She began eating it. Then, in the middle of eating, she asked, 'Would this food still be here if I was outside the safehouse, but in the hostel?'

Taking the plate, she opened the door of her private house, and went back into the hostel, where Donald was sitting at a small table.

'Oh, there you are,' said Donald. 'Can I have a bit?' He leaned over and took a quarter sandwich off her plate.

I turned Donald's table into a magick restaurant table, and encouraged him to think of something he wanted to eat. He immediately produced a plain sandwich, identical to the one that Mia had chosen.

'I heard there is something else that looks like a wooden box, that does things,' said Mia. 'What does that do for you?'

I produced a mini-cupboard, and explained that it did clothes, and that if you put your fingers in it, it could help with illnesses, and with physical appearance.

'Give me that,' said Donald. 'I'd like to be thinner and younger.'

He snatched the hollow wooden box and putting his fingers in it, said:

'Make me thinner and younger.'

The result was rather surprising. The colour came back into Donald's cheeks, he looked about forty, and his hair colour was now brown.

'Give it back,' said Mia.

She seized the box, and with her fingers in the hollowed-out part, said, 'Make me thinner and younger.'

The same thing happened to her. Mia's hair became longer and the colour was now dark ash blonde. She appeared to be in early middle age. At that moment, two cheerful black girls in their thirties, Kelsey and Janice, came in.

'Whose getting thinner and younger?' asked Janice.

'Yes, I want to hear about this,' said Kelsey, taking the mini-cupboard from Mia. 'What is this for?'

The wooden box was passing from hand to hand, and I was trying to get a word in to let them know that you could make another box by looking at it and saying, 'Make another,' but it was just impossible to intervene.

So, I made three more mini-cupboards. Now at least everyone had their own. I left the four of them experimenting with their boxes.

AFGHANISTAN POPPIES

It was lunch time, and the radio was covering the news headlines. There was a feature about the effects of hard drugs on addicts in the West. It was rather gloomy. No one seemed to have a solution to the problem. I thought to myself, 'If there were no poppy flowers, that particular problem would not exist. Perhaps someone could genetically modify poppy plants so that they never flowered.'

I haven't ruled that out, as a possibility, but the plants were already flowering for this year. My mind hovered over the vast poppy fields of Afghanistan. They looked very beautiful, with their huge, extravagantly-petalled pink and white blooms. Having tried to grow poppies from seed myself, I know that it takes a year of nurturing and constant watering to get the plants to the point of flowering. But perhaps that's because I'm still a beginner gardener.

In Afghanistan, the plants grow profusely, and there are armed guards in the poppy plantations, so valuable is the crop. One particularly colourful plantation caught my attention. I created a huge electromagnetic sack above the fields.

'Let every bud, flower and seed pod now go into that bag,' I decreed.

The poppies poured in. There were so many that I had to keep expanding the size of the bag. It hung like an enormous hot air balloon, blocking out everything else in the sky. In the fields below, the farmers stood, looking up, their legs shaking with fear. I realised that their whole livelihood, representing commitments to numerous dealers downstream, was at stake. Part of me relented, and wanted to make it up to them. So, using a public address system, I announced to the farmers, 'I am taking over your production system. From now on, you only supply my drugs. If you do that, you will lack for nothing.'

The farmers stood together in a circle, looking at me. I came down to their level.

'We know all about your drugs,' said one of them. 'Our dealers already supply them, and they say the quality is better than ours. You are putting us out of business.'

'Have you tried these devices?' I asked, producing several mini-cupboards.

'Oh, so that's what they look like,' said another farmer. 'I've heard of them, but never seen one.'

'Help yourself,' I said.

Then the farmer said the one thing I would have preferred him not to.

'Does it do cars?' he asked.

I was ambivalent about making cars from the mini-cupboards, because it could have an impact on countries' economies, and on car manufacturers.

'I don't know, I've never tried,' I replied.

A minute later, a large truck was standing there, much to the delight of the farmers. Then there were four more. The men talked excitedly amongst themselves. They were not particularly wedded to heroin production, which was labour intensive, and relied on the right weather conditions. These men lived in basic accommodation. In the summer, they set up tents by their plantations, so that they could guard them day and night. Now, that would change. They would have a better quality of life. I explained how to make another cupboard from the first one. The head man solemnly created one for each of the farmers and their sons.

'You will need these as well,' I said, setting up some large magick restaurant tables, showing how they could be re-sized.

The men took it all in their stride, and began making new clothes for themselves. It occurred to me that they had given no thought whatsoever to the women in their families. So I went to look for them. The women spent their days away from the men, working together on cooking, cleaning and care of children and old people. They were sitting in a large, communal work room when I went in. All of them were dressed in black, with black headscarves. I am told that Afghan women do not have to wear black, but these farmers wives were rather conservatively dressed. At least I blended in, in my black puffa coat and hood.

'Hello,' I said. 'I have just given gifts to the men in your community, and I am now doing the same to you,' I turned all their tables into magick restaurant tables, and handed out mini-cupboards to them all, showing how they could be used.

'Oh yes,' said one woman. 'We know about these.' They set about using them.

'The mini-cupboards can be helpful for illness and old-age,' I said. 'Older people can now retain the wisdom and experience earned from a full lifetime, while being physically in their prime.'

'Oh,' said the head woman, and she got up and left.

She went into an adjoining building where a very frail elderly woman with white hair was lying in bed, attended by a younger female member of the family. The head woman leant over the old lady, taking her hand and whispering to her. She placed the old lady's fingers in the wooden box, along with her own, and wished her mother in good health, in the prime of her life.

The old lady could barely lift her hand, but she listened attentively to what her daughter was saying. Then she raised her head, and I could see that her hair was no longer white, but dark, with a few lighter strands. Her face plumped up, and her eyes looked larger and firmer. Then she reached out her hand and stood up, throwing a black cloak around her.

I left her and her daughter together, and returned to the main room, where the other women were now using the magick restaurant tables to create rich meat dishes with delicious sauces, and other delicacies on smaller plates. The women carried the food out to where the men were sitting. The men had already made a modest choice for their first magick table meal, just soup and bread as usual. When the women came out in procession, with the plates, they looked very surprised.

'What is this for?' said one.

At that moment, the head woman came out and addressed the men, 'Today is a day for celebration! Our mother has regained her health, and is back amongst us.'

All the men looked up in astonishment.

'Come and welcome her back,' said the head woman, beckoning the men into the communal room where men and women were permitted to sit together as a family group.

The men filed into the low-ceilinged room, where the mother was now standing, smiling, surrounded by the other women. She embraced family members, and greeted neighbours warmly.

After the men had withdrawn to eat their feast outside, the mother presided over the women's meal, catching up on news of children and grandchildren. Then she set about changing things, using the mini-cupboard.

'The goddess has given us this for a purpose,' she said. 'So we should make the most of it.'

I was somewhat embarrassed to be described in such terms, but remembered that in Asia, from time immemorial, people with more advanced technologies than the rest had always been referred to as gods and goddesses.

As I was leaving, I looked back on the group of men sitting outside their tents. What a transformation! They had let themselves get a bit carried away. Each senior man now had a chair that was more like a throne, and they all had richly coloured head gear, with coats of red and purple velvet, and baggy trousers that glinted with gold thread.

A GLIMPSE OF HELL

It happened that I was away from home for twenty-four hours. The North American and IRA terrorists, who operated the business of making money through access to me in the electromagnetic environment, had not been aware of that. As a result, they had sold morning, afternoon and evening blocks to various groups who came and went without making money. They had to be compensated for their trouble. The local terrorists were unable to demonstrate to their masters in North America that they were managing to control me, and they got negative feedback for that.

Their senior managers in the United States decided to intervene. I had just finished lunch, and stood up to clear the table, when I was hit by an array of one hundred oscillators. This was not something I had experienced before, and if I had not been using shielding devices, I would have been seriously incapacitated. It was clear that the attack had been mounted by US technical specialists, so I merged all the unit rooms in the British Isles, and selected all the technical support staff in them. Then I removed all their shielding devices, and announced, 'Let all those selected return to the United States.'

The entire country was emptied of technicians. Replacements would be imported automatically from any members of the terrorist league that were still speaking to the North Americans, if there were any. But so unexpected was the withdrawal of labour, that there were none left, apart from one or two groups on the extreme wings of terrorism. It was several hours before the first of these arrived. In the meantime, I was busy sweeping leaves off the patio, and tidying up the garden.

After my evening meal, I heard a string of abusive comments that I have come to associate with old fashioned psychological warfare, as taught by North American faeces groups. This was first heard in my last mission. I looked out into the terrorists' garden amphitheatre, and saw a range of tiered seating. Several men and women were sitting in rows looking towards my house, wearing face masks to conceal their identity.

'We have got her trained now,' said an older woman. 'She will get up and take her plates into the kitchen, and then our men will make sure she has to visit the toilet in a hurry.'

The two other women burst into peals of derisive laughter. I was quite used to such approaches, but in this case, they were incredibly out of date. For a start, no terrorists were ever able to make me run anywhere, least of all to the toilet, as I had all kinds of shielding devices. But these people were unaware of that. Secondly, the woman who spoke, sounded very like an elderly Jihadette called Esme, who had once been the terror of Pakistan's ISIS women's movement. This woman had to be of the same vintage.

'She sounds as old as me, and I'm over seventy,' I said to myself.

'Seventy,' said the Jihadette. 'She is nearly my age.'

'They sound like a bunch of old torturers and murderous bandits from Pakistan,' I thought.

All the men and women gasped at that.

'I was told our masks would conceal our identity,' complained one.

'How did she find out? It's your fault,' another shouted at the North American supervisor.

'It is true, I've tortured and murdered more than any of you, in my time,' said the elderly woman. 'But I've come here for healing, and *she* is going to give it to me.'

The old woman pointed a gnarled finger at me. I reached out and removed the youthful mask of the woman was wearing. She looked very like Esme, with heavily wrinkled skin and a grim expression, under a black and white Asian headscarf.

'You'll get nothing from me, so you might as well leave,' I said.

The old woman got up and left, followed by her middle-aged companion. I could hear them muttering to themselves, as they went out of the amphitheatre. After they left, the remaining younger woman spoke to an Asian man in his fifties standing on top of the gantry used by terrorists to embark in flying Pringles. He was the manager in charge of this unseemly attack, and he intended to stay close to the Pringle, in case he needed a quick getaway. His younger female companion said, 'I'll soon have both the older women finished off, and you can get rid of the men. Then we will run things between us.'

This announcement was delivered in a confident manner.

'What a horrid little schemer,' I thought.

'Arms off, legs off,' I said.

The young woman fell from the stand onto the grass below. She was now no use to the terrorists, and a North American henchman came out with a rifle and fired it at her head, killing her instantly. The henchman stood there impassively. He was only doing his job. Just then, a man from West Africa came running in.

'I told the old lady, it's not my fault that the mini-box wouldn't work,' he shouted at anyone who would listen.

Then he turned to me.

'It wouldn't work, and I paid good money for it. The old woman was not healed.'

The old woman returned and sat in the stands.

'It's a complete waste of money,' she said, directing her comments at me. 'I'll just have to throw it away.'

I guessed what had happened. The African trader had not realised that mini-cupboards did not operate in the British Isles. I had decreed that they should stop working in the UK, after North American terrorists had bought the services of a private hit-man to attack on me. They paid him by selling drugs that they created from the mini-cupboard. But this African's business dealings had nothing to do with me, and I was not disposed to assist the Asian woman, who had been extremely rude.

The African now turned his attention to the Asian manager standing on the Pringle gantry.

'You're behind all this,' he said. 'You knew she wouldn't help us, but you pretended to me that we'd soon have her under control. It's all your fault.'

He raised his fist in a threatening gesture. The Asian manager took out a rifle and shot the man through the heart.

The African fell to the ground, and the North American henchman impassively dragged his body away.

As if nothing had happened, the middle-aged Asian woman appeared in a small turret on the opposite side of the garden. She was now wearing a dark apricot satin gown, and a brown velvet cloak. With her back leaning against the wall, for dramatic effect, she looked towards me and said, 'Healing, I need healing. I've heard you have the gift, lady.'

She stretched out her hand towards me. Then she leaned back against the wall, sighing heavily. It was so stage-managed, particularly the quick change of clothes from the last scene, that anyone could see that she had been primed to try and get something out of me. If one method didn't work, she would try another. Really it wasn't that different from the aggressive methods used by professional beggars in some countries. I had plenty of things to occupy my time, and I lost interest in the play.

Then the elderly Asian lady scuttled in and sat down next to the impassive henchman. She offered him a bag of what was meant to be money, to use his good offices to make me do her bidding. But as a stage prop, the bag lacked credibility. It was a bit of scruffy, dirty cloth, which she drew from her bodice. I opened up the bag and emptied it onto the grass. It contained several safety pins, a bit of metal and a British 2p.

A Middle Eastern man, wearing a white robe, came in. He informed me that he held the rank of Chief Torturer, and could force me to heal the two women, even though, it must be said, they did not look particularly ill. The man then told me that he had friends in high places, a Djinn, no less, who would make sure that I became their servant. As he spoke, I picked up what was in his mind. It was a picture of an ancient road, lined with high stone walls.

I recognised it as a place in Lebanon, near the Temple of Baalbek, which I had read about. The book described how some Middle Eastern people had gone through rituals in order to try and get evil spirits to do things for them. It reminded me of the story of Aladdin and his lamp. The people in the book belonged to a secret society which they called "The Brotherhood". I know there are many political and religious groups which call themselves "The Brotherhood". but this one was an esoteric group of some kind.

'Are you members of The Brotherhood?' I asked.

At this, all the remaining members of this bizarre group stood to attention, saying, 'Yes we are — the Dark Brotherhood.'

They really believed that they had got a demon to come and sort me out. If this was so, he had ripped them off, as he was nowhere to be seen. But there you go. The moral of that is to have no dealings with demons. Things had got incredibly surreal, and the Asian group were pushing their luck. I shot the murderous Asian manager, who had just killed the African, and selected the Chief Torturer and the two women, saying, 'Return to Pakistan.'

It was not the first time I had sent people back to Pakistan. In fact, I did it quite frequently. The country of Pakistan is well defended against electromagnetic attacks, having a special invisible net stretched over the full extent of their country to stop people entering in electromagnetic mode. But I mentally reduced the returnees to subatomic particles, and they filtered through easily, returning to normal on the other side of the net.

On this occasion, I decided to see what was going on, after the returnees arrived. Two soldiers from the Pakistan military had caught the Chief Torturer. They pushed him up against a wall and asked him why he had been sent back. His answer cannot have satisfied them, as they hit him in the kidneys, and he fell to the ground. I thought I should clarify what had happened, so I appeared, explaining that the ghastly group had tried to control me through a Djinn. The Chief Torturer confirmed this.

At that moment, the local military commander came out of the building behind us. On seeing him, the elderly woman started asking for healing again, complaining to him that she had bought a mini-cupboard that didn't work. I explained that mini-cupboards *did* work, but not in the British Isles. The old woman began scrabbling in her bag, and eventually located her wooden box. She tried again. This time it worked. She gave herself the energy and appearance of a woman of forty. She and her female accomplice then left.

'Well, thank God for that!' I thought.

I presented the commander and all the soldiers with mini-cupboards. The commander said that he had heard about the magick restaurant table, and would like to have one for his family home, which was in the building behind us. So, after presenting all the soldiers with mini magick restaurant tables, I accompanied the commander into the building.

On the first floor, was a large table, which could easily have provided for twenty people. I changed it into a magick restaurant table, and the commander called a junior female member of his family to come and try it out. She came in timidly, and after some encouragement, produced a bowl of rice. Satisfied that the table worked, the commander thanked me, and I left. I looked back to make sure the table was performing properly, as one bowl of rice didn't seem quite enough. But it was all right. The whole family were now sitting round the table, which was covered with dishes.

When I got back home, a local terrorist henchman was on guard on the Pringle gantry. A very thin man in his early twenties was standing next to him, drawing on a cigarette. His body was shaking. I thought he needed a fix urgently, so I made him a bag of white powder. He tried some, and lay on the ground with an expression of satisfaction. Three other thin young men came running into a room adjoining the gantry and tried some powder as well. Then they all lay on the ground. I thought they must be hard core drug addicts in the last stages of their lives.

Then I went into the terrorists' garden, where another very ill-looking young man was sitting. He was too weak to stand up. I asked him if he wanted some food, and he told me that he was not allowed to eat today.

'Who says so?' I asked indignantly.

The young man pointed to the other side of the garden, where a tall, heavily built man with thick dark hair was marching up and down in front of some undernourished youths, giving them a lecture. Then another youth arrived. Presumably he was late, because the man hit him, and he fell to the ground. My anger boiled over, and I selected the bully in a magnetic field, 'What you put out is what you get back,' I said.

The evil man started writhing and screaming on the ground, and we could all see what he had been doing to other people for a long time. He died soon afterwards. Another man, similar in appearance, but younger and thinner came out. It was the monster's second in command. He started talking to the young men, who were looking rather shocked at what they had witnessed.

At that moment, the electromagnetic ceiling opened up, and I saw Michael and Tanya from H.M. Special Prison Services looking down.

'What language is that man speaking in?' asked Michael.

I could see that they felt they ought to rescue the starved young men, but their terms of engagement only permitted them to get involved with people from the British Isles, the Irish Republic and North America. I asked a henchman standing nearby what the language was.

'I think they are speaking Croatian,' he said.

Michael and Tanya looked disappointed, and they withdrew. I selected all the men, and their assistant manager, 'Return to the Irish Republic,' I said.

The men all appeared in the arrival area, and received brains that were "the cleverest in the universe" automatically. Members of the Irish Constabulary gave all the men mini-cupboards and showed them how to make themselves fit and healthy. Then they were taken to a large magick restaurant table nearby, where they had their first full meal for a long time.

The assistant manager in charge of them was taken into custody, but as he also now had the cleverest brain in the universe, he accepted his fate. He too had been on a restricted diet, so he probably counted as a victim, which would be taken into consideration.

I was wondering where these men had come from. Having visited Croatia myself, I was not convinced that they were from that country. I looked up the languages of that region on the internet, and it seemed possible that the men could have come from several neighbouring countries, and still be speaking something like Croatian. Tuning into the frequency of the evil man who had just died, I tried to find where he had come from.

The terrorists' garden disappeared, and was replaced by a wood of big dark deciduous trees, with a clearing in the middle. About thirty terribly thin young men were standing or sitting in the clearing, smoking heavily. They did not seem to have anyone in charge of them, so I created a large magick restaurant table, with chairs round it, and invited the men to come and eat. The men pointed to their mouths. They had plastic palates inside their mouths, attached to their teeth, to stop them eating. I selected all the men and said, 'Remove the plastic.'

Then the men came forward, and I helped them to choose food and drink. They rushed their food, constantly looking over their shoulders, like frightened animals.

'What are you doing in this wood?' I asked.

'We are waiting to be called in, to fight in the British Isles,' said one of them.

It did not look as if any of them were capable of walking far, let alone fighting.

'How did you get to be here?' I asked.

'They kidnapped us from our home town,' said one of the young men.

'Where is that?' I asked.

'Bihac,' he replied.

I checked on my iPad, and found that Bihac is in the Federation of Bosnia and Herzegovina.

I had just taken a group of young men from the same unit to the Irish Republic, so the best thing to do seemed to be to bring in the others as well. On arrival, the men were helped by the Irish Constabulary and reunited with the first group.

Thinking back over the events of the day, with the Pakistani Brotherhood, and the Bosnian bandits, I wondered how these people had got themselves involved with our terrorists. Our Group had been chucked out of the International Unity Guild, but they still had an informal arrangement with other mafia and criminal groups. Even so, the people they were calling on were bordering on the criminally insane, rather than terrorists. It looked as if Our Group were running out of people to call.

That evening, I had just gone to bed, when I was attacked by an American mafia technician, wearing a long trench coat and a dark trilby hat. I could see a troop of similar attackers being imported automatically from North America by the terrorists' computer system. The man with the trilby used a non-standard laser gun, which had a much deeper chamber, providing greater electronic power, with increased capacity to inflict pain. Such weapons breach UK laws, and, no doubt, the laws of other NATO countries as well. I selected the guy and his weapon, and picking him up, went to the back garden of the NATO Special Services building. Even though it was night, there was always someone on duty there.

I banged on the door. A scientist in a white coat appeared.

'Look at this man's weapon,' I said. 'It's something new. There are about twenty more villains just arriving from the United States.'

The scientist in the white coat returned with a large plastic container.

'Can you put him in there, please, and we'll have a look at him.'

The terrorist with the trilby was in a miniaturised electromagnetic state, about two feet high. He fitted easily into the plastic container. The scientist picked up the plastic container and took it away.

I got back into bed, and was just settling down, when I saw several British soldiers rounding up the rest of the trilby-hatted Americans. The soldiers looked over the electromagnetic wall into the terrorist unit next-door, which was normally occupied by weapons group infantry soldiers.

'Look at that, there must be four hundred of them,' said one of the soldiers.

'Oh, don't worry,' I said. 'I'll remove them.'

The British soldiers left, and I selected all but one of the trenchcoated invaders.

'Return to the United States.'

I knew that the US had an electromagnetic security net in place, with a device that pulled all the terrorists into it, if they tried to enter the States in electromagnetic form. The terrorists would be picked up by US Military border controls.

I wanted the British and American Authorities to take more notice of what was going on. They seemed to think that I could handle whatever came my way, but I did not see why I should have to do that. I decided to leave one terrorist still standing.

The man was looking rather anxious about his safety. When I picked him up, he looked even more concerned. I took him to a place in California, where I had seen a large terrorist centre for technical support staff, and deposited him on their doorstep.

'Yippee,' cried the man. 'I'm home and I'm safe,' He started running around, firing his laser gun into the air again and again until all the power had been used up.

Two minutes later, an American military helicopter appeared. A soldier let down a hook, attached it to the terrorist's trench coat, and winched him up into the chopper. There wasn't really room in the chopper for anyone else, but I wanted to talk to the soldiers, so I appeared, balancing in the doorway.

'I just returned this terrorist from my home in the British Isles,' I said, 'because I want to highlight the fact that four hundred of these men, all armed with similar weapons, were sent in to attack one poor old senior citizen.'

The soldiers were busy tying up the exuberant trench coater, who was looking somewhat less exuberant now. One of them turned to me.

'Point taken, ma'am!' he said.

I went back to bed and tucked myself in. As I rolled over, I thought, 'That really was one hell of a day!'

PROPHESYING WAR

It was high Summer, and I went to visit some friends who lived in York. After a pleasant day in the Yorkshire countryside, followed by a good meal at an Italian restaurant, I checked into a hotel for the night. My visit had been planned some time in advance, and the terrorists knew all about it. They had connected with a group of terrorists living in the North East, and arranged for them to have a reception party waiting for me. In fact, the reception party had followed me around all day, by WIFI satellite, but opportunities for close-range attacks were limited. To compensate for that, they had invested heavily in staff and technical support at my hotel.

The attacks followed the usual pattern — electromagnetic oscillators aimed at my body, combined with microwave beams to the head, lasers sniping at me, and non-stop synthetic telepathy practitioners wittering away, trying to attract my attention. As usual, I selected a group of these people, and shouted, 'Armless, legless.' Then, I explained to them that they had a choice between being shot in the head by their own lot, who had no further use for them, or taking the escape route to the Irish Republic. The York manageress, who was called Margaret, began talking to a colleague, unaware that I could hear her, 'She seems to be trying to help us. I don't feel comfortable about continuing with this. Why did the North Americans call us in. Two of them are up here with us. I will speak to them. They should be on duty now. Where are they?'

Margaret sent an assistant to ask the technical support team to locate the two North Americans. By "North Americans" she meant the people from where I lived, who called themselves "Our Group". But the two North American men who had been sent to oversee the organisation of the York attacks could not be located. If they had been at home down South, their absence would not have been noted, but here, it was.

'I'm going to raise the matter with their superiors,' said Margaret.

She dialled up their boss and reported the two men absent while on duty. A few minutes later, the men appeared, looking rather shamefaced. They had been hiding in a flying Pringle, and only came down if anyone asked for them. Apparently, they always did this, to ensure that only visiting terrorists ever got hit by me.

But they couldn't hide from me even if they were in a Pringle. In fact, I made a point of removing the North American managers first, wherever they were, while rescuing the junior ranks. This had become such a routine, that the juniors would queue up in the garden, knowing that they would soon be rescued. If I happened to be busy for a moment, they would start complaining, 'Where is she? I was told she would be here.'

I would then remind them that they already knew how to free themselves, and as soon as they remembered, they immediately left for the Irish Republic on their own initiative.

Having established that the North American terrorists were hiding while on duty, Margaret noticed some of her staff waiting in the wings to take over instead of them. She called her staff in and asked them why they had done this, when they were not scheduled for such work. The men said the North Americans had bribed them with cash, which, as they were unemployed, was a reasonable incentive.

'Show me the cash,' I said.

The men took wads of dollar notes out of their pockets.

'If you look carefully at the paper,' I said. 'You will see that it is counterfeit. Real dollars have different paper from that. These are fakes, printed from a computer near where I live.'

Everyone could see that this was the case.

'Why did you fall for that?' asked Margaret.

The men were silent.

'I think the North Americans microwaved their heads to confuse them,' I said.

Margaret turned to the North American pair.

'Did you do that?' she asked.

'We always do that to everybody, including our own staff,' they replied.

'That is appalling,' said Margaret.

'I'm surprised you were not aware that nearly all the British terrorists always get killed whenever they come to the North American Unit,' I said. 'Surely some of the survivors made it home, and passed on a warning to the rest.'

'Ah,' said Margaret. 'That wouldn't happen, because all those called to attend the North American training unit down South have to sign a clause promising not to discuss or pass on anything that takes place during training courses or any other visits to that unit.'

'Then you really set yourself up, didn't you?' I said.

At that moment, I became aware of an unusual higher-frequency presence in our midst. It was like a cool fresh breeze. I think it was a military representative from one of the bodies within NATO. The military have access to a range of high radio frequencies not available for commercial use. The presence did not identify itself and did not use words to speak. Instead it used subvocal communication — referred to within the synthetic telepathy community as "evoked potentials".

What the presence said was, 'The North American Unit have a secret strategy to kill all the British terrorists, so that they can take over the running of the British Isles as a North American colony. Their plan is to use the British Isles as a stepping stone to Europe, as part of the European Theatre of War.'

When the presence said that, it was as if scales fell from our eyes.

'Of course! So that's what they were doing,' I said.

'I see it now,' said Margaret. 'I am never going to work with the North American Group again, and I will pass the word on to all the other British units.'

After that, Margaret called her staff off, and they left me for the night. I went to sleep and returned home the next day. From then on, no British terrorists came to my area down South. The North American group were forced to fight on their own.

I found out that the North Americans had convinced some international investors to back their work in Surrey, on the grounds that they would soon have me under their control, and with my "amazing" powers, they would be able to conquer the world easily. They decided that where I lived would become the capital of their New World.

They persuaded their financial backers to fork out for an extravagant city architecture, a bit like Washington D.C., with high Perspex domes, tall sky scrapers, sinister underpasses, and a mass of spaghetti representing electromagnetic pathways to all parts of the globe. The piece-de-resistance of this conspicuous construction was an exact replica of the United States Capitol Building.

When I discovered their city, it took about two seconds to demolish it. But, as it had been built by the North American secret scientists, they could reinstate it just as quickly, by saying, 'Copy and Paste,' from their original blueprint.

It was about this time, that some of the old IRA staff who had created the original strategy in support of the European Theatre of War, were forced out of hiding, and onto the battle field. They only came out because there was nobody else left that their bosses could call on. They remembered when I was first kidnapped, and told me that not only was I set up on all terrorist computer systems, but that I was attached to another worldwide computer system.

The worldwide computer system to which I was, apparently, attached, had an extensive knowledge, owing to its intelligence-gathering activities. The computer was said to be the US National Security Agency Government computer. The terrorists said that sometime before 2010, the US mafia had infiltrated the NSA, and gained access to the IT development side. Secretly, they started entering some of their key personnel onto this advanced computer system.

Apparently, early IRA founders of the electromagnetic terrorist movement were also set up in files on the same highly classified computer server. Being set up on the NSA computer enabled powerful electromagnetic enhancements to be applied, which meant that anywhere in the world would be in range, a bit like cellphone roaming.

The reason I was on the system was that the original IRA founders thought I had skills they could use, relating to my former occupation, and that I could be persuaded to work for them. But the people who worked for them locally lost touch with all that. As far as they were concerned, I was just another person to be targeted and trafficked, and if that didn't bring in a profit, I was to be killed.

To my mind, the real culprits behind electromagnetic terrorism were the North American scientists, the international investors, and the top team of terrorists running the show. The top team never came down to Earth. They lived in circular buildings, high within the Earth's atmosphere. I had crashed them several times, and killed the occupants, but they always reformed. I now decided to go after the international investors. Drawing on data held within the NSA computer, and recent technology enhancements introduced by NATO, I announced, 'Let the people funding the terrorists now appear before me.'

Two groups of people showed up on video screens. On the first screen, I saw a palatial building, filled with people in Arab dress, in Morocco. They wore pure white. The VIPs within their midst sat on thrones and were shown the greatest respect. By now, I knew they were funded by terrorist sympathisers from within a community of wealthy Qatar businessmen, whose influence extended beyond the Middle East to Indonesia, and to parts of Europe.

On the second screen, I saw two mafia families. The first family had several large villas in Bosnia. One of them was located in the countryside, below some wooded hills. They also owned a private lodge. There was a pleasant lake nearby, and the area was popular with tourist in the Summer months. I looked on the internet, and identified the location as the town of Fojnica, and Prokosko Lake.

The second family had a townhouse in Rome, and a palace in the hills above it. They also had centres near Milan and Verona. The men were impeccably dressed by Italian tailors. They tended to favour camel suits and brown leather shoes. The women, many of whom were elderly matriarchs whose husbands had already died, were expensively and conservatively dressed. One of their villas in the country had marble pillars and domes, covering two pools, one enclosed within the architecture of the house, with a domed ceiling, and the other outside, a few feet below the first pool.

Both these families included men who had responsibility for overseeing the funding and direction of attacks on the British Isles within the European Theatre of War. The Bosnian family gave this responsibility to the younger generation, to allow young bloods to prove themselves worthy of higher office. The Italian family did not allow younger members to hold such responsibilities. They allocated such duties to senior members of their group.

From then on, whenever North American terrorists attacked me, I removed the responsible member of each of these families. This happened every day, and the families began to be unwilling to take on such responsibilities. My hope was that they would be discouraged to the point of no longer providing funding.

I also set up a system which arranged that every time a terrorist attacked me and I hit him back, all the terrorists involved in authorisation of that attack, right up to the level of funders, investors and partners, got it. Also, if a terrorist got a benefit, like the cleverest brain in the universe, and freedom to start a new life, then all those directly involved in authorising his activities, right up to the top, benefited as well.

This approach was more successful than I expected. For example, if terrorists tried to void my bladder, using a laser beam, I would select all the perpetrators on the computer system, and void their bladders and bowels in return. Once that happened to funders and partners, they were not happy at all, and started ordering their staff to stop doing it. And when these terrorist VIPs suddenly got the cleverest brain in the universe, because their junior staff had got it, they stopped being terrorists, and started helping other terrorists to stop as well.

INVASION OF THE CHANNEL ISLANDS

It was five-thirty in the morning when I woke up. Two assistant managers from today's visiting terrorist unit were talking to each other.

'I don't know what's going on,' said the first. 'Why didn't the locals prepare us better for this.'

'They seem to have made themselves scarce,' said the second.

The men must have given the order for attacks on me to start, as a weapons group perpetrator tried to void my bladder. I identified the perpetrator and his boss, and killed them. The visitors were taken by surprise, as they had been told that I was just an old person, who needed to be taken under control. Some of the visitors' senior staff, who were hiding in a Pringle above the building, got hit as well. One of them went on the public address system and called out, 'Attention all staff, you'd better go back to the Islands, as we can't work here.'

'Islands?' I thought. 'That must be the Channel Islands.'

I knew all the terrorist buildings in the Channel Islands, from long experience, and whenever they sent visiting groups to attack me, I would retaliate with attacks on their senior staff.

Now I headed for their VIP Headquarters building to see what was going on.

Normally, Mr and Mrs Mafia Boss would be standing there on duty, drinking cups of tea, looking frightfully well dressed, and rather relaxed, while their troops were on the battlefield. Today, I could only see Mrs Mafia Boss, looking extremely harassed, as she tried to hold her tea cup, while a platoon of North American terrorist infantry marched at a fast pace through her living room. The infantry took over the rest of the unit. Something was wrong. The Chanel Islands terrorists would never have agreed to this. They would never have sent their crack troops to the UK to attack me if they had known this was coming. Did someone plan to get them out of the way? And what had happened to Mr Mafia Boss? He had disappeared.

I decided to return all the North American terrorists to the United States, so I asked Mrs Mafia Boss to get out of the way, to avoid being caught up in things.

'I can't, I'm stuck here,' she said, waving her tea cup.

Next moment, she, and all the invaders, were on their way back to North America. The North American Military have achieved total lockdown as far as electromagnetic terrorism is concerned. That meant that if any electromagnetic people tried to enter the locked down area, they were magnetised into a vortex that took them down to a reception area in the United States. I often wondered what it was like, but never had a reason to go there. Now was my chance.

When I arrived, I could see five American military staff standing at tables, working with computers, and looking at surveillance screens. On the floor below, there were three more people, and behind them was a large vat of dissolving fluid. If any terrorist arrived in electromagnetic form, and fell into the vat, he would disappear forever in about two seconds.

On the floor above, the American military had spotted the terrorists that I had sent from the Channel Islands, coming their way, on their surveillance screens.

'Now, let's see what we've got here,' said one of them. 'Probably another lot of poor raggedy people.'

The returnees poured in through the vortex, and the American military staff started picking individuals, and asking them who they were, before letting them in. Mrs Mafia Boss was there, waving her arms wildly.

'I never wanted to come here. And now *they*'ve taken over our place,' she said, pointing to the terrorist infantrymen who were being funnelled through the system.

The American military were fully clued up, and knew all about that, so I went to York, to visit Margaret, the head of the North East British terrorist group. Margaret was sitting at her desk, reading a newspaper. She got a shock when I arrived unannounced, and shrank back, expecting something bad to happen.

'It's all right,' I said. 'I've come to tell you that there is going to be trouble in the Channel Islands. The North American terrorists have invaded the local mobsters there, and taken them over. Please can you make sure all British terrorists keep away from the area. NATO will sort it out.'

Margaret looked stunned.

'Thanks, I'll let everyone know,' she said.

I went back to the Channel Islands to see what was going on. As I hovered over the area, I saw about thirty flying Pringles, packed with North American troops, surrounding the islands, looking like seagulls about to pounce on a crust of bread. I headed for the local terrorist's infantry building in Alderney. The place was in confusion as I arrived, with men arming themselves, and running about. When they saw me, their leader shouted, 'Help! Help! The North Americans are coming.'

I was just about to pick them up and take them to the Irish Republic, when I heard a familiar sound like a rushing wind.

'It's all right. NATO are just coming,' I said. 'I can take you to the Irish Republic if you like.'

'Can you make it quick,' said their leader. 'The North Americans are at the back door!'

I looked round, and saw a body of men from North America, arriving. They had made their electromagnetic magnification larger than life, so they looked huge. They were wearing summer military uniform, as it was a baking summer day.

Just then, the sky opened and long hoses with suction attachments appeared.

'It's NATO!' I shouted. 'You'll be all right now!'

The NATO rescuers hoovered up both the local terrorists and the North Americans, so I guess they all got to go to the Irish Republic, which was the best solution, as they could be sorted into their respective national groups there.

At that moment, Elliot, the white-coated military scientist looked through the electromagnetic ceiling.

'What's going on?' he asked.

I showed him the mass of Pringles gathered in the sky over the Channel Islands.

When Elliot saw the Pringles, he jumped into his computer chair, and blew a high-pitched whistle. A minute later, men in white coats started running in, and sitting down at their computers.

'Looks like the balloon's going up,' I thought.

A moment later, NATO airborne craft were in the sky. Again, I heard a noise like a mighty rushing wind, and a whole lot of grey suction devices attached to wide hoses, appeared above the Pringles. They hoovered up the Pringles, one at a time. Half an hour later, the sky was clear.

I went back to the Channel Islands terrorist HQ to check whether all the North Americans had gone. I got there just in time to see Mrs Mafia Boss, talking to some NATO soldiers, 'Thank you so much for saving us. I don't know what we'd have done if you hadn't arrived,' she said.

'Terrorists thanking NATO?' I thought. 'What next!'

TYING UP LOOSE ENDS

The Chanel Islands were now safe, but the North American terrorists had moved on to Europe. I went to check what was going on in Poland, where I had recently seen terrorists ready for action. When I looked in on the Polish terrorists' headquarters there was nobody there. Last time I went there it had been full of staff. Now it was empty. Tuning in, I went to a large forest of tall pine trees. The forest was dark, which made it hard to see, but there were thousands of North American troops hiding in there.

It looked as if the North Americans had arrived in Poland in advance, to start the European War, fighting alongside their Polish counterparts. I watched as thousands of men in black electromagnetic uniforms, with black helmets, started to come out of the forest. They had been given orders to move on Krakow, prior to taking Warsaw. Then the noise of a rushing wind shook the forest, and the troops rose up into the air and flashed past me. NATO had arrived and was removing the invaders before they could get started.

Those people in the Special Services building next to H.M. Special Prison Services had not just been sitting around. They knew all about the terrorists' secret plans to attack Europe, and had developed measures to counter them. I thought of all the terrorist bases that I had visited in Europe and North Africa. I hurried to see what was going on in different locations around the European Theatre of War.

First, I went to the clearing in the trees in Bosnia, where the starved youths had been rescued from a terrorist unit. There were no terrorists there now, just an empty magick table restaurant, standing on its own. There was a noise of people coming through the woods. Soon, a troop of British soldiers appeared, led by a major from the British Army. It was a hot day, and the men had been busy removing terrorists from the area all morning.

'I say, is that a magick restaurant table?' asked the major. 'I've heard about them.'

He went and stood by the table, looking at it. A cool pint of real ale appeared.

'Come on, men, let's make the most of this before we move on,' the major announced.

The men gathered round and were much refreshed. Then they were on their way again.

My next stop was Algeria. I went to Al-Qaida's Algerian research base, which had been staffed by North American scientists. The place was closed. There were NATO soldiers, who came from Spain, standing guard outside. The same was true in Tunisia.

I went to Sardinia, where I had seen terrorists building the latest of their secret bases, including an electromagnetic bridge between Sardinia and Corsica. Now the bridge was down, and there were NATO soldiers guarding the entrance to the base.

'What about Marseille and Calais?' I thought.

There were IRA bases in both ports, where they could track their drug and arms imports across the Mediterranean

Sea. Marseilles was empty and closed. As I got to Calais, NATO were just arriving. They went straight to the top of the building, where the IRA boss had his office. Several NATO soldiers came in through the skylight, carrying laser rifles. The IRA boss put his hands up, and left the office. He was escorted down the emergency stairs along with the rest of his staff. Outside the building, a large van was waiting to take them away. Then two NATO soldiers were left on guard outside.

'How soon will it be before NATO get to Britain,' I wondered.

I looked out of my window, into the terrorists' garden, and saw several North American henchmen with their hands up, coming down a secret stairway that led into the trees above. There were NATO soldiers coming up next door's garden path, where an Al-Qaida drugs dealer rented accommodation to North American terrorists. Two Asian drug dealing managers came round the corner of the house, with their hands up. Then one of them turned back, and aimed a punch at the soldier behind him. The drug dealer fell dead instantly, with a laser bullet through his head. The other Asian was marched to a waiting van, and taken away. As I walked down the road, there were NATO soldiers standing guard outside the IRA houses. They had taken away all the occupants.

'What about the International Unity Guild building in New York?' I thought.

My mind was racing ahead, trying to locate where the terrorists might still be fighting back. The I.U.G. building was still standing, but it was empty. There were no soldiers visible, but the main entrance had been boarded up. It looked as if the electromagnetic war was over. There might be pockets of resistance, but after such a walkover by NATO, I could not see how the war could continue. The only advantages the terrorists had on their side were secrecy and invisibility. Once NATO were on to them, it was all over for the terrorists, owing to NATO's far greater capability in weapons technologies.

Why didn't NATO wipe them out before? I suspected that it was because when military personnel looked at the strange assortment of different terrorist groups, in their invisible miniaturised forms, they dismissed them as not significantly serious a threat to justify taking action. Damage done to civilians by a few ISIS suicide attackers could be felt and seen by everyone in the world, and clearly qualified as war. Thousands of invisible, miniaturised, electromagnetic terrorists, whatever they were doing, did not. And yet, I knew from my visits to targeted individuals in North America, that there were hundreds of thousands, if not millions, of suffering victims of electromagnetic attacks at home, whose plight was being overlooked.

Perhaps that was because electromagnetic weapons did not, generally, breach the terms of engagement which would have allowed the military to become involved. If so, that meant that North America, and many other parts of the world, were full of victims who would go on being targeted by electromagnetic terrorists, even though it appeared that the European War was over. I admired NATO's efficiency in dealing with the attack on Europe, but I was frustrated that nothing had been done for targeted individuals.

I went to the back door of the Special Services building, and looked in. The white-coated scientists were all sitting at their desks. They had played a key part in NATO's successful prevention of war in Europe, which was highly creditable. and yet, I felt anger rise up inside me, because they ignored the suffering of their own people at home. Selecting two of the scientists sitting at the far end of the room, Jeff and Glen, I said, 'Let these two men experience everything that I experience at the hands of terrorists from now on.'

Then I went up to the top of the building, where senior staff worked, and entered the rooms of Cameron, the head, and Gerald, deputy head of the Special Services.

'Let these two men also experience everything that I experience at the hands of terrorists from now on,' I said.

The men concerned were all North Americans, making a significant contribution to NATO. But I did not regret my actions. I felt sure that after a few weeks, the military would begin to understand what it was like to live in the invisible virtual prison camps run by the North American mafia, who formed a major part of the terrorists' electromagnetic army. At that moment, some local terrorists attacked me with oscillators. Glen, one of the two scientists now linked to me, moaned and threw up.

'I feel so ill,' he gasped.

Staff from the medical centre that Special Services shared with H.M. Prison Services came to Glen's aid. I guessed that the rocking motion of the oscillators had given Glen sea-sickness. Then a terrorist tried, unsuccessfully, to void my bladder. Jeff, the other scientist, shot out of his seat.

'Oh no, I've been attacked. What a mess!' he said, in disgust.

He went to get changed. Elliot came out to look for me.

'Have you done something to our men?' he asked.

'Yes,' I said, and I explained why.

'Well,' said Elliot. 'It might be no bad thing if we kept Glen and Jeff under observation here, so that we could learn at first hand, what it is that targeted victims go through. But it would be embarrassing if our top bosses were hit. Is there something you can do about that?'

I shook my head.

'It's the top bosses that need convincing most.' I said. 'But if you happen to find a way to extricate them, then that will be good news for all targeted individuals too.'

Elliot went off to make arrangements for Glen and Jeff to be re-classified as research subjects. Later I went to see them. They were sharing a large hospital room, and both were tucked up in bed. Their laptops were on the table so they could work in there if they felt up to it, but at the moment they weren't interested.

Some North American terrorists followed me into the sick bay. I could see one balancing precariously on the edge of a window, as he leaned in with a laser weapon. He aimed it at the side of my body. I was quite used to that, and it had little effect on me, as I wore shielding devices. But Glen let out a yell, 'Ow! That hurt,' he cried.

Jeff felt it as well, though not as much.

'I hope this is going to stop soon,' he said. 'I'm not enjoying any of it.'

I went upstairs to the top offices. Cameron, the head of the office, had been throwing up, like Glen. He was being helped by staff from the medical centre.

'I don't understand it,' said Gerald. 'He was perfectly well a few minutes ago.'

Then the terrorists, who had followed me up to the top offices, directed a pulsing electromagnetic beam, at Gerald's left lung. This is not as dangerous as it sounds, but it is designed to make the victim think he is having a heart attack.

Gerald clutched his chest, 'It's my heart, I think they've got me,' he gasped, and fell on the floor.

The interesting thing about that, from my perspective, was that I didn't get the same thing. That meant that the terrorists had started targeting men from the Special Services building as separate individuals. They might have lost me to some extent, but they had now gained four sons.

'I want to go home,' said Cameron.

'Good idea,' said Gerald. 'It's safer there.'

The two senior men made their way out of the building. I went to check back on Glen and Jeff. Several terrorists wearing black wetsuits were now lined up on the ceiling, where an electromagnetic gantry had been quickly constructed. They were firing laser guns at the two invalids.

Elliot was standing listening to his colleagues' complaints.

'I just got hit in the arm,' said Glen.

'That's nothing,' said Jeff. 'I just got hit in the butt. Excuse me, I've got to go,' and he got up and ran to the bathroom.

'Their missing half the fun, because the terrorists are invisible to them,' I thought. 'Let all four men now have the ability to see and hear the terrorists the same way that I do.'

'Look up there! Did you see that! I can see one of them,' cried Glen.

'I know what I'd like to do to the fucking varmints,' said Jeff.

Then he spotted one of them.

'Aha!' he said. 'Just a minute now,' He aimed a punch at a black uniformed offender.

The terrorist fell to the ground dead.

'Did you see that, Glen,' said Jeff. 'I showed him!'

The two scientists clearly had hours of entertainment ahead of them.

Next day, Cameron and Gerald made their way up to their offices. They decided to work in the same office for now, so that they could share solidarity.

'Did you sleep all right?' said Gerald.

'Yeah,' said Cameron. 'Everything was fine till about four in the morning. Then I heard this oldster wittering away in my ear. Totally insane stuff. The old guy was banging on about how monoliths all lived in Finland and migrated to the UK by air in formation every Summer. Then when he thought no one was listening, the old guy started muttering to himself in a demented way about his bosses. He said, 'I wish my nose hadn't been bleeding, otherwise, I'd have shown them... did you have any of that?'

'Thank God, no,' said Gerald. 'I got to hear some tart calling me a big boy and lisping obscenities for a while but I went back to sleep, so it wasn't too bad.

'Welcome to the world of targeted individuals,' I thought.

ATTACKS IN THE UNITED STATES

Next day, Glen and Jeff were still sitting in bed. Glen had taken some sea-sickness medicine, but it wasn't working too well. One of the black-suited terrorists crawled along the ceiling architecture that was now fully in place, and started to target the lower bowels of both men, filtering gas into their intestines. Glen cramped up, gasping, but Jeff stretched out calmly, munching on toast and reading the newspaper.

'What's your secret?' asked Glen.

'Oh, it's just this little thing,' said Jeff, removing his shielding device and waving it in the air.

'Give me that!' shouted Glen, and he grabbed it from Jeff.

Then the black-suited attacker targeted both of them again, and they raced for the bathroom, still fighting over the piece of shielding material.

Things were developing according to plan, but it seemed to me that the impact of this research exercise, which was being monitored and recorded by a scientist in the next room, was limited. We needed something bigger than that to draw attention to what North American targeted individuals were going through. My mind turned across the Atlantic to the United States National Security Agency in Maryland.

'Why not?' I thought.

I selected that renowned building complex, with its smoked glass exterior and said, 'Let all those inside this building now hear and feel the same terrorist attacks as I do, and anything else that comes their way.'

I took care not to say "hear and *see*", as targeted individuals usually cannot see their attackers, and I wanted the experience of agency employees to be as realistic as possible. Then, in my invisible form, I went into the building through the foyer, and down some stairs into a large, underground room with terracotta walls. About sixty staff were sitting at computers with headphones on. I don't know what they were doing, but listening seemed to be an important part of it.

The local terrorists in my garden were sitting up and watching with interest. To get to the United States, and in particular, to the NSA, was their ultimate dream. They regretted signing up to attack me, now that such a prize was before them. But how could they get there? They couldn't follow me in through the NSA foyer, because they could not get past the United States border controls.

I went upstairs to a part of the NSA building within the smoked glass area. There was a fine view from all the windows up there. As I came onto the landing, about two thirds of the way up the building, I saw a black-suited spiderman attacker waving at me from outside the glass.

'Let me in!' he shouted.

I carefully created a tiny access point in the smoked glass. It was hard to detect, but it was enough. He was in, followed shortly by twenty others. They scurried about, sussing out where the air conditioning ducts were, before they began exploring the rooms. I was not sure where they had come from, but for my purposes, they seemed to have the right idea.

On one side of the landing, a glass door led into a large communal room, with many people sitting at computer desks. Opposite the stairs, there was a smaller room, where a senior official was working. On the other side of the stairs, there were two doors. One led directly into the room of a top-ranking official, and the other led into the room of his personal secretary, next to the double-doored lifts.

I went into the room of the senior official. An invisible black-suited attacker was already crouching on a rail he had built across the ceiling. The senior official scratched his leg.

'I've been bitten by something,' he said, looking up from his laptop screen.

'So far so good,' I thought. 'I'll go down to the listening centre.'

As I went downstairs, I could hear terrorists from my local psychological warfare section at home muttering to themselves;

'It's not fair, I could be in the States, earning so much more than here.'

I looked into my garden and saw ten men in long frocks, watching me. I selected them all, picked them up, and deposited them in the NSA's listening centre. Then I noticed several weapons group men in black wetsuits, sitting in the garden, looking rather glum. I transported them across to the NSA as well. Twenty more men in frocks were queuing up, and they all got the dream of a lifetime, to go to the United States.

Looking out of the agency's smoked windows, I could see a black cloud, like a flock of birds, heading for the top of the agency building. They had been selected and sent there remotely by their controller. But there was no way they could get in. I went up to the top of the smoked glass and smashed it open. The people inside would not notice, but there was now a gaping electromagnetic hole in the top of the building. The first black-suited attackers climbed in. They looked like spidermen. These guys were the North American terrorists' "A Team", not the sort we ever saw in the British Isles. They could crawl up walls and abseil down buildings.

Outside the agency, in roads nearby, unmarked terrorist vans were being discreetly parked, their engines running. Technical support terrorists were moving into position. I went back down into the listening centre. Two girls were sitting staring at computer screens with their headphones on. Then they started giggling. One of them took the phones off and passed them to the man sitting next to her.

'Listen to this,' she said.

The man put on her phones and listened. What he heard was, 'Aren't you the darnedest, cutest little woman I've set eyes on?'

The man's face puckered, as he tried not to laugh. The voice went on, 'I could lick you all over...'

Another man took off his headphones. He was listening on a different channel.

'That's the grossest thing I ever heard' he said.

'Give that to me,' said his female colleague, seizing his headphones.

As she listened, she heard, 'Are you the man with the big balls that I saw just now. I'd love to give you a rub down...'

Staff were getting up and talking to the supervisor. Then an announcement came over the public-address system, 'Would anyone wishing to report problems with their receivers please go the helpdesk outside where...'

But at that moment a gravelly male voice broke in, 'Have you got the sweetest, little pussy…'

The public address switched off with a sharp click. The room emptied, as all the staff went to report problems to the helpdesk. A few minutes later, some NSA technicians marched in and started listening to the terrorists' telephone sexperts on their receivers. They checked the skirting boards with electronic equipment. An Our Group terrorist in a long frock opened a door and looked in. Seeing a technician bent over on the floor, s/he reached her hand into the back of the technician's pants.

'Shit,' said the technician. 'Someone's tickling my testicles.'

The long-frocked terrorist quickly darted back behind the door.

'Only doing my bit for the cause,' s/he said, tossing back her hair.

Two elderly French-Canadian henchmen, located in my garden, were listening intently, trying to peer over my shoulder.

'Wasn't that succulent,' said one of them, wistfully.

They were sorry to be missing all the fun.

Upstairs in the NSA's communal technical section, black-suited terrorists were on the ceiling, sniping at staff with laser weapons. The top-ranking official's door was open, and he was lying on the floor, shouting in pain, as two members of the terrorists' A Team hit him with enhanced pain infliction weapons and brain-freezing microwave radiation beams. His secretary was on the phone calling the first aid team, 'Please come quickly, he seems to be having a seizure,' she called.

Men came running up the stairs, and when the lift doors opened, a team of medics appeared carrying a stretcher.

Outside the building, NSA technicians were scouring the area, trying to find how the terrorists had hacked into the building, and where the WIFI for the invasion was located. They were unable to pick anything up.

'Must be a private satellite,' said one of them.

'We'll have to call our Special Detection people,' said another.

Three ambulances drew up outside, and senior men from the agency could be seen being stretchered into them. Then, a large dark van appeared, and ten men from the Special Detection squad got out. They wore black helmets and goggles, and carried electronic weapons. They looked up on the roof of the agency, where some spidermen were standing.

'Look,' said one of them. 'We've got ghouls on the roof.'

The men raked the sky with scanning equipment, checking for a signal from a private commercial satellite. A military helicopter appeared overhead, in telephone contact with the Detection team below.

'Looks like we've got the WIFI source now,' said the helicopter pilot, on his intercom.

The Detection team went into the basement of the building to hunt for "ghouls", and started to work their way up. After a while, there were spidermen on the roof trying to escape. A large Pringle zoomed into view and hung suspended above the roof. Several rope-ladders came out, and the spidermen climbed up. The noise of rotors could be heard in the distance, and soon two Chinooks came into view. The Pringle whizzed off. It was full by now, but there more spidermen left behind. The Chinooks positioned themselves above the agency roof, and as the doors slid back, teams of US military personnel came down on ropes. The soldiers were armed with advanced electromagnetic weapons. They had no difficulty getting to grips with the terrorists, and after a short struggle, the military put cuffs on the spider men, and winched them up into the helicopters.

By now, terrorists from "Our Group", that I had imported from my garden, were being escorted out of the building by the Special Detection team, their hands tied behind their backs. They were loaded into large dark vans and taken away.

'Well,' I thought to myself. 'Let's see what difference that makes to targeted individuals. Some changes in the law would be a good start.'

The un-readiness of the NSA for an electromagnetic attack was a surprise, as was the ease with which I was able to get into the building unchallenged. That suggested to me that civilian law enforcement agencies in the US were not equipped to deal with attacks from invisible electromagnetic terrorists. It was likely that police in each US State would be equally unaware of the invisible threat, which was why there were so many targeted individuals. If you can't see the perpetrators, how are you going to arrest them? I began to wonder about the preparedness of US defences at the highest level.

'I know,' I thought. 'Let's see what happens if terrorists try to get into the Pentagon.'

Picking up a villainous terrorist manager, who controlled electromagnetic access to a set of buildings opposite me, I dropped him in the corridor of a section of the Pentagon. A second later, five armed security guards jumped on him, and forcibly took him away.

'Wow!' I thought. 'That's impressive!'

'Thank you, ma'am,' came the subvocal response, a nanosecond later.

The response came from Ryan, one of the Pentagon guards. I had never met a computer system with such a powerful Central Processing Unit as the one in the Pentagon. It was much faster than the one I was running on, so much so, that I had to stop for a moment, and think, 'Where would you store a computer system that operated faster than the speed of light?'

There is an answer to that, but it was not something I wanted to contemplate right then. It meant that the system had to be located at a higher level of frequency than humans can normally tolerate.

'Was that guy we picked up bothering you?' asked another guard, called Justin.

Justin put his head through the electromagnetic wall that separated my environment from his. A moment later, I was in the corridor with the men.

'Oh, I get lots of them, and they all bother me,' I said.

What bothered me more was who could protect American citizens from electromagnetic terrorist attacks. The Pentagon guards were the first I had met who seemed to have a good grasp of the issues. The men all nodded. They fully understood the point I was making, and a lot more beside. I realised that they could not only read my mind, but also my gut reactions, in record time. There would be no secrets between these guys, and no secrets between them and me. Luckily, I was used to that, after several years of synthetic telepathy intrusions by the terrorists.

'We heard about the NSA incident,' said Ryan.

'Apparently the ghouls have been giving you a lot of trouble,' said a third guard, called Owen. 'We read about it.'

Owen reached behind him into a sliding cupboard in the wall, and drew out the book '*Terror in Britain.*' The men were very kind and friendly, so I felt I ought to offer them something.

'Did you hear about magick table restaurants?' I asked.

'We heard, Martha,' said Justin.

'Would you like some?' I asked, scattering some mini magick tables in front of them.

'Can you fix it for our bar to have some tables?' asked Ryan.

'No, we can't have them in the bar,' said Owen. 'That would reduce the bar staff takings.'

At that moment, a tall senior officer, whose name was Wyatt, appeared along the corridor. He had been watching everything on CCTV.

'What's this, men, talking in the corridor? Get back to your duties, please.'

The men were not intimidated by Wyatt's comments.

'We've got a visitor,' said Justin. 'And she wants to give us some magick restaurant tables. We were just discussing the best place. We can't use the bar. Do you have a suggestion, sir?'

Wyatt considered for a minute. Then he said, 'I know, it can go in our recreation room.'

He led the way along the corridor, down some stairs, and into a spacious, pleasant room, with a large wooden table in the middle. Immediately, I turned the table into a magick restaurant table, and all the men tested to see if it worked, which, of course, it did, producing the famed real ale to order.

Then I presented Wyatt with a mini magick restaurant table, for his personal use.

'Do you know about these?' I asked, producing some mini-cupboards.

The men picked up the cupboards.

'I heard these boxes produce drugs that are legal and help addicts,' said Ryan.

'You heard right,' I said.

Using the mini-cupboard, Wyatt made some white powder in a plastic bag, and handed it round to the men, so they could tell how different it was from lethal drugs. I could see they approved. Owen looked at the mini-cupboard in his hand.

'How come we don't have anything like this?' he asked.

'Maybe some of your military do,' I said. 'But it isn't widely known about. I can tell that your capabilities are far greater than mine, so you must be able to do everything I can, and a lot more.'

At that moment, I began to noticed the atmosphere in the room. It had an intense high frequency about it, combined with a deep magnetic "pull", which affected me as if I had drunk several straight gins. I could see frequency lines waving and shimmering, like a mirage, in front of my eyes.

'Don't worry,' said Wyatt. 'You'll get used to it. It's our natural environment.'

'Is it true that these things can cure diseases?' asked Justin, pointing to the boxes.

I never make formal claims about the mini-cupboards, as whatever may be happening, it has certainly not been scientifically demonstrated.

'Well,' I said. 'They seem to help.'

'How would it be if you could fill a container with those things?' asked Wyatt, 'Then we could offer them round to our colleagues.'

I created a large box of mini-cupboards, and explained how they could self-replicate. Then I remembered something.

'There's another thing they can do,' I said. 'But I don't know if smart gentlemen like yourselves would benefit much from it.'

'Try me,' said Owen.

'Hold the box, and repeat, "I have the cleverest brain in the universe".' I said.

While Owen was doing that, I created an easy chair right behind him, so that he would fall back into it, rather than onto the floor.

'I can't miss this,' said Ryan.

'Me neither,' said Owen.

Soon, all the men had the cleverest brain in the universe. That seemed to be enough for one day, so I thanked the men for their hospitality and went home.

Back home, the local terrorists were hiding, having seen one of their managers taken into custody rather firmly by the Pentagon guards. But once they were sure I was on my own, they came charging out, all guns blazing. I despatched a few of the bad guys. Then a technical hit man appeared. The terrorists' bosses had hired him. They had no money to pay him with, but they promised him false papers to enter the United States.

The man had specialist equipment which he prepared and aimed in my direction. I watched him standing there. Then, he began to shimmer and fade, and the last echo of his appearance floated away into nothing. I looked up and saw Ryan standing there, holding a device in his hand. He smiled and waved.

'Thanks for the rescue,' I said.

Ryan surveyed the surrounding area, and located the defunct clinical research base across the road that had once been the North American terrorists' local powerhouse. Lifting up the top of the industrial site, he looked in.

'What happened to this?' he asked.

'Our military finished them off,' I said.

'That's good,' said Ryan.

He got up, as if to go. Then he turned and looked at me.

'Those spidermen in the NSA building, do you know where they come from?'

That really surprised me.

'I thought you guys would know all about that,' I said.

'We've never been asked to look at it,' said Ryan.

I turned my face towards a high-level view of the USA, and searched for the strongest frequency of the spidermen. I tuned into a place somewhere between Idaho and Wyoming. There was an underground base. I went down into it, looking for spidermen, and saw hundreds of them walking about in an inverted turret construction.

'There are some down there,' I said.

Ryan had changed into the goggles and helmet, and was holding an electronic weapon like the ones the Special Detection squad had used.

'Oh yes, I see them,' he said, looking in.

'But that isn't where the frequency is strongest,' I said.

I withdrew my gaze, and searched the surrounding area above ground. Then I saw it! A young man aged about twenty-five, sitting in a small room, working on his laptop. The intensity of the frequency coming from the laptop was incredible.

'There it is!' I cried. 'He's doing it all by himself.'

Ryan and I looked at the young man's laptop. It had technical drawings of spidermen, and an automated process for enabling spidermen to enter the electromagnetic environment, with all the capabilities that went with this special upgrade.

Ryan pounced on the man, and compressed him into a small space, using technology I had not seen before. Suddenly, Justin and Owen were there too, disarming the man, and removing him, with his laptop, for questioning.

'How could one young man be doing all that by himself?' I asked myself.

'Secret scientists next generation kids,' said Ryan, answering my unspoken question.

'What are your people doing about this?' I asked. 'With all the technology at your disposal, why is it still going on?'

We were now sitting in a clearing in Wyoming, with the mountains behind us.

'You see, Martha,' said Owen. 'The way it works, rescuing civilians from an internal threat is a matter for law enforcement in each State. But when it comes to electromagnetic technology, no one at State level has the technical know-how to do that. The police know hardly anything about ghouls, and intelligence staff have not been given the tools to detect them. The technology is only available at federal and military level.'

'Then no one can help targeted individuals,' I said.

Wyatt's lanky form appeared from nowhere. He had been keeping tracks on us.

'It's up to each State to pass laws about prohibition of electromagnetic weapons,' he said. 'Most of the politicians don't understand enough to see the risks. In some cases, there is mafia resistance feeding into the political arena. But we cannot interfere with the democratic process.'

'Shouldn't the military be briefing your Senate or something like that?' I asked.

'If its perceived as a military threat, yes.' said Wyatt. 'But thousands of targeted individuals scattered across the States, do not necessarily constitute a material risk in any individual State.'

'Well, OK,' I said. 'But look at the spidermen upgrade. Look what they did to the NSA, without any forward planning. What if they got themselves organised? They could take over your country, and run it invisibly through people in politics they controlled, and no one would be any the wiser. You could even have a political puppet in the White House…'

'Our military are subject to the laws of our country,' said Wyatt. 'If we are given the order to intervene, we do so. Otherwise, not.'

'But surely there are military advisors to the politicians,' I persisted.

'If something is seen to be going wrong, they will act,' said Wyatt. 'But up to now, we've not had anything to point to as something going wrong…' Then his face creased up in a smile. 'Until, that is, you came along and let all those ghouls into the NSA. Now, I wouldn't be surprised if that didn't make our military sit up. After all, if one old senior like yourself could cause so much trouble, we may have to re-think our risk and threat assessments.'

'I guess I'll have to be content with that for now,' I said. 'But targeted individuals are increasingly banding together, lobbying and seeking redress at all levels. Wouldn't it be worth starting to retrain and arm law-enforcement agents at State level, so that when new laws on electromagnetic crime are passed, the police are ready to implement them.'

I was starting to sound like a political activist, something I certainly am not, as I'm far too lazy. Then I had an idea.

'How would it be if you guys were to start passing on "the cleverest brain in the universe" to all the people in your outfit, and to the committees where politicians meet the military? That would be a start, at least.'

Wyatt took my hand, 'Martha, I promise we will do our best.'

So, that was where we left it.

SHOOTING DOWN SATELLITES

It occurred to me that I might be able to disconnect the North American terrorists' WIFI communications systems all over the world, by shooting at their commercial satellites. I knew that they shared these satellites with a number of other terrorist groups. Our Group had lost access to their commercial satellite some months ago, because they could not keep up the monthly payments on the service. The satellites orbited the earth on a continuous basis, and each satellite took two hours to pass across the local area paid for by the North Americans.

But how to find the satellites? I did not know what they looked like. I had seen pictures of things with solar panels attached, and imagined they might look something like that. Thanks to NATO's greatly enhanced electromagnetic environment, I could throw out words into the ether and get something back, so I had a go.

'Select the terrorists' satellite and let me look at it,' I announced, mentally.

What appeared in my mental view was not what I expected. It was a large, blue-grey pod that looked like a whale without a tail, although it had a couple of tiny fin-like tail panels. I mentally shot a laser beam at the under-belly of the whale, and watched as it slowly lost altitude, and turned its nose towards the sea below.

The local terrorists on ultrasound synthetic telepathy duty let out a howl which I could hear with my physical ears, after which their Syntel communications became silent. In a few minutes they had reconnected via a local hand-held transmitter, but for the next two hours, they were out of contact with their friends in the United States.

'Why stop there?' I thought. 'There must be at least twelve of those things flying around in the sky.'

'Select all terrorists satellites up in the air,' I announced.

This time I could see six. There were reasons why I could not see all twelve, one being that it depended which computer system I was announcing on, as to which satellites I could select. I could switch between computer systems at will, but for now, I decided to go with the six satellites I had got. I dumped them all in the sea. Then I went to look for the people who had launched them.

Immediately I saw a neat industrial business park with white flat roofs, and blue-tinted windows. It looked hi-tec, which together with the bright sunlight and blue sky suggested to me that it was somewhere in California. I homed in on the main building, and saw a man wearing blue workwear and a blue hard hat, standing at an IT communications consul. He was looking at a plasma screen display which showed six satellites diving into the sea.

'It could be worse,' he said to an unseen colleague via an intercom. 'At least they are not in the main shipping lanes, and they are damaged, so the data will be unreadable.'

I could hear the local terrorists bewailing the loss of their operational data, including their reports on work completed.

How would they get paid if their reports were not processed? One terrorist said that there was a master copy of the terrorist data which was kept permanently in the sky, as it was too sensitive to store on the ground.

I decided to see if I could catch an undamaged satellite, and present it to the British Military's Special Technical Services Department, which adjoined HM Special Prison Services. I sent out a search for one, and selected it in an electromagnetic envelope. It felt a bit like catching a fish. I could reel it in, but there was a risk that if I put it on the ground, it might fly off again. Perhaps, if I could prise the thing open, before landing it. That might stop it operating.

I carefully laid the satellite on the garden doorstep of the Special Technical Services Department, and prised open the front of the satellite. It opened like an oyster shell. Inside, I could see a lot of pale pink communications media, with black marks on it, wound into large circular packs. The satellite mechanism seemed to be picking up data by WIFI, and translating it into the black marks. The mechanism was still whirring away to itself.

Elliot, the white-coated senior scientist came out.

'I know what that is,' he said.

'Is it of interest?' I asked, knowing how busy he always was with his day job.

'Oh yes,' he said, and he called two white-coated junior scientists to carry it inside.

I went back to the California business park, to see what was going on.

The man at the consul had just launched six replacement satellites, and it was business as usual. I did not seem to have had much impact on the terrorists' satellite operations. I looked into the main business hall. There were men in blue uniforms everywhere. Some were sitting at tables, preparing the circular packs of data for input into the satellites.

'Really, this is a matter for the US Military,' I thought.

I selected six more satellites out of the sky, opened them up like oysters with pearls in them, and deposited them on the grass in the field in the Irish Republic where US NATO representatives were based. Two of the US military men that I usually dealt with came out to have a look.

'Are these of interest to you at all?' I asked, tentatively.

'Oh, yes,' said one of the men, whose name was Haden.

'Would you like some more?' I asked

'Yes, please,' said the Haden.

It seemed to me that it would make life a lot easier for the US Military if they had some of the blue-uniformed terrorists to explain how the satellites worked. So, I went back to the California industrial estate, and selected the men sitting at the table, who were preparing the contents of the satellites. I brought the table and chairs they were sitting on as well, and carefully set them down in the field. Several US military personnel came running out.

'Ah, that will be helpful,' said Haden.

I watched as the blue-uniformed men were led away into to the top security area. Then I returned to the business park, where men at the satellite consul were launching more satellites. There was no way I could go hunting for them all individually. So I tried making an announcement, 'Let all satellites go to the US NATO base in the Republic of Ireland and land themselves carefully in a neat line on the grass, with their lids open,' I announced.

The satellites all obediently changed course and set off for the Republic of Ireland.

'Shit,' said the consul operative.

He kept launching more satellites. In the end there were about two hundred of them lying on the grass in the Irish Republic.

'That's it,' said the consul operative. 'We're all out.'

I looked into the main factory hall, which was full of blue-uniformed men and announced, 'Legs off, clothes off, voices gone, pass it on.'

Instantly, all the men were sitting on the ground, silent and unclothed. Their legs were still there, but they were disconnected for electromagnetic purposes, and no longer able to move. I went out to the entrance of the industrial park. There was a large building which looked like a van maintenance business. There were car wash areas, machine testing areas, and sales areas. The building was on two levels. In the basement there was a side entrance, where staff arrived for work. Some of them walked through a door into an underground corridor, which led to the satellite production plant.

I placed a sonar tracking device on the main building. Then I returned to the satellite construction hall. Men with motorised pallets were handing out uniforms to their now-naked colleagues, hooking them up onto the pallets through their uniforms and taking them away. Suddenly, the ceiling of the hall broke open with a crack, and a number of armed US military personnel appeared. They had been tipped off by their NATO contacts. They had followed my tracker to the industrial site where the terrorist satellites were made and burst in to clean the place out.

There was chaos on the floor of the industrial hall. Sirens were going off. A man with a loud speaker was ordering all staff to evacuate the building, and men in blue uniforms were running for the exits in all directions. There were US military personnel on the roof, and many more all over the industrial site, putting handcuffs on men, and leading them away.

I decided to make one final check for satellites in the sky. I picked up something, but it was bigger than the previous ones. I guided it down onto the NATO field in the Irish Republic. It had a transparent top over the standard shell, made of a shielding substance to prevent detection. As I brought it down, Haden and three other men came out.

'There it is,' said Haden, pointing to the satellite. 'That's the master copy. Now we have everything. Thanks, Martha.'

Haden and the three other men picked up the master satellite between them and carried it into their operations area.

THE END OF THE TERROR

That night it was hot. I took off my night-time crash helmet and left the bedroom door open. I was lying in bed, and the North American terrorists were mounting microwave attacks on my brain, in retaliation for the loss of their satellites and their data. I felt dizzy and confused, and too tired to fend off the attack.

'I guess I'll just try to sleep,' I thought, pulling my pillow over my head.

At that moment, I saw something moving in the terrorists' electromagnetic environment. At first, it looked like mountains in the distance, then huge men dressed in the uniforms of Roman Centurions could be seen coming towards us. They were full size, despite being in the electromagnetic environment, where scaling-down in height normally applies. There was a gasp from the terrorists. They switched off their equipment and went very quiet. They had seen the centurions before, and they knew that there would be no more attacks while they were around. No one knows who they are, but they must be something to do with our military.

'Get the microwave equipment, it's up there on that ridge,' said one centurion.

I looked up towards a high hill, and saw an array of microwave transmitters, partially camouflaged by some trees. There were a few operatives up there, trembling behind their technical kit. I wondered if the centurions would confiscate the microwave weapons. As if in answer to my unspoken question, one of them said, 'We can leave the kit, it's the people we want.'

The centurions started seizing groups of terrorists, putting them in bags and loading them into trucks. Then they reached up into the sky of the electromagnetic environment and began clearing out hundreds of terrorists from a kind of false ceiling up there. The centurion uniform was one commonly used by the North American terrorists, and my rescuers appeared to have adopted it in order to blend in unobtrusively with the terrorist community. A bold Irish terrorist youth stood on a rock and began asking the centurions questions.

'Why have you come?' he asked.

'We are here all the time,' replied the centurion. 'We always come when we are needed.'

'Did she call you?' continued the youth.

'We don't need to be called,' said the centurion. 'We decide when to intervene.'

As I watched, a group of centurions picked up the underlying structure of the terrorists' amphitheatre architecture, and began rolling it up like a carpet. Any terrorists still in there were rolled up too. The soldiers folded up the carpet and put it in the back of a truck. Then they moved off down the road towards the next terrorist installation.

A couple of hours later, a full-size, senior terrorist administrative technician in a dark suit appeared in the garden area near my house. A rabble of reduced-size low-level terrorists from the Irish mafia group were gathered there, attempting to shout at me via a handheld synthetic telepathy parabola, which looked like a small TV satellite dish. They had nothing else, now that their WIFI satellites were down.

'Get out now, it's all over,' said the administrator.

The Irish terrorists refused to move. The administrator picked up a stick and started hitting the rabble. The he seized one end of the grassy floor which formed their amphitheatre and began rolling it up. The terrorists screamed and fell on to the ground below.

'Who is going to come and look after us?' they shouted.

The man made no reply and walked off, leaving the rabble squeaking and scrabbling about on the ground.

Next morning, I woke up to the sound of the radio. I always slept with the radio on, as it tended to drown out the terrorists. As I was waking up, I heard the voice of someone on the radio, 'It's over. There is no need to fight any more.'

The radio was just broadcasting an early morning "Thought for the Day", but a group of terrorists that were listening took it literally, and got up and left the area. Over the years, there had been a number of strange coincidences in radio broadcasts, such as the radio saying exactly the same words that I, or the terrorists were saying, at the same moment, or seeming to answer a question that someone had asked. Whenever this happened, the weapons group terrorists would get up and leave, being of a superstitious frame of mind.

That night, a large number of children appeared in the terrorists' garden. This was a sure sign that several groups of Asians were due to take over the night shift from midnight. Michael and Tanya put their heads through the electromagnetic ceiling and gave me an enquiring look.

'I was just about to send them to the Irish Republic,' I said, and I selected a batch of twenty kids and sent them over.

The children were aged two years or less, and though now possessing the cleverest brains in the universe as soon as they arrived, still needed to be cared for a lot. There were gasps when the tiny tots appeared in the arrival area. A soldier got on his cellphone and asked if there were any women soldiers on duty. Three women soldiers came running in. I created a low wheeled transporter, padded like a cot, and the women soldiers put the first ten tots in there.

'Can I have lots of nappies, please?' said a woman soldier.

I created piles of them and put them on the transporter. Then a man from the emergency services pushed a hospital bed in, and put the protective rails up. The other ten tots went in that one, and the women wheeled them off to the medical centre outside.

'Do you know where they are from?' asked the soldier on duty.

'No,' I said. 'But I can find out.'

Selecting the children in a magnetic field, I said, 'Let each child have a loose, plastic wrist band, with the name of their home town written on a label attached to it.'

But I didn't have time to check where the kids came from. Back in the terrorists' garden, there were now even more children. I doubted if the soldiers in the Irish Republic would be able to cope with them all.

Michael and Tanya put their heads through the electromagnetic ceiling again.

'Do you know if any of the are British?' he asked.

'I haven't found out yet,' I said. 'But there are so many here, would you be able to take them even if they are Irish.'

'Yes,' said Michael. 'We have facilities to route them through.'

'Go on, bring them in to my area!' cried Tanya.

I selected the remaining children, in two groups of twenty, and delivered them into the upper garden area of H.M. Special Prison Services, where Tanya normally took delivery of child victims. They were at the toddling stage. Tanya and several other women prison officers took two children each and led them by the hand into a large room which was used for leisure activities. Several men prison officers came to help as well. I created a large, low table, with little chairs, and made it into a magick table restaurant, so that the kids could have something to eat, as it would take time to arrange transport to the place where the children would stay the night.

With help from some women prison officers, the kids worked out how to use the magick table. They made themselves chocolate biscuits and orange juice in child drinking mugs.

Then Tanya asked, 'Please can we have some of those wooden boxes that create things? I've heard they help with physical problems.'

I made some mini-cupboards and handed them out to the women prison officers. Several prison officers suffered from chronic back pain. Tanya's friend, Pam, began taking the boxes round to them, and their pain went away. Michael came in. He was totally exhausted, as he had been working in his own time, rescuing kids, when he should have been home in bed.

'Give one to Michael,' I said.

Michael tried the box, to see if it could help him. One moment he was slumped in a chair, and next minute, he was bright and refreshed.

'This box is great!' he said. 'Can I take one home for my family?'

'Everyone can take as many as they like,' I said.

At that moment, Tanya had a call on her cellphone.

'It's Elliot,' she said. 'He says can we send some boxes over to his place.'

His place was, in fact, the building next door. I created a large cardboard box, full of mini-cupboards, and a prison officer took them across.

Now fully refreshed, Michael took a look at the forty toddlers sitting round the table, with men and women prison officers attending to them.

'Any idea where these kids come from?' he asked.

I created wrist bands with labels showing the home town for every kid. Tanya went to read the labels. Then she put her hand over her mouth, her eyes wide with astonishment. She gave Michael a nudge.

'Take a look at this,' she whispered.

Michael took a look.

'Phew… Hey, Jack, come and look at this.'

None of the prison officers would tell me where the kids had come from. But I found out the next day, when Tanya admitted to me that they all came from round the corner, in the same town as H.M. Special Prison Services.

At that moment, Elliot and several white-coated scientists came in. Elliot was carrying a mini-cupboard full of some liquid. He ceremoniously placed it in the centre of the children's table. Then, as if by magic, the liquid in the wooden box lit up, producing a flame. A glorious silver tree, decorated with exquisite pink, gold and pearl crystal balls appeared and grew up from inside the flame. The children were entranced. One of the children was able to reach up and touch a crystal ball. It came off the tree, and the child picked it up and started licking it. The other children's faces said it all.

'Where is *my* crystal ball?'

Quickly, I created replica crystal balls for each of them.

Then Tanya said, 'Can you make the kids have the cleverest brains in the universe, it seems a shame they should miss out on that, just because they didn't go to the Irish Republic.'

I selected all the kids and gave them the cleverest brains in the universe. But I forgot to let the prison officers know that it was a "pass it on" decree. Anyone who touched the toddlers would also become great brains as well. Almost immediately, the men and women helpers, sitting with the kids, fell backwards on to the floor, in a state of temporary shock, as they started to see everything from a completely new point of view.

I wished I could join in and get my brain fixed too, but it was not to be, as the way the electromagnetic system works, you cannot personally receive things from the level that produced them. Tanya leaned over a tiny tot to help it recover its crystal ball, which had rolled out of reach. When she touched the child's arm, she slipped to the floor with a thud, as she suddenly received the cleverest brain in the universe.

'Are you hurt, Tanya,' I asked. anxiously.

'A bit,' she said, rubbing her back.

I quickly brought her a mini-cupboard and the pain in her face disappeared. I blamed myself for not warning her. But Tanya was now back up and running again.

'Come over here, Elliot,' she said, giving me a wink.

The senior scientist came over obligingly.

'Did you want something, Tanya.'

Tanya stretched out her hand and patted his arm. I could see what was coming, and I quickly created a comfy padded armchair behind him, just in time, as he sank into it. I was not sure if he would notice the difference to his mind, being such a great brain to start with, but apparently, he did.

Soon, all the white-coated scientists were queuing up to shake Elliot by the hand and enhance their brain power. A party atmosphere took over. Some of the women prison officers started using the mini-cupboard to make changes to their physical appearance. Tanya was now a size twelve, and looked a few years younger.

'It will be a shock for her husband,' I thought. 'But they say that love is blind, so perhaps he won't notice.'

Next day, I was mulling over what had happened the night before.

'What a difference it would make to the world if everyone could benefit from the positive side of electromagnetic technologies?' I thought.

I noticed that when terrorists went to the Irish Republic and gave themselves the cleverest brain in the universe, their personalities became human again, and they no longer wanted to hurt people. So, I decided to select any terrorists that were on the computer system at that moment, across the world, and let them have the cleverest brain in the universe, including the funders and investors who were behind the attacks on the British Isles.

Everything went quiet for a while, and I wondered what had happened. I located the Arab terrorist funders base in Morocco, and took a look. The Arabs were no longer wearing their long, white robes. They were carefully folding them up, and giving them to a servant. Underneath, they were smartly dressed in expensive-looking modern clothes, more like the Italian mafia men I had seen. From their appearance, you would never guess they had ever been investors in terrorism.

Then I heard a noise up above me in the area where the local terrorists worked. A group of managers were walking down the stairs, and telling their staff they could all go home. Their staff, who had only just been uploaded onto the computer system a moment ago, took this as a hint that they could now go to the Irish Republic. That was something which, up until then they were strictly forbidden to do. They all disappeared there at once, where they were able to have their brains enhanced in a similar manner.

As the terrorist area emptied, the computer system automatically called replacement staff in. These staff had not been selected by me earlier for brain enhancement, as they were not on the computer system at that time. They set about organising themselves in to groups to carry out written instructions on how to attack me. But before they could get any further, one of the Arabs I had seen earlier, arrived in a flying Pringle. He got out of the crisp-shaped airship, and stood in front of the terrorist buildings.

'Come out, everybody,' he said. 'I want you all to share in what we have received.'

The terrorists did not dare to disobey, but they were afraid something bad was coming their way, and they stood at a distance.

'I want all of you to gather round and touch my hands,' continued the Arab. 'As the benefits can only be passed to you that way. Then go and help your friends.'

This was remarkably out of character for a high-born Arab. Normally, they scorned all contact with the rank and file of the terrorist community. One young man came forward, but he did not feel it right for him to reach out and touch such a senior person. Cutting through all protocol, the Arab put his hand on that of the young man, who fell to the ground, in shock.

'My head has expanded,' he cried.

Then he sat up.

'It's all right everyone. Go ahead and touch him. What he says is true.'

The lowly terrorists began to crowd round the Arab, respectfully touching his hand. They were all transformed, immediately and dramatically. Once they had got over the initial impact of having an incredibly improved brain, they started walking down the hill to where their compatriots were waiting to come on duty. They found their friends and passed on the benefits to them as well.

This worked so well that I repeated the process across the world, for each terrorist shift that came on duty. I had never thought that braininess and goodness were the same thing, so I was a bit puzzled at how much kinder the terrorists became when they had a new brain. But it could be that working in the terrorist version of the electromagnetic environment, where they all had their heads microwaved regularly to make them compliant, had removed their humanity, and getting a new brain turned them back into human beings.

As more terrorists were returning to the Irish Republic and being helped back in to the community, and as an ever-increasing number of terrorists all over the world were becoming the cleverest person in the universe, electromagnetic terrorism began to decrease significantly. Everyone could see that being a terrorist was not a smart thing to do. There were so many more enjoyable ways of passing the time, especially now that their basic needs of food, clothes and shelter were being met through devices like the magick table and the mini-cupboard.

I now have more time to devote to my own pursuits. Exploring the universe is high on my list. I have visited many beautiful worlds, some inhabited and some not, but I never found any that had humans living on them. A question that particularly interested me was whether there was anything outside of space. One day, I decided to try and jump outside space and see what happened. So, I did, and I found that... there *was* something else. At the moment, that is all I can say, but from now on, there is something new to be explored, and that is where I'm going next.

NOTES

Video on Synthetic Telepathy

It is really worth searching the internet for a YouTube video of Dr Joseph Pompei of MadLabs — 'making his own private racket in the library' — because it demonstrates how synthetic telepathy works.

See also: Sound from Ultrasound — Wikipedia — how Dr F Joseph Pompei of MIT developed a technology he calls the "Audio Spotlight".

Reference books:

'1996' by Gloria Naylor, Third World Press, US. (1 Dec 2005)

'Nine Lives: My Time as MI6's Top Spy Inside al-Qaeda by Almen Dean, Oneworld Publications, (7 Jun 2018)

'Shooting Up: A History of Drugs in Warfare by Lukasz Kamienski, C Hurst & Co Publishers Ltd, (31 Mar 2016)

'The Shock Doctrine: The Rise of Disaster Capitalism' by Naomi Klein, Penguin; 1st edition (May 2008)

'The Ordeal of Gilbert Pinfold by Evelyn Waugh, Chapman & Hall, (1957). This book is considered by some to be an early record of a synthetic telepathy attack.

CPSIA information can be obtained
at www.ICGtesting.com
Printed in the USA
LVHW091354240719
625173LV00001B/100/P

9 781788 303804